WHEN DREAMS TRAVEL

GITHA HARIHARAN's first novel, *The Thousand Faces of Night*, won the Commonwealth Writers Prize. Since then, she has published a collection of stories, *The Art of Dying*, and a novel called *The Ghosts of Vasu Master*. She has also edited *A Southern Harvest*, a volume of stories translated from South Indian languages. Githa Hariharan lives in New Delhi.

GITHA HARIHARAN

WHEN DREAMS TRAVEL

PICADOR

First published 1999 by Picador

This edition published 2000 by Picador
an imprint of Macmillan Publishers Ltd
25 Eccleston Place, London SW1W 9NF
Basingstoke and Oxford
Associated companies throughout the world
www.macmillan.co.uk

ISBN 0 330 37299 8

3 5 7 9 8 6 4 2

A CIP catalogue record for this book is available from
the British Library.

Typeset by SetSystems Ltd, Saffron Walden, Essex
Printed and bound in Great Britain by
Mackays of Chatham plc, Chatham, Kent

For Latha

Contents

Contents

Acknowledgements

All quotations from *The Thousand and One Nights* are from the Penguin Classics edition of *Tales from the Thousand and One Nights*, translated with an introduction by N. J. Dawood, 1954.

The quotation from 'Nightmares' by Jorge Luis Borges is from *Seven Nights*, New Directions, New York, 1984, p. 26; and from 'The Garden of the Forking Paths', *Labyrinths*, New Directions, New York, 1964, p. 23.

'. . . we cannot examine dreams directly,
we can only speak of the memory of dreams'

Jorge Luis Borges

PART ONE

TRAVELLERS

IN THE EMBRACE OF DARKNESS

'Do you not know that a feast cannot be merry with fewer than four companions, and that women cannot be truly happy without men?'

THE CURTAIN RISES. Darkness, that furry old familiar of night, spreads itself on-stage. It means to stay, this sinuous, long-tailed night, moulting its woolly skin again and again, a thousand times if necessary. Or a thousand and one times – a safer measure of uneven infinity.

There are four figures in this night's embrace, two men and two women. One of them, a man, sits apart from the other three, kneeling behind a screen or a door. He holds a plaything in his hand, an ancient, blood-dripping sword. His back is straight and rigid with waiting. Though he is well armed, his wild eyes brim with fear. Who knows what unfathomable, magic-tainted visions he must sit through, what terrors of the night he must strike down before they unman him? This is Shahzaman, sometimes called Zaman, Sultan of Samarkand.

Of the remaining trio, two are on a low bed. Two, a man and a woman, Sultan Shahryar and his most recent bride, Shahrzad. Here too there is a sword, but this one seems a mere ornament. It is a grand, showy thing of gem-encrusted gold; and it lies on the floor, almost innocent, almost forgotten. Not far from this pointless spectacle is a modestly robed and veiled woman, Shahrzad's younger sister. She, Dunyazad, crouches monkey-like on the floor, waiting for her cue to ask a question, or exclaim piously, or gasp, or groan or sigh at the right times. Her eyes concentrate on Shahrzad, her words and gestures, on the whole scene – with the man, the woman and the bed – as if she will never let go of it.

The bed is a moist, rumpled mess of sweaty silk. Though the half-naked man on it is a fastidious king, he does not seem to have noticed the hint of slime and stickiness on his sheets. He is seated, propped up against pillows, this Sultan Shahryar, listening. His eyes are fixed on the talking woman, his new wife, Shahrzad. Her head is bare, her hair hangs unpinned and dishevelled down her back. Her hastily worn robe does not quite cover her damp neck, or the breasts with the fresh, red marks swelling on them. But her sultan does not see any of this though he is staring at Shahrzad as if ready to devour her. He is willing himself, this king with the lion's appetite, to *see* her words, flesh them out; draw strength from them once he has confirmed their trustworthiness.

Shahrzad, the woman who is talking for her life, does not look frightened. She must be though, how can she not be terrified? This could be her very last performance. Even now, dawn is making its way up the palace walls, considering the window where it must bare its sword-toothed yawn. The sultan may say this morning, or the next: 'That's enough storytelling! Off with her head!' Shahrzad does not betray her fear, but as night nears morning, she stoops now and then, lifts the hem of her robe and wipes the sweat on her neck and face. Or she throws back her neck, holds her goblet high and drinks deeply, eyes shut. What she does not swallow she holds for a moment or two, rolling the liquid in her mouth as if she is tasting it for the last time. Then she wets her lips with her tongue and begins again.

Dunyazad's lamp lights the room. Its small but stubborn

flame is a mirror that stalks the woman who is never still. It picks up her image and stretches it across floor and wall, a second Shahrzad, elastic, shadowy, massive; a matriarch of impressive proportions.

Shahrzad appears to be the only person in the world gifted with movement. The three other figures in the scene hold still as if bewitched into their waiting, listening postures. But Shahrzad, though solidly built – her breasts heavy domes, her legs palatial pillars – flows in one continuous glimmer of movement. Her words are not always elegant or apposite or even her own. But for the space of the night at least, all that is vital in this palace is here, in this sweating, exhausted, ambitious body. It is she who holds the scene together. If she stops, if she collapses, if she loses Shahryar's interest or attention, the roof could cave in, and with it, all hope of the city's deliverance, or its sultan's redemption. Sometimes, mid-sentence, Shahrzad pauses as if to take stock of her audience. Her eyes move from Dunyazad on the floor, crouched like a suppliant, to a half-naked, half-believing Shahryar on the bed, to the unseen Zaman, kneeling behind the door, his breath wheezing with impatience as he waits for her to finish. Shahrzad's eyes turn shrewd; she begins again.

*

This self-absorbed scene lives on, shamelessly immortal. It unfolds itself every night for a thousand and one nights. It could be the entire play itself, all of life compressed into a permanent entanglement – so self-contained does it seem, so complete its power over the players who make up its four limbs. But this scene is only the heart – though the hungry, searching heart – of a much larger body. The scene lives in the shade of a ragged, porous umbrella of a story, a wandering story, said to haunt travellers on the roads leading to paradise.

This story is propped up by a pair of upright, stallion-mounted brothers. Two pillars, tall, firm-backed, standing apart from everything around them. Each holds a kingdom at the crown. Each brother rules, not over mere cities and fields, but over his property. Not over men and women, but over his subjects.

When the story begins, the brothers have already enjoyed their royal status for twenty years. Since we are to know them so intimately for the next twenty or more, we look to the storyteller for clues to satisfy our curiosity about our heroes. There is, for instance, a father, 'a Sassanid king who lived in the lands of India and China' and who 'commanded armies, courtiers, followers and servants'. But it is not clear what role he played in his sons' lives except to provide their kingdoms when he died; his own for the elder son, Shahryar, and Samarkand for the younger son, Shahzaman. So the story-teller is vague about the father, and indeed about geographical location, beginning with the familiar all-encompassing realism-resisting formula, 'It is related – but Allah alone is wise and all-knowing . . .' As for the mother (or mothers), the storyteller is completely silent on the point. Surely even Shahryar and Shahzaman must have required the services of a mother before they mounted their steeds, snapped their fingers to summon waiting slaves?

The two brothers, when we meet them, are orphans. We also know they care for each other, because when the story begins, Shahryar, not having seen his younger brother for twenty years, feels 'a great longing' for his presence. It has taken him a while to notice that he misses Shahzaman. But when he does, he is quick to act. He summons his right arm and guardian angel – the wazir we will accompany on his hard and solitary journey as minister, father and upholder of the faith. Shahryar orders this wazir, his trusted chief minister, to travel to Samarkand immediately and invite Shahzaman to his city.

Till this turning point, a longing and an invitation that will alter the fate of many men and many more women, the brothers – our elusive storyteller tells us – are happy. They are happy in their legacy, the legacy to rule, having been taught to mount, steer, lord over, from the day they were born. They are renowned (particularly Shahryar) for their horsemanship, having sat on haughty white stallions before they learnt to walk. We know nothing of Shahzaman but his cleverness with a horse, and his rather ambitious name, shah-zaman, shah of time, ruler of the age. But the principal heir, Shahryar (shahr-yar, friend of the city, master of the city), is also reputed to govern his kingdom with such justice that all his subjects love him, such as the love of a subject is. So, two kings mounted on their thoroughbred horses, from that height surveying the world around them, dispensing what is right and wrong. Shahryar and Shahzaman must have become aware quite early in their lives of their entanglement with justice, and that they, with the advantage of height, could dispense it as they chose.

Between these two oases of justice lie unconquered deserts and wildernesses. Shahryar's wazir makes a dangerous journey to deliver the invitation that will reunite the brothers in more ways than they expect. We are not told if this is the same wazir who will one day be equally famed as minister and as father, but for our purposes his courageous journey may provide the clue. What are deserts and wildernesses to a man who has already fathered a martyr-in-the-making?

The wazir delivers the message of brotherly love and longing from the just king Shahryar. Shahzaman is properly overjoyed, and with alacrity appoints his wazir deputy ruler and sets out with 'tents, camels, mules, servants, retainers'. So much is the background, the necessary (if sketchy and moth-eaten) setting of our tale.

*

Shahzaman is in a camp a few miles from his city. The gates, closed for safety, are still in view, though somewhat diminished in size and grandeur by distance. Zaman wakes; and finds he cannot sleep again. He emerges from his tent and meets night. Zaman encounters the deepest part of night, the unadulterated splendour of moonless darkness. There is something about this velvety, cloud-textured universe that is not so easily escaped or domesticated; especially when a man is alone and naked, without the twin crutches of city and palace, under a vast, brooding sky. For a minute Zaman is overwhelmed by the size, the depth, the blackness of it all – this world which he has always believed wore his kingdom like a proud and substantial jewel. Zaman's throat is clogged by a little lump, just the size of an insignificant nut. He blinks, swallows with difficulty. His eyes water.

The storyteller turns sly here, as if suddenly sensitive to royal privacy. We are left to imagine why Zaman who commands 'servants and retainers' chooses to go back to his palace alone; or why he leaves the camp secretly; or why he enters the palace through an entrance known only to him, up to his rooms by a hidden staircase. There is some half-hearted mention of yet another gift for Shahryar, a gift conveniently forgotten in the palace. The storyteller would have us believe perhaps that Zaman, like any of the subjects he rules, would go fetch it himself. Or is the gift so valuable, so essentially private in nature, that only he can set eyes on it?

In that moonless darkness that so disturbs Zaman, he wakes up and his memory summons a great ruby that lights up in glaring crimson the unknown terrors of the night. He goes back, he *must* go back, to find the ruby himself, see for himself what this terror is that has woken him so rudely, dared to plant its seed of doubt in his royal heart. He must make the unknown known, tear it from the embracing arms of darkness.

His ardour for knowledge, a dusky, beckoning secret, is richly rewarded. In the heart of night, he finds his room. The pale gleaming body of his wife lies on his bed. Two muscular arms – though he can just about make out the ebony contour of one elbow – hold her in blissful sleep. A deeper shade of black flows into the room. A sword dangling limply wakes at the touch of a quick hand. It moves forward and pierces, slices all the flesh before him. Zaman's vision of the foul woman and the black slave is dying as a wet blanket spreads itself between his eyes and their locked embrace. Now he can see only blood, all of it an identical belligerent ruby red so he can't tell whose it is. Swiftly he wipes the sword on the bed and races back to the camp. He wakes up his men and orders them to set out immediately. Though his queen will probably wait patiently for him now, he is in a hurry to get to Shahryar's city.

Shahryar, hearing that Zaman is at his city gates, hastens to meet him in style. Feasts and other entertainments begin. But Zaman is pale and preoccupied. In answer to Shahryar's enquiries, he can only say, 'I am afflicted with a painful sore.' (The sore in one version of the story is black; in another a giant; but always a slave. And in all of them Zaman is struck by the fact that he is barely out of his city. What did the woman plan to do once he had actually left?)

Shahryar suggests a therapeutic hunt, but Zaman remains behind in the palace. Alone, he trails from room to room as if in search of something. Then he finds himself at a window overlooking the royal gardens. Zaman takes a deep breath and trains his hungry eagle eyes on the scene below.

It is day this time, but almost on order, a door opens, and not one but forty slaves, twenty women, twenty men, emerge. Zaman sees his brother's wife among the slaves, leading them to the fountain. She looks up and he retreats quickly, but even from behind the lattice screen he can see her undressing, then stretching out naked on the grass. All around her clothes pile up in satiny bushes, the whole world is shedding trousers, robes, veils. A naked circus cavorts before Zaman's eyes, its hungry, panting contortionists twisting themselves into imposs-ible shapes. Zaman watches. His face has turned bloodless, as if all their hands are round his neck, squeezing.

Though he is far above the garden Zaman can hear the queen's invitation to one of the slaves. Her call, 'Come, Masood,' must be a familiar one because he sees the man go to her promptly. As on a signal the others grope for each other, the remaining twenty women and nineteen men, though Zaman is not keeping count, smothered as he is by their grunting, saliva-dripping kisses. But then he pushes their sweaty bodies off him and his head clears. He is soaring now, relief has given him light wings and saved him. *He* is not the only one; in fact, his brother's wife is worse than his. He turns away from the window, feeling a sharp, healthy hunger. It is time to break his fast and enjoy his brother's hospitality.

Naturally Shahryar is surprised by this sudden return to health and good humour. But at first his questions draw out only the Samarkand part of the story. Zaman pauses, giving his brother time to let the images (and their implications) sink in. Shahryar is now alert. He can feel his body bracing itself to meet a blow, from an enemy he still cannot see though he can recognize the smell of its treachery. He listens to Zaman describing the orgy in his own garden in all its inflaming detail. Zaman hangs his head in sympathy. Shahryar is still officially a just king, a Friend of the City. He refuses to believe it till his own eyes have played witness; but the brothers feel very very close. Zaman, with his recent experience of clandestine operations, suggests that Shahryar pretend to go on another hunt, but actually conceal himself in the room with the view. The two brothers will then confirm together, inevitably, that women, even *their* wives, *their* noble queens, are tainted with untrustworthy desire.

Now it is Shahryar's agony which is in the limelight. Our storyteller tells us he is 'half demented' at the sight of his wife and slave women cuckolding him in his own garden with his own slaves. Unlike Zaman he does not draw his sword and drown the disgrace in blood. But that he is truly Zaman's brother is revealed by his proposal: that they renounce their royal state and roam the world till they meet another king who has been equally (or more) dishonoured.

The brothers travel far till they reach a seashore. While resting under a tree, they see the waves part and a huge black pillar thrust itself skyward. In terror they scramble up the tree and watch a gigantic jinni come to the shore with a chest, open it up and remove a box. The box in turn opens to reveal a fresh-faced girl rising like a pale and trembling moon. The jinni, her supernatural master, gazes at her with satisfaction, lays his head on her knees and falls asleep. The girl looks up and spies two pairs of awestruck eyes that barely blink, afraid they may miss something. So wide open and receptive are these eyes that they seem to have mastered, instantly, the entire language of gestures.

In the girl's look and moving hands they now read, 'Come down, he is asleep.' Then, 'Come down or I will wake him up.' Her mime is so effective that she gets immediate results. They slip down the tree trunk one after the other. Again she tells them without a word (and what signs these must have been, these unnamed gestures that issue a sexual invitation with the postscript of a threat) that if they do not sleep with her ('pierce her with their rapiers') she will wake the jinni.

She pulls her clothes deftly over her head without stirring a muscle below her waist. She arranges the clothes in a nest on the ground. Then she lifts her jinni's head, gently, gently, a ripe and bloated pumpkin that will fall to the ground and hurt itself if she is not careful. She smiles lovingly at the tranquil bald head gleaming on his new pillow. Then she turns to the brothers, spreads her legs.

The brothers still their trembling bodies and meekly take turns mounting her. It is a swift, silent business, a novel experience for both men in more ways than one. When she has had enough of them, she reaches for the jinni's sleeping head and her clothes. She removes a large purse from a pocket and pulls out a string weighed down with ninety-eight rings. She takes Shahryar's ring and Shahzaman's and adds them to her collection. The ravished brothers shudder. In this moment, in what appears to be a sudden rush of insight, they are convinced they can read a life in a face. They read the girl's story now, in the gloating face she wears as she looks down at the jinni, his head back on her knees. The jinni carried her away on her bridal night when she was still a virgin, but since then she has been unfaithful to her master a hundred times, always in his presence and without ever being caught.

What comfort to discover a shame larger than one's own! The brothers recover as if they have been fed a magic potion; what are they doing in this desolate witch-infested spot by the sea when a palace, a city, a whole kingdom waits for them? They turn back, their freshly polished pride crowning their heads again. Once in his palace, Shahryar has his wife, her women slaves and their black lovers killed. (He, unlike Zaman, retains his royal fastidiousness about messy blood and sticky hands.) Perhaps it is the same fastidiousness that dictates his new harem policy. Women (or wives, or queens) are necessary; celibacy never occurs to him. The ideal plan: find a fresh virgin every day; marry her for the night; in the morning, there are eunuchs, wazirs and executioners who will see to the dangerous woman whose desire has just been awakened.

The plan flowers into action. Brides enter the palace and

even before the inmates have learnt their names or faces, they are meat for the executioner's hungry axe. Shahryar does not know it, but he has ensured that his name will be inscribed in myth and history much longer than his palaces, monuments or his conquests.

*

Three years pass. The city thins; even loyal subjects may prefer flight to giving up their daughters. Shahryar's wazir is reduced (or so our storyteller would have us believe) to confiding in his daughter about the severe shortage of virgins in the city. Shahrzad, he must know, is an ideal candidate. He has named her well, shahr-zad, born of the city. Not only is this child of the city chaste but clever, ambitious and quick-tongued. The wazir tells Shahrzad a somewhat double-edged cautionary tale, almost confident that she will not take fright. Once she volunteers to be the bride – though she talks of being a saviour or a martyr, not of bridal delights or dreads – there is a chance that this bloodthirsty story will head towards a happier ending. At the end awaits salvation, and to get there Shahrzad must reconcile the sultan to the hard lot of men. With the help of her silent sister Dunyazad she must coax him to repent, and acknowledge that all women need not be killed. A thousand and one nights later it is all accomplished. When we part from them, the brothers are united with the sisters. The story ends on-stage. Off-stage it has just begun.

ON THE WAY TO PARADISE

'O, Shahrazad, this thousand and first night
is brighter for us than the day.'

THE DAY AFTER the thousand and one nights, two couples sit in a shady bower of the royal gardens. The palace looms behind them, a grim-faced chaperon who has seen much blood swept away but not shed any himself. The couples have, for the moment, taken refuge from the palace, its vast pompous halls, its forbidden rooms that hold fast the past. But even here, where they have escaped for an hour of peace and quiet, they can hear the rattling drums of the marketplace, the trumpets blaring in celebration everywhere in the city.

With an effort the couples shut out both palace and city. They turn inward towards each other, members of a secret society. They form two teams, children at a game of hide and seek; or seek and capture, a game of power. The team of two brothers versus the team of two sisters. But the teams exclude, dissolve, expand. Now it is a contest between siblings, now between couples. The brothers glow with reborn faith. Though it has bared its cruel fangs before, love has been rediscovered as wise, chaste, eloquent. It is capable of succour once again; of providing a well-deserved rest from the cares of ruling. The sisters, surprisingly, sit quietly, their hands clasped modestly on their laps. It would seem they need a sword, a sharpened axe before them – waiting – to loosen wits, tongue, memory.

'Shahrzad,' asks her sultan, Shahryar, 'where did all those stories come from? Shahzaman and I have read and studied more than you have. Certainly we have travelled more, seen marvels and lands and wickedness you can only imagine.'

She who the repentant sultan has crowned with the words chaste and tender, wise and eloquent, replies, 'I don't have a sword, so it seems I cannot rule. I cannot rule, I cannot travel, I don't care to weep. But I can dream.'

'Tell us,' say the brothers Shahryar and Shahzaman in chorus. 'Now tell us – of your own free will – your secret dreams, Shahrzad!'

Shahrzad smiles and shakes her head. 'My dreams? They're nothing – just a rubbishy pile of rough, uncut stones.' She turns to her sister, Dunyazad. Between them passes a swift, secretive look. 'Besides,' adds Shahrzad, darting a teasing look at Shahryar, 'only those locked up in hovels and dungeons and palaces can see and hear these dreams. Only those whose necks are naked and at risk can understand them.'

Though the sultan is persistent, Shahrzad, free from the fear of imminent death, is able to say: 'No, my king, no crude and fragmented dreams will mar this happy day of redemption.' And she falls silent. The time for storytelling is past. The saviour of the city, the sultan's redeemer, gets to her feet and walks back to the women's wing of the palace. The sultan and his brother watch the receding figure with admiration. Slaves, eunuchs and waiting girls greet her with devoted fervour as she walks past them to her chamber. But from a distance, from where Dunyazad sits, Shahrzad moves slowly, an odd mixture of grandeur and clumsiness, as if her feet have suddenly grown heavy. As if now that her arduous travels are over, she will be weighed down with her good works, her wandering feet firmly bound to the palace, to partake of its eternal delights.

*

The thousand and one nights are done. At the end of the play, a bloodthirsty drama in which swords pierce soft, yielding flesh, a happy conclusion is announced. The sultan, powerful, noble, deluded, has seen the light. He has been brought to his senses by a woman; and with, of all things, her stories; her ready tongue, her cleverness. In this abnormal climate where imagination – through the medium of the word – asserts its power over the bloodshedding sword, everyone forgives everyone.

A happy ending demands a celebration: a marriage would be ideal. Or an alliance – to seal the peace accord and ensure its validity. Though it is a new beginning for them, the sultan and his begum cannot marry each other again. (There are three children already, conceived, nurtured and delivered in official silence.) But we have the queen's sister and the king's brother, and they are not mere onlookers. These participants in the play, Shahzaman and Dunyazad, are drafted to provide the required marriage. Meanwhile the couple that have undergone a fiery trial sit in the background, ready with blessings. Their trusted minister, again an intimate connection, stands by, his face too wise to gloat, but lit all the same with a righteous triumph. The wazir's eyes take in the usual mundanities of a celebration – wine, meats, sweets, fruits. But he has seen to it that the pervading air is that of a religious festival. After all, they have just witnessed no less than the tussle between power and salvation.

The story – or stories – have been told; the immediate purpose achieved. Shahryar, through understated repentance, is back on the road to salvation. The team of redeemers, the wazir, Dunyazad and Shahrzad, get their rewards. The wazir's ministerial position is enviably secure, his position in court unrivalled. So is his unbending standard of morality. His flag of chastity flies proudly from the ramparts of his mansion. Dunyazad is married. Now it is her turn to taste the delicious nightly reward of flesh caressed. She can, while remaining chaste, give away her virginity, the burden that has been growing heavier by the hour as she waited outside the royal bedchamber night after night. And Shahrzad: she has gained martyrdom even before death. She has nothing to do now but enjoy the benefits of redemption.

Yet in some years, say fifteen, twenty, the news travels to Samarkand, to the recently widowed Dunyazad, that Shahrzad is now ready for her final reward: a martyr's tomb lovingly built and embellished by Shahryar.

*

The thousand and one nights are done, or so they tell her. Dunyazad carries those story-laden memories like festering wounds, not in some safe, reticent organ, but in a permanently deformed tongue weighed down by memory, memory laced with fantasy. The thousand and one nights have run their course, peace and prosperity reign like the gargoyle and griffin on either side of Shahryar's palace. Shahrzad, invincible warrior, terrifying sister, has weakened. Off the battlefield, she has died an ignominious death from petty bodily causes. A pure white marble monument is being built over the body that cheated the regal sword. Dunyazad, sister, heiress, amputated sorceress, waits in a magnificent palace, that man-made testament to power and grandeur. There is no end to her waiting, she sees, unless she lifts those pretty, useless feet and steps forward. Dunyazad, never far behind, seeks Shahrzad's new haunting grounds.

Dunyazad takes to travelling. She carries the weight of an unwritten history, the entire apparatus that unfolds accordion-like to reveal its shifting games of well-constructed lies. But on Shahrzad's trail, she can flaunt the resourcefulness of an intrepid explorer. She too can lead an expedition, sometimes more than one, every night to lands beyond seas and mountains – China, Africa, India. Dunyazad savours the names before they slip off her tongue. The names are charms at the head of vivid scenes, harbours, palaces, hovels, cluttered markets. They summon heroic deeds that can stretch puny forms to a dazzling breadth of endurance. Or they conjure the evil form, changeable, now small enough to lie dormant in a lamp, now as insubstantial and deadly as a smoky vapour that cuts off oxygen. Whatever its size and shape, evil stuns the curious eye with its brilliance; its kinship with magic; its truck with desire without limits.

Years ago she, like her famous sister, learnt to be an effortless traveller, a traveller who can set off at a moment's notice, unburdened by anything less portable than imagination. It helped that their tastes were not yet fastidious. At the outset of their joint career they could hardly be expected to be discriminating. Any road was acceptable, any sea; mount and vessel were chosen in a hurry, choices sometimes made blindfolded. Navigation was spontaneous, haphazard. Chance was a constant, respected member of the crew. The object was to go, go out of the bedchamber in the dungeons. Levitate above the earthbound palace with its dark heart where ticked a sharpened sword.

But the journey before Dunyazad now is more frightening. Not just because she is alone till she finds Shahrzad or her ghost, but because all impending journeys are curiously subterranean. No map exists for the ridiculously small, dark space she has to travel within, a dingy mildewed dungeon which once housed a marriage bed. There are iron chains here, iron bracelets from which prisoners were hung and tortured. The veteran traveller, sister of the famous and glib explorer, stands now on the border of a new country. She has sighted the land that lies so alarmingly close to home, and amazingly, she sees that it is a place which no one has entered, conquered, then returned unmarked.

On these travels, Dunyazad follows, with the wisdom of hindsight, the many routes a virgin can take to martyrdom. She learns what it is to be Shahrzad's descendant; to be Shahrzad's sister, her trusted maid and accomplice, her most passionate lover. And Shahrzad too is travelling again in uncharted territories, the kind she likes best. Though she remains invisible to the naked eye, she can be stalked; Dunyazad, that loving spy, walks in her footsteps. At the tail end of this caravan of a thousand and one camels is a third woman, the youngest of the trio. This woman, as yet unknown to the royal sisters, has the strange notion that she is the natural companion, or descendant, of Dunyazad. She follows far behind, a sunstruck traveller in an alien desert. Like her illustrious forebears, she is given to dreaming; fabricating concoctions of travellers, virgins, martyrs. The powerless must have a dream or two, dreams that break walls, dreams that go through walls as if *they* are powerless.

The caravan inches forward over the years. Women, dreams and stories are transported from India to Persia to Arabia to France to England and back to India. Looming over them all is a shape-shifting woman, a woman with many names. Her father saw – prophetically – that her fate was tied up with her city's well-being. He called her the cityborn, Shahrzad. But there are other names that attach themselves to this storywoman. There is, for instance, the exotic Scheherazade, a name that means nothing more than pretty tinsel in a child's treasure chest. But this name, unpacked and reconstructed by men across the seas, is persistent. Sometimes it is coupled with the rumour that Shahrzad was beautiful; or that she was simple-minded; or that she told innocuous bedtime stories dressed in fabulous clothes.

But Shahrzad, like her own story, is a survivor. The travelling tale undergoes a change of costume, language and setting at each serai on its way. It adapts itself to local conditions, to this century or that, a permanent fugitive from its officious parent, legitimate history. And Shahrzad – she too has learnt the lessons of the tales she told. She is now a myth that must be sought in many places, fleshed in different bodies, before her dreams let go of Dunyazad or her descendants.

KNOTS IN THE
AFTERLIFE

'When I am received by the King, I shall send for you. Then,
when the king has finished his act with me, you must say:
"Tell me, my sister, some tale of marvel to beguile the night."
Then I will tell you a tale which, if Allah wills, shall be the
means of our deliverance.'

1

It is mid-afternoon. The city is in the clutches of a dream. The columns of marble and slabs of grey stone reflect the glare; their edges blur into sunlight. From this distance the city is nameless. Or its hushed, remote appearance, its muted suggestion of opulence and ruin, beauty and decay, conjure a range of identities. Samarkand, Basra, Isfahan. A city that can, if it desires, elude the moorings of dates and milestones. Alexandria, Ctesiphon, Baghdad. It is difficult to pin a single name on to it, locate this mirage-city on a coded map. The eyes must be shut, its jaded vision shed, to colour the physical features of a city which stands on the ancient, shifting soils of history. To define the limits of its ruins, not venerated but lived in.

Towards this city dreaming in the embrace of the afternoon sun moves a modest train of camels, mules and horses. Though the caravan has slowed down since the city has come into view, the animals' hooves still raise dust like devious gusts of wind. The city is only a few miles down the road. But it is hard, from this vantage point, to hold still its trembling image on the dusty horizon. To say, 'There it is at last – the city of beautiful palaces and tombs where fame, honour, love and memory are solidified in stone and marble. The journey is over.'

For the travellers on the backs of camels and horses, or within the tents of the caravan, only the swirls of dust seem alive and capable of movement. Every now and then, strips of sand rise from the ground, whimsical jinn who hide and reveal in turn, road, domes, minarets.

The sun retreats behind a cloud for a moment. Suddenly the dust is more dense. One sheet takes to the air decisively, and wraps itself round the walls of the city like a fantastic serpent whose intentions are clearly malevolent. It extends its hood to the city gates. When the sun emerges, the scene is again suffused with white light. The insubstantial serpent dissipates. The city gates melt back into view.

The travellers move towards one of the gates of the legendary city, showpiece of wealth and high culture, pillar of the surrounding countryside that works hard to sustain it. The kingdom needs this nucleus and the fantasies it breeds, both beneficent and otherwise. Though tens of centuries may go by, though this city be reduced to rubble and a successor and yet another be built in a distant place, its grand design, of honour and chastity – and power – will never be left behind.

So close to its gates, even this mythical city demands a name. The travellers choose Shahabad. In the close-up view of the city and its earthbound reality, it is possible to discount the hallucinatory aura that haunted the earlier view from down the road. The hint of the aberrant, the mystery of the unknown, are now – with an equal measure of relief and disappointment – ascribed to an unruly imagination. Now the view includes the narrow winding gullies of the bazaars, the grey pockmarked walls of the old hammam, and the only too familiar cobbled streets and partially hidden gardens of the richer quarter. Already visible is the heart of the city, the palace round which it is built. Or at least its upper storey windows can be seen, narrow vertical slits that wink in the sunlight. The grey domes above balloon dourly over the city. At this range, neither dust, sunlight, nor the safety of distance – a long-range perspective – can wish the structure away. It sits there, squat, worn, splendid, a memory that will not go away despite years of neglect.

The city is still silent. But in this smaller frame enclosing the party of travellers, there is an occasional creak of wheels, the padding of spongy camel's hooves, the impatient neigh of a thirsty horse. The animals instinctively come to a halt at their usual resting spot, the serai outside the wall-flanked gates. They head towards a tank of murky water.

A man on horseback turns his animal around and rides up to the tent on the camel cart. In the camel cart, holding the tent's flaps open, stands a figure. He is smooth-shaven and his turban covers all of his hair and part of his forehead. His features are a shade too large for his long bony face. The effect is of a reticent but hard man; the kind who is not easily given to complaint, but who also does not forget his grudges, storing them up. On the other hand, his eyes, set rather close to each other, give him a surprisingly womanish look, the sharp, experienced look of a middle-aged woman.

His dark, well-shaped eyebrows meet in a frown now as he considers his fellow travellers and the city before him. The man on horseback asks him, 'Shall we stop? The animals are tired and thirsty.'

A silence follows. The traveller in the cart moves his hand and lets it rest on the short scimitar tucked into the sash of his robe. Then the man on horseback hears the imperious command softened by a husky voice: 'No. Move on. We must get there before the afternoon siesta is over.'

The traveller stands there a little longer, holding the tent flaps open, as if to ensure that the reluctant animals and their masters do not linger outside the gates. The man on horseback speaks to the city guards in a low voice; the gates swing open.

The visitors' train enters the city. It takes a winding route on the last lap of its journey, along rough, sandy backstreets. Though the route is longer, its purpose is served. Scarcely anyone other than a few ragged children, a blind beggar and a porter nodding off on the job notice the party unwilling to draw attention to themselves. In a city where the sun beats down with its all-seeing glare, its people have learnt to cover themselves in thin, loose robes, tents in the shade of which grow many damp secrets.

The flap of the tent on the camel cart is fastened. The tent seems empty. Even the animals sense the need for swiftness and secrecy. Not a neigh or grunt is heard from the burdened beasts; nor a single whip raised by their masters. Hooves are muffled by sand; the most sluggish mule treads the common trail meekly.

At the palace gates, the guards are waiting, their eyes scanning the curve of the over-lit road. The gates swing open like a miracle, completely noiseless, and a hooded, rotund figure detaches herself from the group of strong-limbed guards. Her face is veiled, but from her walk, the torso and padded hips jerking from side to side like a fat pendulum, it is apparent that she is not a young woman.

The camel cart with the tent is suddenly surrounded. For

the next few minutes, the entrance of the tent is not visible. As if by accident, the bodies of the guards and fellow travellers make a human wall around the tent as they unload the mules, camels, horses. Through the chinks in this wall, through a fleeting gap between a moving arm and a bending back, there is a brief glimpse of the traveller on the camel cart. He alights, is met by the veiled fat woman, and he follows her into the palace. They disappear into the building so quickly that it may well be an illusion, or a trick of the afternoon light, because when the wall of men falls away, and the animals stretch and grunt and neigh impatiently now that their stables await them round the corner, the camel cart is empty. Only the tent sits on it, its hanging flap waving innocently.

Inside the palace, the two walk quietly, the traveller following the veiled woman. Her hips jerk crazily from side to side as she hurries down vast carpeted halls. So close behind her, the traveller feels a touch of dizziness at the sight of this relentless see-sawing motion. Once they are in the long windowless corridor that divides the palace into men's wing and women's wing, the woman stops. They have been walking so fast that the traveller now bumps into her. He puts out an arm to steady the breathless woman who has turned to face him. The woman pulls back her veil in a swift movement and looks into the traveller's face eagerly.

'Sabiha?' the traveller asks. She nods. Her hand moves to his face.

'You've changed,' she says with a wondering surprise. 'There is something new about your face. Almost as if—' and she breaks off, looks around.

He does not ask her what the something is. 'Which room are you taking me to?' he enquires instead.

Sabiha looks at him, her shrewd beady eyes veiled for a moment with compassion. 'Not any of the old ones,' she replies. 'Come, you must be very tired. Please follow me.'

The two walk on, the man following the woman up a narrow winding flight of stone steps. They climb till they reach the highest floor of the palace. Sabiha leads the man to a corner room, far to the left. The two slip in like shadows and the door shuts behind them.

The man looks around to place the room he is in. It is large, and where it meets windows, closets, an adjoining little passage, arches edged with elaborate carving turn stone into delicate filigreed borders. High up a wall, a small window frames a minuscule portion of sky and spires, a remembrance of the world left behind once in the palace grounds. The room has one more window, large and elegant, overlooking a private palace garden, a formal one with a fountain gushing out of its belly. From the window, the pool into which the fountain empties itself is a circle of glimmering movement. Its glitter seems deceitful, as if it calls attention to its surface only to camouflage what lies underneath.

The traveller moves away from the window and turns to a long mirror on the wall across. The fat woman, Sabiha, pants, perhaps from unaccustomed exertion, as she lays a hand on the man's dusty turban and begins to unwind it. The hair spills out, a basket of coiled snakes suddenly turned upside-down. Released from its binding turban, the traveller's hair hangs down to his waist, flattened and matted. Fine strands of grey thread in like silk into the dull, coarse black. Sabiha lifts this hair, unhooks and unties the man's robe. The robe falls to the floor where the turban already lies uncoiled. Sabiha peels off the damp, long silk shirt next to his skin.

The man is like a dummy in her hands. The decisive navigator of caravans, the imperious commander of journeys in the desert, is gone. Hair unbound, the traveller has exchanged one face for another. The naked neck and shoulders belong to this new face; as does the body below, now being divested of its last layer of clothing, a thick bandage of cloth tied tightly round the chest.

The traveller is now a woman. She has long matted hair, drooping, pear-like breasts and pale smooth thighs. She sits on a low sofa. Sabiha disappears behind a screen and comes back with a basin of cool, fragrant water and wads of soft cotton and cloth. She begins to wipe the woman's face, the sandy crust around her eyes, nose and ears. Then she discards the dirty cloth and picks up a fresh wad as she moves below the neck.

The silent woman – till so recently a man – considers her revealed body with detachment. Her face is unreadable as she watches it being wiped, scrubbed and perfumed. As a man, she was impressive, though smallish and smooth-chinned. The tight knot of her turban, the eyebrows meeting in a frown, the hand resting with deliberate casualness on the scimitar at her belt: the overwhelming impression was a sense of control. Now with her breasts unbound, her hair freed of grime and knots with a wet comb, her allegiance is to a lesser-known species. She is unfettered, naked as she is. But without the dissembling crutch of masculinity, she has slipped into a world where speculation is the mother tongue. Where story and myth and legend pinion her body with their overturned bowls of flesh.

Sabiha has left, taking away the traveller's robes. The desert sand and grit – and any other detritus of the journey – are also gone with the basinful of dirt-choked cloth. The visitor remains behind in the room. She is dressed like an ageing princess. She stands up, walks slowly to the window with a stiff self-consciousness. After an all too brief respite, her body is trying out once more the posture of a regal bearing, this time in a woman's guise. Dunyazad, weighed down with hips, breasts, walks to the window like a brand new mother careful of her wards, vulnerable flesh and blood.

2

She mouths her name softly, as if to remind herself that it is she who has accomplished the sandy journey to the old palace. Dunyazad, she whispers.

Dunya-zad, born of the world. The Queen Mother of Samarkand, widow of Sultan Shahzaman. Dunyazad, sister and accomplice of Shahrzad of the sinuous tales. Once she waited on the couple hidden in the damp folds of their marriage bed. She was the audience, the prompter, the chorus, the heckler. Together she and Shahrzad womaned that puppet creature in its fabulous robe that went so very near the sultan's sword; that touched its pointed tip and survived to vanquish him.

Now she is back in Shahabad, in the palace where her sister proved her mettle as a warrior. She is back though the battle is over. She is back, perhaps, because the battle is not over.

Dunyazad looks around the room. Fat Sabiha is right. The room is not one of the old ones. There is something open-faced and bland about this room; it is too well-lit to hold secrets. Dunyazad walks around, picks up ornamental trifles, feels silken sheets and carpets like an assessor. She moves to a closet, draws aside the flimsy curtain that covers the brick shelves built into the wall. She runs her fingers across the folded clothes kept there. White muslin, silk, lamb and camel wool. The textures are familiar, but the clothes are not. All these robes and veils – she can't remember wearing any of them in those days, nor does she recall seeing them on Shahrzad. Dunyazad suddenly pulls back her arm. Her fingers tingle. The room, the palace, her return to Shahabad: what can she be thinking of, stroking clothes in cupboards when she has returned for a less nostalgic purpose?

She moves to the window, sits, and tells herself: Plan now. Think. But the needs of the present refuse to come forward and take charge. Instead she considers the two figures she can see from the window. They are, inexplicably, pacing up and down the other side of the watery curtain made by the fountain. The two are very young women. Girls really, though one seems to carry herself like someone older. The young women, Shahrzad and Dunyazad, are walking up and down, reciting at each other in rehearsal for a play.

Dunyazad hears a knocking at the door; a discreet cue has arrived from the wings of the stage. She does not turn away from the window, but calls over her shoulder, 'Enter!' Sabiha waddles in, wiping her sweaty face with her veil. Dunyazad watches her silently, waiting for her to catch her breath.

When she speaks, her voice is hoarse and rasping as if it is permanently starved for fresh air. 'Princess,' she begins, in a tone of such tender affection that Dunyazad feels she is young again. Perhaps she will always be a girl in this palace, wonder-struck and frightened in turn.

She pushes the thought away and turns to the business at hand. 'Sabiha,' she says, 'what is the matter with you? Your face is grey and swollen, and your voice – you can hardly talk! Sit down. Go on, sit,' and she waves impatiently at a plump brocaded cushion when she sees the woman's hesitation.

Sabiha groans softly as she lowers her ample frame to the

floor. Dunyazad looks searchingly into her face. 'Your name came back to me the moment I saw your face, but – you were the nursemaid, weren't you?' she asks, wondering at this new dimension of memory. Beneath its taunts with the unforgettable, it has this sieve-like frailty like any other living creature. 'You looked after the children when—' and Dunyazad pauses, not sure if she can acknowledge aloud those days and their unnameable nights.

Sabiha, unexpectedly, smiles with pure pleasure. For her those days were the best years of her life, spent as warden of the royal begum's children, offspring of a martyr-in-the-making, even a possible saviour. 'Yes,' she says and sighs. 'But the palace has not needed a nursemaid for many years. Such a noble mansion, so many rooms and people, but no children!' She wipes her eyes with her dirty veil, remembering the premature death of two of her royal charges; the estrangement of the lone survivor; and the sultan's lack of progeny despite a well-worn marriage bed.

Dunyazad feels impatience return to her. She can barely remember her dead nephew and niece. As for the surviving one, Prince Umar, her only interest in him is that Shahrzad must have loved him. Or she hopes her sister did, a little better and more generously than Dunyazad does her own son, an imbecile who requires constant watching.

She paces up and down the floor. She wants to interrupt Sabiha's nostalgic fit which has rapidly deteriorated into whining, but she does not know where to begin. She steels herself, comes to a halt, and suddenly drops to her knees in front of Sabiha. 'What happened?' she whispers, her voice as hoarse as Sabiha's now, 'how did my sister die?'

The woman's mouth shuts like a trap. In her eyes Dunya-zad sees the stirring of fear – a trembling half-formed thing, a spluttering flame she has not come face to face with for many years. Sabiha's sudden silence and the accompanying look of shifty terror wakens her suspicion, a suspicion she has barely articulated to herself yet.

Suddenly she is enraged. Her unbending stepson, the ruler of Samarkand, will be displeased when he discovers that she who groomed him for the throne has made this unsanctioned journey to Shahabad. She has forced herself to approach this palace again, lay herself open to its infection of memory, and is she to be foiled at the very beginning of her mission?

'Tell me,' Dunyazad snaps now, 'tell me what you know.' It seems natural to assume that no one in the palace knows the whole truth, save one perhaps. Already she is remember-ing and using fluently the language of the besieged palace.

'She suddenly took ill,' murmurs Sabiha. 'It was all over before we knew what was happening.' She is sweating again as she heaves herself to her feet. Dunyazad does not stop her. She is considering this series of overlapping images: a drooping Shahrzad, a swift raging fever, the rapid onset of delirium, then silence. That face with the wandering eyes and restless, mobile muscles still as marble.

'Did – did you see her after—' but Sabiha does not let her stammer her way to the end of her question.

'No, it was too sudden and I was sick.' She seems now to remember how painful it is for her to breathe. 'Malika—' she brings out with difficulty. 'My lady,' she repeats herself, 'I must go. My days are numbered. I came up to tell you that the sultan is sending one of his favourite slaves to wait on you.

She will be here soon, and you can send him a message through her.'

Sabiha recites these words like a parrot that has memorized its lesson. She bends and kisses the floor before Dunyazad formally, in a manner quite different from the earlier tenderness and voluble excitement. Dunyazad lets her go. What is the use of pressing her? She is only a sick old woman, probably deaf and senile. Yet – yet – the nostalgia, the fear, the shrewd knowing look accompanying the stiff little speech – pile up like disconnected clues, though Dunyazad cannot see, or acknowledge, what the mystery is about.

*

Alone in her room, Dunyazad paces up and down, a movement that prods memory. She has paced like this before in this palace, in its rooms, terraces and gardens, a simmering volcano trapped in a small, artificial lake. She holds back this train of thought. She of all people should know the pain-tipped pleasure of anticipation, what it is to whet the appetite all day, wait for the sun to set, prepare to do justice to the orgy of delicacies that night.

Dunyazad pauses. It is not anticipation that fills her, but fear. This fear is something diffuse and cloudy; it is not possible to mourn for Shahrzad in this room. It betrays no sign of her having been here. What must she do to find her? Change windows, wander from one room of the palace to another, slip down, down till she is in the bedchamber in the dungeons? And when she finally finds her, when Dunyazad, her sister's tremulous shadow, embraces Shahrzad, the distance between Shahabad and Samarkand will shrink in that instant for ever. The distance – a winding, dusty road of memories, lovers and husbands, sister, fellow warrior – will fall dead on their old, common battleground.

Suddenly Dunyazad hears a clear, peremptory knock on the door, and before she can recover herself, call out, the door opens slyly. She sees a slavegirl standing there, bending low. The bent head says, 'A message from the sultan, Malika. Will you see him tonight?'

Dunyazad pauses, uncertain, but the slavegirl has meanwhile raised her head. Dunyazad shrinks back a little. The girl has a large date-shaped mark to the right side of her mouth. It is coated with a dark brown fur, sleek and glistening, unlike the dull mass of black hair on her head. Dunyazad remembers her regal training, resists the urge to snap at the girl, Get out! I can't bear to look at a face like that! Instead she smiles carefully, covering up confusion and guilt with kindness. 'What is your name, child?' she asks, realizing even as she moves towards her that the stranger is no child despite the slight, girlish body.

The girl's face changes. She looks cunning, a wily woman older than her body, or an ageless witch. She considers Dunyazad as if she has been asked to part with a secret. 'Dilshad,' she finally says. Dunyazad is struck by the irony of the name. This insolent slavegirl, with a boyish body even thinner than her own, and the disfiguring mark of a beast on her face, is called Happy Heart! Perhaps the girl is lying, but why should she?

Dunyazad turns away from her to think out her answer. Should she meet Shahryar so soon? Or should she familiarize herself with the palace again, its old and new secrets waiting to be discovered?

With a word she can accelerate the pace of her mission. Shahryar is waiting for her. The sultan Shahryar, ruler of Shahabad. Lord of this palace, its dome-shaded terraces, arch-windowed upper rooms, its hidden dungeons. Shahryar, lord of Shahrzad. The widower Shahryar, her brother-in-law, awaits her in the neutral strip between the men's wing and women's wing, the hall of song and dance. He will, perhaps, have sent the singing girls away; the drummer and the tambourine man may have found their way to the girls in the servants' hall of the palace, entertaining themselves for a change.

Dunyazad could go down the stairs, dressed like a dignified widow, a pious middle-aged woman. She will meet Shahryar in the silent gallery built to amplify every whispered grief, every drumbeat of the heart. Perhaps they will – in the shock of seeing each other's faces – move towards each other, towards an embrace. Behind his shoulders she will see Zaman on one side. Shahzaman, the sultan best known for his campaign against night and its dark terrors; Shahzaman, her old enemy and lover, now bone stripped of flesh in his modest and neglected tomb in Samarkand. By the side of this skeleton parading as flesh-and-blood memory hovers her sister, not as she was when they lived and plotted together, but as she must have been when she died. Will her eyes be open and staring with fear? And those eloquent lips – do they part in pain or desire?

Dunyazad draws in her breath sharply and her face flushes,

perhaps with shame. She hears her stepson or her own father, the wazir – the voices that ring in her head every time she reprimands herself. 'This is grief, life and death, no drama concocted for an idle woman's entertainment!'

She can feel the slave's eyes on her back. She turns around abruptly and catches her in the act of an open stare. The look that she intercepts is so coolly speculative that she is, for a moment, completely unnerved. She can't have this freakish woman waiting on her, shadowing her fearlessly, dogging her every move with unashamed curiosity! She blurts out on an impulse: 'I will wait on the sultan soon – not tonight – but as soon as I have recovered from my journey.' She is composing a brief apology as well, something that will be dignified and not too cringing; words that will not reveal anything of herself, either her newly stirred fears or the depths of her grief.

But Dilshad interrupts her: 'The sultan is going on a hunt tomorrow. If you don't see him tonight, you will have to wait for several days . . .' Dunyazad looks at her sharply, and the girl adds almost as an afterthought, 'Malika.'

'I will wait then,' Dunyazad says in a decided voice. 'And, oh – convey my deepest respects and heartfelt condolences to the sultan.' She stops – there is so much to say, but now, and through this stranger? But Dilshad is smiling at her. The smile has transformed her face so that she looks friendly and pleasant, almost attractive. Her eyes though seem to tease Dunyazad as she kisses the ground before her and says, 'I will deliver your message now, then wait for your word – whenever you need me.'

3

Dunyazad lies in a strange bed waiting for sleep. To lie waiting in a bed which is not her own – she has done this before, though it was many years ago. Her body then seemed to have been made for waiting; young and impatient, but condemned to wait. Now when her body no longer evokes desire, she knows how to wait. She has learnt deviousness during the time of peace.

Dunyazad sleeps. The palace is silent, but it sleeps like a guard dog – or a eunuch – with eyes open. When all the lamps are put out, every door securely fastened, one of its long, shadowy arms stretches and glides forward. In the dead of night, the presiding spirit of the palace sleepwalks its way up the stairs, up, up into Dunyazad's room.

The arm floats in through the door and comes to rest by her bed. A hand with long thin fingers reaches out; strokes her hair secretively.

She does not stir. In her sleep she is slipping into a tunnel lined with interminable steps. A querulous whooshing sound echoes round and round down the length of the tunnel; she has stepped into the centre of a trapped storm. She bends her head, thrusts herself forward into this desert wind that has wandered into the wrong place.

It is so dark that she is unable to say whether the steps lead up or down. But she can feel the tightness in her knees from constant bending as she climbs five hundred steps, then down another five hundred. All along the sound of the wind grows till it is a raging monster that wails and roars in turn, angered by its imprisonment. Her ears ring with the unfathomable words of this companion with two equally repugnant voices.

She is at the end of the tunnel now, and before her stands a vast iron door. Though she does not know where it will lead, she must open it. Travellers in the desert see a mirage when there is no oasis in sight. She moves back a step, gathers all her panting strength, falls against the door. It gives way with a terrible clanging protest.

Before her eyes can register what lies beyond, she takes a very deep breath, a breath full of silence. Behind her the tunnel melts away. Then she finds herself standing in a palace; a palace so still, so palpably silent that its only occupants seem to be tombs, tombs full of air that has lost its tongue.

In the large, desolate hall where she now stands, there is a throne of black stone. She is drawn to it because it is the only dark, restful spot in the room which is a mass of glittering white marble. She shades her eyes with a hand and goes to the throne. She sees an inscription shining in blood-red letters on the wall above the throne:

> Rest, O traveller, on this seat of stone.
> Take comfort in its hard, homely skin,
> its rough and friendly touch.
> Leave your heart in its care, O traveller!
> For down these passages
> lurks that old spellbinder,
> the fiend of the flowing waters.

Dunyazad, a woman given to caution, trained to be alert to the mysteries hidden in words, goes through this inscription carefully. She considers each ruby-tinged word, its solemn, almost dispassionate invitation to part with her heart. And where is the heart that can be given away at will, whole and intact, for safekeeping?

She turns away from the black throne with a shrug. So close to the promised flowing waters, to the passages that lead to the fiend of fiends, it is impossible to take precautions. Can you stand on the edge of a cliff or on the outskirts of the desert and say, 'I will take the plunge into life, but gently; there are bodies, bodies which house hearts and souls, that may be hurt?'

She is impatient now, no longer willing to float and drift about on marble floors. Her feet are shod for a more rough terrain and they move briskly to one end of the hall, her footsteps loud, clear and regular. The passage is not unlike the tunnel she travelled so recently; except this is quiet, ominously quiet.

She sees many doorways, passes entrances to chambers as she walks down the meandering passage. But she does not stop till she reaches an alcove where a dull silvery glow hangs like a lantern at the door. She stops here and gazes at the door, taking stock of her opponent. As she had suspected, there is an inscription here too. But this is in graceful gold-hued calligraphy, and it is a brief question: 'What,' it asks with elegant flower-bedecked swirls, 'is the power of love?'

She feels a tremor then, and before it can overcome her, she pushes the door open. She goes in.

Around her she sees the riches of a kingdom. But these

gems, these silks, gold, pearls, camels and magical stallions are unlike anything she has seen before. They are as alive as she is, but they are cunningly inlaid on the floor so that she sees before her a spread of marble, veined with everything precious. A sheet of living gems from one end of the room to the other, a sheet that lilts with a subtle, rhythmic movement, like a carpet of flowing water.

She hesitates, but it is now too late for doubt or safety. And she has also seen a small rectangle in the centre of the room, an island of stillness in the chamber of flowing waters.

She takes a tentative step forward. Before she can determine her next move, identify the shortest route to the island, she is swept away by a surprisingly strong current. She thrashes about, then swims. When no longer able to keep up the struggle, she floats. I am not wet, she tells herself over and over again like a charm. It is all a vision – nothing but a vision and a dream.

But when she is thrown ashore on the long hard earth of the island, she has to lie there for a while, eyes shut, gasping for breath. She can feel the smooth, dry marble on her cheek and hands. Her right foot stings. It feels wet and sticky as if it is bleeding. She stretches the foot and it comes to her in a flash that it is not blood she feels but a tablet of China steel, the kind found on tombs.

She pulls herself up with a start, looks around wildly as if she has just woken up and remembered everything, and calls, 'Shahryar!' Her voice is shrill, girlish. Unlike her waking tone, there is a touch of hysteria to this frightened call, as if she expects no response.

Dunyazad crawls on the tomb till she reaches the tablet.

She reads the words: 'Here lies Shahrzad, Beloved Consort of Sultan Shahryar, Daughter of the Chief Wazir to the Sultan of Shahabad, Mother of Prince Umar and the departed Prince Jaffar.' Dunyazad sees her grief, a menacing wave swelling and rising. It will crash down on her any minute now, but like an imbecile she is feverishly searching the tablet for her own name. She searches not only with her eyes, but with her fingers, which trace the letters as a groping, blind person would. At the very instant she realizes the search is futile, that there is not even an incomplete phrase beginning 'Shahrzad, sister of,' she sees the wave come down on her. She hears herself scream as she rises to meet it.

4

When Dunyazad opens her eyes the next morning it is barely dawn. That swelling orb setting the sky alight – how repetitious it is, this desire to chant the same words of hope, the same words in praise of faith! Yet looking at the view from the small upper window – all sky if a few stubborn domes are deliberately blurred in the lower end of the frame – Dunyazad feels a single-minded fervour warm her, a fervour that reminds her of the wazir. She remembers her last visit to Shahabad, the only one since her marriage to Shahzaman. She sees the wazir in his deathbed, surrounded by religious leaders, admirers, citizens. It is an auspicious death, accompanied by the recitation of holy, blessed chants. People gather, ordinary men and women too, to see a good death and be enlightened. In the bed is the man who has lived a long, full life, a man who has weighed the odds and chosen the wise path. A man, thinks Dunyazad, who gambled and won.

The room fills up. It is stifling inside and everyone is sweating, breathing hard, just as the wazir is. His rasping breath stops for a few seconds, there is a horrible retching rattle as if he is choking on phlegm. Then the whistling and panting begin again on a softer note. Dunyazad moves to the door. She hears, on her way, a girlish wail rise shrilly, then sink to the floor. An old woman bent double picks it up and flings it to the waiting air. 'Look your fill, sisters!' she calls out. Her voice draws a thin sharp line down their hearts. 'He hardened his father's heart and saved our daughters and granddaughters. All we can do is wail and beat our breasts. But look at him – don't you see he is on his way to paradise?'

*

The door shuts on Dunyazad but she hovers outside like an inquisitive kitchen girl. She strains her ears to catch every word, both voices. She hears her father first. He is saying to Shahrzad: 'This is a dangerous mission, my daughter!' Dunyazad knows his narrow eyes bore holes into her sister's face with their intensity. And having warned her, signalled his love in the only way he knows, he goes on quickly: 'Have you made up your mind? Do you have to go to the palace tomorrow?'

Now the wazir is examining his pupil's face from behind his solid ministerial armour. He is considering this unexpected discovery he made not too long ago, a promising pupil from the women's wing. He has trained and nurtured her till she has crossed over to firm ground, exiled herself from the shifting, unreliable sea of a feminine enclosure. Today he waits for Shahrzad to have the last word. He waits for her to pay him her pupil's fees in full measure.

'Yes, Father,' says Shahrzad. 'I must go. Nothing can change that, I know.'

The wazir nods, turns his head away. But first he lifts her hand to his cheek and lets it rest there for a moment. 'I will see to the arrangements,' he tells her, his voice curt and businesslike. The wazir leaves for the palace; the sultan must be told right away. On the way he must see to a significant detail himself. There are many shroud-makers in the city, but he has to find someone to make the most dignified, elegant shroud Shahabad has ever seen, a shroud fit for martyrs.

*

Dunyazad shuts her eyes. The wazir's body has been bathed in cold camphor-laced water and gently packed in five pieces of white cotton, the shroud that has come from the palace as a token of royal favour. The shroud carries the wazir away. Dunyazad can no longer hold in view the limp bundle of her father heavy on other men's shoulders. Instead she sees two girls sitting together, not facing each other but the open expanse looming before their terrace. Two girls, Shahrzad and Dunyazad, look intently into this womb of possibilities. The sky is all but dark. Somewhere in the distance, a thin strip of red slits the heavens with a knife-wound. The gash is a slim bracelet of pink and vermilion beads. Two virgins examine this hint of blood in the darkness before them and see their bridal nights. When they speak, it is not of those amorous games they have sensed, the results of which they have seen in the heaving childbed of the women's wing. Instead they ask each other: What does a martyr look like?

This is a new game they have made up, a simple but useful entertainment. They can use a range of props and costumes – pearl-bordered veils, riotous fields of flowers or a dagger like an elongated star – all to be had for the asking since most of them are imaginary. All they need to play is the desire to be a heroine. The sisters have a few cousins and friends who may have played the game well, but many of them are under lock and key in their own homes, their fathers having publicly denied their virginity. Others have been smuggled out of Shahabad.

The game is called The Martyr's Walk and each player describes herself as she makes her way to the blade-holding hand that waits for her. Minor variations are allowed. Sometimes the waiting doom is to be dealt out by a hunter; sometimes an executioner or an evil jinni or a king old enough to be their father. But it is always a man who waits for them and he has something sharp in his hand, something that draws blood. Otherwise where is the terror and the excitement and the hard-won martyrdom?

On the terrace the two sisters play instead of praying. Dunyazad says in a voice she hopes is the right pitch for poetry, 'I see myself in a long, silky robe. My flowing hair (I have just washed and scented it) touches the small of my back. I look delicate, but my back is very straight as I walk, no – as I float – towards the hunter. As I drift nearer and nearer, he and everybody else (because there are crowds of people to witness it all and say goodbye) look into my heart as if my face and figure are flimsy curtains they can see through. They look and they know I will die for my dreams.'

Dunyazad is a little afraid that she has got carried away. She looks at her sister warily – is that a smile stretching her mouth, is she going to laugh at her? (Though laughter is not part of the game, they break this rule quite often.) Shahrzad does not laugh. She too has a vision in her grip. Her martyr trembles to the surface, her broken, uneven features emerging to life as Shahrzad's eyes hold her. Like Dunyazad's martyr, this one is passionate but less willing to die. She is naked but still she sweats; her sweat reeks of fear and excitement. She walks in measured steps though she has never been naked in public before. Her executioner appraises her with interest. Their eyes meet. He thinks he can vanquish her with a simple dagger. She can feel something hard and unyielding in her stomach; it pushes its way up to her chest, her head, till there is a firmly clenched fist behind her eyes. They stand face to face, he in his glinting armour of metal, she in hers of angry skin. She looks at him steadily – at the man who will be her lover and tormentor. Her hands move to her breasts as if gesturing at an offering. The sun is in his eyes but he can see through the glare a little hoard of sparkling red jewels. Her daring, her tenacity, her love of power and danger, and most of all, her greed for life.

*

Shahrzad played The Martyr's Walk with consummate skill, but the path has outlived the martyr. That is an old story; for now, in Shahabad, Dunyazad knows she cannot put off seeing Shahryar any longer. The slavegirl Dilshad has already carried a message to Shahryar. Dunyazad sits before the mirror, waiting for assistance in her preparation to meet the sultan face to face. Though she will be suitably robed and veiled, it is important to get every detail of her toilet right. It is her fortitude she wants on display, not the ravages of time or grief, evidence that can evoke only pity. Dunyazad leans forward and looks deep into the solemn, reflected face before her.

As always in this palace of memories, her image does not remain alone for long. She sees Shahryar in the mirror, tracing a finger down the curve of a young, vulnerable neck. Dunya-

zad sees Shahrzad holding her body still, all the better to feel
the trail of gooseflesh that snakes down her throat to her bare
breasts. In the silence, a story (or a third person, a watch-
woman) hangs like a band of saliva between them. Shahryar
pauses, his finger stilled. Shahrzad stirs. They stretch, look
around, searching for the ghostly interloper. They speak to
each other in whispers lest they disturb Dunyazad who lies
hidden nearby. Dunyazad hears them but remains where she
is, the third presence required to complete every nightly
encounter between husband and wife. She waits on them,
allowing herself to doze only when she hears Shahryar's
whistling snore followed by Shahrzad's even, regular breathing. But these fits of sleep are all too brief and restless. Her
ears, sharp as the steely edge of the executioner's blade, pick
up every hint of a moan or a sigh. Bodies stir to life, resigned
to the fact that life, and its nightly business, must go on.

Shahrzad and Shahryar are at work in the sultan's bedchamber. Dunyazad is awake and waiting for them. Through
the thin partition of wood and silk that hides the sight from
her, Dunyazad hears them. She hears a grunt. His, she thinks.
Then a gasp like a long-drawn-out departure and an interminable interval when everything is muffled. Flesh and bone
interlock, a mouth meets a thigh, limbs shift, skin slips.
Dunyazad hears the secretive silence of legs and back clamped
together.

If she were to move forward, put her head on the other
side of the partition, they would not see her. Or seeing her,
face flushed, veil slipping down from head to shoulders,
disordered by emotion, they would not know her. If Dunyazad
gets up from the bed where she waits for midnight, if she

accosts their sweaty embrace and says, 'Look, this is too much, I can't wait any longer,' what would she see? Two bodies wrestling. A man and a woman in a grappling embrace, though it is hard to say which is man, which woman. In the many-limbed creature writhing on the bed, the carpet, against the wall, Dunyazad cannot see where the man and the woman are. Shahrzad and Shahryar, sister, king, sword, story are all in the monster, filling it up from mouth to foot.

When the creature is overcome by satiety, when it tears itself apart from the weight and pressure of its captives, Dunyazad sees them again. There is Shahryar – Dunyazad's first sight of a man in the thrall of desire. Or desire fulfilled. Eyes glazed, jaw hanging loose, Shahryar moans like a stag that has escaped the tiger only to die of its wounds. And there, there is Wise Shahrzad, her skin dripping with sweat and slime. Lying on her back, breasts splayed, legs thrown apart. Her eyes are shut. She looks incapable of saying a word again.

*

Dunyazad is in her room getting ready to meet Shahryar. To her own surprise, she has again called for Dilshad, this time to help her get dressed. Though the girl is unpredictable – coaxing, wheedling and insolent in turn – she is a relief from the bland, official politeness of everyone else in the palace: all is well, life goes on as before; though all is not well, we must mourn in dignity, in keeping with palace doctrine. Dilshad makes her feel her secret desire is not hopeless. That she will, she *can* unearth the details of Shahrzad's death, and in some irrevocable way, avenge it.

For now, off the battlefield, Dunyazad dithers, surrounded

by robes, veils, jewels, a clutter of plausible costumes on the floor around her. She has forgotten the pleasures of colours and textures, the satisfaction of a length of fabric cleaving to her breasts and legs like a bright skin. She has always had to be modestly dressed – first as a handmaiden in the background to Shahrzad and Shahryar, then as Zaman's wife, then as widow and guardian of the boy-king of Samarkand, cynosure of a thousand spies' eyes. Zaman with his innumerable jealousies, with, in his last years, his deranged fear of darkness, insisted she always dress in pale, maidenly colours. As if to spite him, and to render herself totally inconspicuous, she has since worn a dull, heavy black. Now she longs for someone to interrupt her fruitless search and say, 'Here, this is what you are looking for. The green silk and the strand of pearls will be perfect for this unexpected replay of the past.'

It is ridiculous to feel this silly anxiety flutter around the solid, substantial mass of her grief. She feels demeaned. Surely her two intimate experiences of men, her spectator's view of Shahryar's grand-scale tyranny, love and redemption, and the quick, furtive, mercifully brief coupling with Shahzaman, have taught her something? But here is Dilshad – and happily her arrival chases this question away. The two get to work in complicitous silence, picking up discarded jewels, matching them carefully with satins and brocades, checking that the last necklace is firmly clasped, the gold-trimmed veil securely fastened. Though they work quietly, Dilshad seems to know exactly what Dunyazad wants.

Dunyazad and Shahryar, under the same roof, in the same room. Though his figure filled her childhood with images of regal splendour, whimsy, tyranny, though she seems to have known him all her life, they do not meet alone. This at least is as it was in the past, except that they meet now without that crucial link between them. Minus Shahrzad, they meet in the small room off the main hall where Shahryar receives visitors every morning. That she has had to come to him, not he to her apartment, has invested the meeting with a formal air. As do their chaperons: Dilshad to see to the sultan's goblet, discreet serving girls and burly eunuchs in the background.

She kisses the ground before her; he invites her to sit. Her heart beats fast, but she lifts her chin decisively. She looks him in the face, hoping that all wounds will be more or less obscured or plastered over by the subtle glitter of costume, ritual, courtesy. They consider each other in unsmiling silence.

(How foolish her excitement and anxiety have been! There will always be an ancient bedchamber between them, a bridal night that never was. And in this room, the real one they sit in now, so very straight-backed, two ghosts are on guard to make sure not a muscle gives way. It is difficult to stir themselves out of their reveries and speak with these two demanding eavesdroppers forever within sight and earshot.)

The sight of the old antagonist shakes her more than she can tell. She knew him first, and best, as a dangerous and exciting enemy. The redeemed sultan she saw only briefly, a newly acquired benevolent brother who saw to her marriage and her departure for Samarkand. And now this new Shahryar, without a queen, without Shahrzad; the features that once inspired admiration, resentment and terror blurred in an ageing body. Regal still, but in a faded, melancholy style, with sunken cheeks, pouches under the eyes, wrinkled hands peeping out of pearl-studded sleeves. Do those grand, despotic desires still live under the skin of this stranger?

'Dunyazad,' he says, reading her face, 'see what time does to all of God's creatures. Time has not respected your love or mine. It has seized those we loved. Why would this monster leave us untouched?'

Though what he says is platitudinous, the sultan's words bring before her such a distinct image of the young Shahrzad, bold, defiant and unruined, that her eyes fill. At least she Dunyazad never saw grow old; would now never do so. She bends to regain control of herself.

'What does love – a rare love – look like?' she then hears him ask, and she raises her head in surprise. Dilshad, her face admirably composed, moves forward, fills his goblet. The sultan takes a small, fastidious sip, then waves Dilshad away. He says to Dunyazad, 'I will show the world how much a man can love a woman. I am building a memorial that will do justice to my love for Shahrzad. And it must do more – it must teach generations to come what a chaste woman is.' Shahryar's eyes glow with undying faith. 'It must remember – for ever – my grief when she left me behind.'

*

59

The sultan of justice, later the sultan of manly and bloody honour, is now the sultan of love. Love remembered in the tranquillity of grief. Dunyazad is coming to terms with the new Shahryar as all their meetings flow into the same conversation, the monologue that is apparently as unchanging as his love and grief. She hears more about the plans for the tomb, the large numbers of people who have been supervising its execution, the brilliant architects, calligraphers, engineers and artisans whom Shahryar has drafted into service as his team. There is one especially gifted calligrapher who has been seized and transported to Shahabad from a distant, captured city. Shahryar has promised him liberty once the tomb is inscribed with the most tender, holy and beautiful words known to man.

There are words and whispers about the tomb elsewhere in the palace as well. Strings of them, tripping up Dunyazad, not all of them tender or holy. An army has invaded the city at the sultan's orders: an army of stonecutters, inlay workers, calligraphers, masons, supervisors. Slaves and freemen who cannot pay the new tomb tax pull carts loaded with bricks, stone and slabs of marble. Their bent backs travel to and from the palace, as Shahryar inspects jasper, carnelian, turquoise, agate, coral, onyx, pearls, gold leaf. 'What colour is a dream?' he is often heard asking himself dreamily. Dunyazad hears a slavegirl whisper to a friendly eunuch – 'How much does this dream weigh? Can it break a man's back?'

The sultan sits at ease in the garden pavilion by the pond, or lounges on his gem-inlaid couch. 'Do you know,' he asks Dunyazad, 'how my father built the city of Shahabad? He was on his way home from a hard but triumphant battle. His kingdom had just grown twofold, but he was exhausted. He had a pain in his back and he could feel the lice crawling around in his filthy hair. It was weeks since he had had a good night's sleep, or a night without nightmares of death or losing his kingdom altogether.'

'He chose the site where our city now stands to pitch his tents for the night. He slept as he had not done for years. And in his sleep, a gentle-faced woman came to him. "Stay here," she said to him. "Build your city here, a city with a golden palace for its heart." She gave him a bronze horseman whose lance would always point in the direction from which an enemy invasion could next be expected. "Your palace of course must have a dome, the most perfect of forms. Place this on your dome."

'Then the visitor from paradise made him a promise. "I will always wait for you," she told him. "I will be as patient and steadfast as the palace you build."

'The king woke up refreshed and looked about him with new eyes. He half-expected the woman to be asleep by his side. But she had gone back into his dream to wait as promised. It was the brass horseman he found in his bed, waiting for him to lay the first brick with his own hand. Then the king called his men and told them, "Build me a city, and may God bless you."'

*

There is a dream-woman in Shahryar's night too, a woman made of memories.

Shahryar and Dunyazad are alone at last, walking up and down a bare room with a large, open window. The evening light streams in and bathes them in its gentle light. 'There is a building,' Shahryar tells Dunyazad, 'a gem like the woman who inspired it, struggling to break free of my mind. I see a place, a monument of pure white marble, a home to love *and* chastity.'

Shahryar comes to a halt by the window. So does Dunyazad, stealing a quick look at his face which has grown sad and pensive. Dunyazad feels something stir in her throat when he says, 'But I ask myself sometimes, can the two ever live together, love and loyalty, amicable partners under the same roof?'

Shahryar has paused. Dunyazad realizes it, just as she can feel her lips stretched in a painful, reluctant smile. The sultan looks surprised, as if he has finally realized who he is talking to.

'Dunyazad,' he says, 'when a long, warm afternoon is over, when the gardener has watered the parched earth and evening rises sweet and moist – do you know the time I am talking of?'

'Yes,' she says in a low voice. 'The hour before the coming of night.'

'Yes, that is it,' he agrees, turning back to the window to gaze moodily into the distance. 'It's in that brief, evocative hour that I see how empty my hands are. I should have sons by my side, filling my evening with a mellow joy. But Umar, our young prince of the people, thinks he can teach me how to rule. He forgets that I too had a king for a father; that I too waited for the throne. As for my beloved wife—' and Shahryar stops. He looks at Dunyazad, his eyes filling with bewilderment. 'Can anyone live without a sanctuary? And how would the harem or the palace or the city be home, be safe, if it is not haram, secure for some because forbidden to others?'

Shahryar's shoulders sag. 'It's a cruel mystery, isn't it? If your father were here he would have unravelled it all for us — what a redeemed life really is, why it seems so empty and pointless.' He sees Dunyazad's face grow wet with tears. He takes her arm. They move closer. She can feel the weight of his head on her shoulders, his beard lying by her neck like a furry tail. She can hear the sound of blood rushing; it is impossible to breathe evenly.

She can also sense someone watching them. She looks up. Over his shoulder she can see Dilshad, lingering at the door, waiting for their eyes to meet. The girl's face is intent; it glows with a signal or a reminder. Then Dilshad disappears. Dunyazad comes back to herself. She lifts Shahryar's head gently, retreats a step. She wipes her eyes furtively as they look out of the window together.

*

The next time they meet, they are alone again, but they are back at the beginning, at his dream-building. 'I have worked night and day to build her a fitting monument,' Shahryar tells Dunyazad. 'She will wait there for me in innocent sleep, surrounded by marble, gold, and precious gems from all the lands of the known world.'

'And Umar, what does he—' Dunyazad begins but he cuts her off sharply.

'It grieves me to hear that your only son is an imbecile. Zaman's son is on the throne, but he is your stepson, is he not?' He sees the flicker of pain on her face before it grows composed again. He chides her gently, 'You and I cannot live again through our sons, Dunyazad. But if you will allow me to get back to what I was saying. To remember Shahrzad, it is not enough just to recall our love; we have to go down that old path she travelled with me, earning my love with her ready tongue.'

Dunyazad listens, head bowed.

'There is still so much to be done, though no one has ever built such a memorial so fast before,' he then says. 'But you, who she loved so much, will want to see it even before it is finished.'

All of a sudden she is enraged by his resigned air, as if the safest beloved is a closed chapter. And who is he to talk of sisterly love, assure her of Shahrzad's feelings for her? Dunyazad's breasts swell. If she sees the tomb, it would be like wishing Shahrzad dead. She wants to shake him till his bones rattle and say, Call it a tomb! You are talking about a dead body, not your love for her! Did Shahrzad escape the axe once only to die in ignominy? Did I assist the priestess at her rituals – did we together hold back the dagger that could have been used long ago, when you slept tamed, satiated, unaware – only for this mediocre epitaph?

'My sister,' Dunyazad brings out quickly. 'How long was she unwell – I mean, what was her illness?'

Shahryar's face loses all animation; it grows quite cool and still. 'It was sudden and fatal,' he says. 'And Zaman, my beloved brother? It's been a few years now, but I recall we had no news of *his* illness before we heard of his shocking death?'

She remains silent but meets his challenging stare without flinching. The two look at each other assessingly, the widow and the widower, the brother and the sister, as if desire must walk forever hand in hand with a shared guilt. Then the sultan waves her away, bringing their meetings to an end, but not before a parting shot. 'Did you have to rush to Shahabad alone? I would have sent word to your son when Shahrzad's monument was ready. We plan to hold a month of special prayers.'

6

Dunyazad's eyes fly open. She is sitting up in bed, her body arched with tension as if to meet an unknown lover in the darkness. In that minute between sleep and wakefulness, she is able to see spirits; the palace-jinni shows her his face in a quick, awful flash. Shahrzad knew how evil could be personified, how it grew in different shapes and sizes. Evil could expand in her stories, be enlarged into a towering monster as tall as the sky; it could shrink, compressed into the tiny recesses of a lamp or a ring. But a structure of stone and brick and marble – can this testament to human nobility, the splendour of kings, have a fiend for its soul?

As the question forms itself in her mind in a coherent string of words, the spirit vanishes. Dunyazad lights a candle and sees that even in its spluttering, shadow-casting light the palace room is bland, ornamental; innocent of the peaks and treacheries of human imagination. She feels cheated. She blows out the candle and gets out of bed. A dark robe, a small lamp, and she is ready.

The dream has wandered into the second part of the night, in this palace where night has always been divided into two acts. In the second act then, stealthy Dunyazad, barefoot, feels her way down an endless series of steps, down to the heart – or bowels – of the palace. She meets no one on the way; not one guard, slave or eunuch, though she knows of old how well the palace is guarded against thieves and intruders. Dunyazad struggles not to lose count of the steps. Her hands are sore from trailing across the different species of palace-skin, from the marble of the upper floors to the rough stone of the dungeon.

When she runs out of numbers, she knows she has arrived. She bends low and slips into the old bedchamber with the sacred marriage bed. She cannot wait to get back her breath before she lights her lamp. She sets it down and looks. This is no dream, just as she is no casually curious visitor. Even before her days in the palace, Shahryar's chamber began its descent. In a palace that drank blood for a daily tonic, glossed over virginal blood with embellished marble, the king must have many bedchambers, and they must be well concealed. Shahryar's bed, weighed down with the tender flesh of virgins, had to be moved from the vast rooms overlooking the royal gardens. It was too exposed, too dangerous. Some of the virgins had angry fathers, shamed brothers, desperate mothers and sisters.

By the time Shahrzad and Dunyazad moved to the palace, a thousand brides had died. Shahryar's bed lay in its dungeon throbbing with its festering secrets, the palace rising like a fort above it.

Dunyazad looks around. She sees that it is now a ridiculously small, dark space, a dingy mildewed dungeon that smells of bats. The iron chains and bracelets from which prisoners were hung and tortured remain; but not the carpets, lanterns, curtains and goblets that altered the dungeon into a cosy nest during its royal tenancy. These props went back to the upper floors once Shahrzad had earned her triumph.

Dunyazad looks for the secret opening leading to a tank of

water. The tank is still there, half full, the water thick and filthy. The lamp burns low; she struggles with its wick. In the dying light, in the imperfect watery mirror from the past, she sees that she was right to crawl down to the dungeon. Here there is no pretence that Shahrzad is dead. Dunyazad sees the trembling face in the mirror, her sister's deathless face.

There is something about this face, some eagerness to push time forward, that makes it so ready to age. Shahrzad's face was ready, already prepared, when the wazir interviewed her in his room. To go to the wazir's room, where books, plans, men and their seductive powers awaited her, she had to cross the invisible line that edged her mother's wing. Behind this shoreline lay a sea of predictable movement, bodies swelling and going flaccid, bodies dripping blood or milk, bodies coming together in sticky embrace, bodies heaving and pushing to come apart. Shahrzad had to leave behind this monotonous, womanish sea, this watery womb, and put her foot on land.

Once on firm ground, once she had taken those steps forward, Shahrzad shed the unfocused look of a yearning girl. And on the bridal night, when she discovered the shuddering appetites of the body, saw what it was to unleash the mind for her purposes, Shahrzad lost what was left of her girl's face. But having stepped forward, daringly embraced that night of ageing and the thousand which were to follow, she seemed to have subjugated age, stripped it of its power to impose one face on another. Having given up her vulnerable face so entirely, Shahrzad would never age again so quickly or easily. She would only grow more majestic year after year.

Dunyazad sets down the lamp and crouches before the

tank. Her moist and oily hand strokes her face feature by feature as if it is the reflection of the face she has just seen. Try as she might she cannot see either face, original or reflection, wrapped up in a shroud. She suddenly realizes how tired she is; how dirty, how sweaty. With her sister this adventure would have been different. Dunyazad turns away, dreading the long dreary climb back to the room fit for princesses.

Dunyazad steals into bed, too worn out to wash her face and hands though they feel clammy and unclean. The sheet clings to her bare legs, slippery slime. She wants to kick it off but cannot make the effort. Soon it will creep up her body, cover her neck, face, head. She should know this; *she* should know something of shrouds and their hunger. But the night's travels have sucked her dry; she is only a spineless puppet now, without a will of her own. Dunyazad succumbs to it all – to the tricks of the palace night, the steady movement of the advancing shroud. She drifts into a fitful, restless sleep.

When she wakes it is to an instant sense of panic. Where is she, what happened to those sombre, spacious widow's rooms where her life has hung in limbo for years? She looks around suspiciously, her eyes darting here and there. When they rest on the window, she remembers. The palace comes back to her. She breaks into a dry-throated sob; suddenly she is terrified of being here; being here alone.

She struggles to her feet. The room swims about her. Slowly, like a worm with an extraordinary burden, she makes her way to the door; opens it; calls aloud.

Her voice echoes eerily. Even as she hears its quavering demand for 'Sabiha' she feels a twinge of bitter isolation.

There is no one left here, no one she knows, ready to offer a hand or a hope at a word. There is, of course, her brother-in-law, but he is the sultan, and a sultan trapped in the role of an ageing, grieving widower. There is only one name which comes to her aid, Sabiha, senile remnant of the glorious, fabled past.

She hears hurrying feet; she feels powerful arms support her, assume the burden of her body. 'Sabiha?' she asks wonderingly, surprised even in her wobbly, melting state that the old woman can be so strong.

A voice she does not recognize, a firm, ringing voice, tells her bluntly: 'The old woman is ill. She can't hear you – she's left the palace for good.' The snapping of this last, fragile link with the known marks her own rapid descent into oblivion. Dunyazad's mouth gapes open, a stupid bewilderment overcomes her, and she goes limp.

There is an edifice in our submerged selves, in that inconsistently lit private world, that we sink to in moments of danger. This is where Dunyazad is now, a deadweight who has sunk without a trace, all the way down to the floor of the sea. She lies on this shifting, sandy surface, waiting for help.

She senses a shadowy figure come up to her and turn her around. She can feel a cautious, regular breath on her face, then she is lifted off the floor and carried into a marble enclosure. She is laid out carefully as if her body is on display. The air fills with a sweet, elegiac fragrance made of dampness, incense and stale flowers. She knows – though not a word has been spoken – that she is to lie there for ever. By her side sits the figure, whom she now recognizes as the smooth-faced palace-jinni, eternal rake and guardian of women. It is not clear, she realizes with mounting unease, whether he guards her from harm or whether he is her prison warden.

Dunyazad, febrile, delirious, cries aloud: 'Am I dying?' And without waiting for an answer, she wails 'No! I can't die yet!' She struggles to swallow the hard lump stuck in her throat so that she can explain why; surely anyone with a little reason will see why? A cool, reassuring hand strokes her forehead. Something wet and peaceful – ah the simple blessedness of water – is being tenderly spooned into her mouth. She calms down; she remembers; she is not on the ocean floor but in the palace, still very much alive. She stirs but the cool hand restrains her. The hand speaks soothingly: 'You're not going to die so easily, dearest! Keep your eyes closed; lie back.'

Dunyazad lies still, listening carefully. What went before was a false dream then. And this new one – will it deliver the saviour she is counting on? That rich, carefully modulated voice conjuring fantastical creatures to do what it wants: it is the same voice Dunyazad hears now, flowing across the emptiness. Dunyazad cannot make sense of the words yet. She crawls in the direction of the achingly familiar voice. She can just make out a stray word now and then – 'folly' and 'fortune' and 'grave' and then a whole phrase: 'Know, my friends . . .' Dunyazad trembles with anticipation when she hears the ubiquitous invitation to share a story. She pulls herself up. The words and the voice that links them draw her like a flame in the damp, lonely darkness. She trains her eyes on this hazy light till she sees a pearly, gleaming pavilion.

Shahrzad is there, Wise Shahrzad, talking as always, ringed by a host of ghostly virgin brides. Shahrzad looks into the distance, sees her. A smile of delighted surprise fills her face and she holds out her arms to her Dunyazad. Though Shahrzad is surrounded, used as she is to leading, she will want an accomplice on equal ground. And she is lonely, having been alone, so alone, since she made the terrible mistake of dying.

All Dunyazad has to do is cross the waters that separate them. She calls out beseechingly: 'Wait! I want to hear it too – how can you leave *me* out?' Her words alight on the water, swallow it up and make it negotiable. She begins to cross, she is almost there, and the vision melts painlessly into obscurity, the voice into silence. Dunyazad waits; then opens her eyes. It was no delusion then. The silky voice has an owner. Dilshad of the teasing eyes and the fur-marked, laughing mouth sits by her bedside, looking down at her. 'Are you feeling better?' she asks and Dunyazad nods, feeling both foolish and grateful. 'Rest then,' the girl says. 'Sleep it off and get back your strength. I've talked you out of your feverish dreams.' And like an obedient child, a role memory tells her she once performed to perfection, Dunyazad finally settles down to a dreamless sleep.

7

Dunyazad hears a soft knock on the door and two maids enter her room. One sets down a laden tray, bows deeply, and kneels before it, waiting for an order to serve. The other maid glides towards Dunyazad to help her dress. The girls are timid and modest; even their breathing is humble, as meek and controlled as all their movements in her presence.

Their mindless servility makes her long for Dilshad. After that unexpected spell of tender nursing, Dunyazad has seen little of her. At first she was surprised – and grateful – for this tact on the younger woman's part. Who knows what Dunyazad could have said in her delirious state, revealing words which may force an intimacy with a slavegirl who knows nothing of the past?

Shahryar ignores Dunyazad, having failed to stir her with his dream-building. Now that she is well and impatient again, she has little to do but wait for Dilshad. She is not sure if the unpredictable girl will be an enemy or an ally in the days to come, but a familiar hunger in her demands that she find out. She could ask for her but she is held back by a ridiculous attack of pride. After all, even if Dilshad is the sultan's slave, she is a slave, while she, Dunyazad . . . She learns to quell this pang of pride and sends word to Dilshad.

*

The little monkey-face trips in with perfect confidence, more unlike a diffident slave than ever. 'It's about time you asked for me – I have something to show you,' she announces, ignoring the frown gathering on Dunyazad's face. She leaves the room, returns a few minutes later lugging an ornate wooden chest.

'What do you think is in it?' she asks Dunyazad with childish glee.

'I have no idea,' says Dunyazad coldly. 'Why don't you open it and find out?'

'That's a clever plan,' giggles Dilshad, putting on a droll stupid-slave face. She opens the chest with a flourish and looks expectantly at Dunyazad. In spite of herself, Dunyazad is infected by her excitement – and she draws forward to look into the chest.

She sees odds and ends, girlish treasures, then with a sickening lurch of her stomach she sees a familiar diaphanous robe, a necklace of red jewels, and a sparkling, invincible dagger.

Dunyazad pulls back. She looks at Dilshad with distaste. Must she be reduced to playing games with this slavegirl? 'Where did you get it?' she asks sharply.

'You mean did I steal it?' says the brazen girl. 'And you – have you never tried to steal anything?

'I'll tell you a secret,' continues Dilshad with a confiding air. 'There's something I've wanted to steal ever since a great lady taught me to read and write. There are these stories – hundreds and hundreds of them – written out in letters of gold, lying unread in the treasury . . .'

Seeing the outrage in Dunyazad's face, Dilshad's mood

suddenly shifts. 'I didn't steal the chest,' she says sulkily. 'The sultan said I could have it.'

Dunyazad is silent and disbelieving.

'All right – if you must know – he lets me take out things from the chest whenever I want. The costume box, we call it. She's gone, and he doesn't need this junk box to remember her by, does he? He's got her embalmed and entombed in marble and gold and all the precious stones possible.'

Dilshad moves closer to Dunyazad so that their faces are just an inch apart. It is difficult to tell whether Dilshad's anger is directed at Shahryar and his grief that is to be eloquently erected for posterity; or whether it is merely a petty spite, directed at all of them. 'He will see her,' she hisses at Dunyazad, '– or where he claims she rests – every time he looks out of his royal window.'

She moves away from Dilshad's face, from its repulsively hot and feral breath, but really, what the girl has said is not so different from what Dunyazad herself has been thinking. This troubles Dunyazad: after all, where is the conspiracy between them?

'Well?' says Dilshad, gloating. 'Go ahead, dip in, touch! They won't bite you!'

Dunyazad draws a deep, calming breath. The embers of the past cling tenaciously to life within her. Why should a few orphaned objects, tawdry and insignificant in themselves, hold any power over her? She looks into the box once more. But there is something else there, something that glints among the pain-stiffened mementoes, signalling her attention. Then as she bends forward, her hand outstretched, it recovers the bland, indifferent look of a stranger. Dunyazad reaches for the ivory-framed mirror that she does not remember seeing before, aware of Dilshad's eyes on her. The ivory is a pale yellow. It unfolds and spreads into two budding wings, one on either side of the dusty glass. Dunyazad holds up the mirror to look at her face, or to screen it from Dilshad's probing eyes. The glass has a slender, thread-like scar, cracking her reflection.

'Yes, it was hers,' she hears Dilshad say though her question was not asked aloud. 'I was *her* slave before the shah noticed me.'

Dunyazad exhales. Mirror in hand, she turns to Dilshad as if seeing her for the first time. 'Then you know?' she begins in a trembling voice. Excitement and a kind of triumph bubble up her throat.

'Where the mirror comes from?' There is a note of warning in this swift interruption, and in the intimate tone of counter-questioning that Dilshad has assumed. They are, Dunyazad realizes with amazement, now talking as equals. Or if there is an imbalance of power, it is she, Dilshad, with her hints of forbidden knowledge, her unknown loyalties, who must dictate the terms of this new footing. She has, after all, Shahryar's ear. Perhaps more, perhaps her flat stomach and narrow hips warm the sultan's aching limbs, fill all the angular, empty spaces in his sagging bed of grief.

'There was a young man,' Dilshad is whispering in her ear. 'A young man who came with the rich merchant Sulaiman, across seas and deserts to the palace of Shahabad. Though a foreigner, he seemed to know our ways, the ways of cities and palaces, as well as Sulaiman, his adopted father. Maybe he was really the old man's son, born of a woman whose breasts ripened by a distant seashore, waiting for her foreign lover to return in his cargo-laden dhow.

'Sulaiman paid rich tribute to the sultan. At his direction, the young man (whom the merchant called Abdulla) unpacked and displayed mounds of cloves, cardamom and pepper. Huge bundles of spices, sandalwood, ivory, and muslin as fine as a sieve. The sultan was gracious to the merchant. But it was Abdulla who really took the fancy of the royals. I don't know whose attention he caught first, the sultan's or the sultana's. But he could, they discovered, not only brave hazardous journeys, but also talk of them. He was summoned back to the palace again and again, almost every day, till he too, like all travellers, departed. But when he was in Shahabad, he was to tell the young princes about his land and his voyages. I remember the day he brought the little mirror with him – the queen and I were there. We often were, she hated to miss a word of his accounts. "Now that my journey is done," she once said to me (though he, on the other side of the room, could hear her as well as I), "I find it strangely comforting to hear of others' travels."'

Dilshad suddenly brings down the lid of the chest with a thud. Her face, almost pretty in this brief foray into girlish wistfulness, turns sulky again. 'I don't know how to finish stories,' she mutters. 'You finish it, you are the malika, I am only a slave.' And she is gone, though the chest – and its contents – remain behind.

*

In the safe and dark cocoon of the night, Dunyazad, alone in her bed, holds the mirror up to her face again. Shahrzad held it like this once – no, not once, but many many times. Like all inmates of a harem, even the royal begum had a secret, a rite that gave pleasure partly because of its forbidden flavour. She too was alone in her bed, now that the sultan's harem was filling up again in tribute to her storytelling efforts. The glass was whole, the ivory still pearl white. She bent, kissed tenderly the pristine frame of the innocent boyish gift in which she could see her own true reflection.

Dunyazad spies on her sister, and sees that the saviour is a mere girl now, caught in a tangle of desire very different from what pinned her down on Shahryar's heavy bed. Dunyazad's lips trace Shahrzad's route, round the minute territory of hard, carved wings. Then her mouth moves to the centre, following the curved path of the crack. Her lips sting. How strange – the desire she just saw on Shahrzad's face has lost all its moist freshness. It is just another dry, dull ache in the pit of her own stomach, a pain ignored too long. She is filled with pity for this stale woman in the mirror. It matters very little to anyone if she sleeps alone, night after night, untouched. It matters very little whether she lives or dies, because her role, her part in the play, is done. Dunyazad jerks herself away from the reflection. The mirror is just a broken little toy; and she is a silly old fool with no special claims to prop her up simply because she is all alone in the world. Why should she assume that the stranger (if there was such a man in the first place) meant anything to Shahrzad? Has she too come to believe that the harem breeds hungry women, a race of cuckolding subjects? For the space of a moment, Dunyazad sees a half-life pretending to be an oracle; she sees a middle-aged woman fleshing out a phantom, pouring into it the banalities of youth and beauty, worshipping it with desire. Dunyazad looks at the mirror in her hand with loathing, then flings it to the carpet. She thinks she can hear it break; she shuts her eyes with grim satisfaction.

But there is skin in her sleep. Young skin, deep brown skin, stretches out and falls into place, a glossy map of sinew and muscle. It is an extravagant spread of delicacies, thighs, eyes, masses of dark curly hair, neat slim wrists. In this dream there is no sand, no sea, no journey. A body fills up every inch of the frame, a man's body. Dunyazad moans, turns over, flings out an arm. She touches empty air.

8

The palace has grown obese, a flabby old man full of stale air. He uses up more and more oxygen as he swells. Dunyazad, as short of breath as the other inmates of the palace, recognizes the symptom. She remembers that evil is not always larger than life. The evil you meet down the corridor is more often than not banal, its faithful companion venal gossip.

Dunyazad's luxurious room has now grown hateful to her. It flaunts pretend-windows that pay homage to a world outside. But they are really there to screen, to enclose, so that she is forced to turn inward, wallow in the past or in the palace's seductive, anachronistic tales. There *is* a present, in which she must act if she is to act at all, and surely that is the point of her dusty, hurried flight to Shahabad?

She wanders from room to room in the women's wing, and when she can, a little beyond. A cautious traveller, she says little but takes in as much as she can. Everywhere she goes in the palace, a ghost of foreboding stalks her. It feeds on them all, this foreboding, a living, breathing thing, on its way to being full-grown. Just as it was in the days when Shahrzad's martyrdom was in the making; in the days before her fate was finally resolved.

Dunyazad senses another shadow dogging her, a shadow resembling Dilshad. She meets rumours, many agile, butterfly-winged whispers. The old bed is back in the dungeon, she hears. The inmates of the harem, recruits in times of relative peace, cannot let go of this bit of news. They worry it to death among themselves till their teeth strike a narrow, twisted bone. If it is true (and their eyes widen with fear, their voices falter with excitement), they may be called to grope their way down, down those stony, forbidding steps. To a chamber where no magical carpet can hide old, tell-tale stains. Where neither perfume nor incense can mask the rusty smell of blood.

Does Shahryar fear for his life? Impossible to believe: the people after all love their redeemed sultan, now more than ever in his grey season of grief. But every time Shahryar is not seen for a few days, his loving subjects speculate endlessly about a royal death. And if Dunyazad eavesdrops at the right place she can hear the echo of one of her own burning questions. How (or why) did Shahrzad die? Only the shah – and a few trusted men slaves – claim to have been there when the queen suddenly took ill. The rest saw the sealed coffin; the sultan could not bear to see, or display, the beloved face dead. And on the border of the women's wing, on the edge of that strip of neuter territory, there is another name that slips down stealthy tongues and stirs to subversive life. The conspiring knots of people in dark corners seem to be linked somehow with the rebellious Prince Umar. His name is never spoken aloud – the sultan has forbidden it since Umar stormed out of the palace. But an air of expectation hangs over all the whispering and rustling, a heavy, rain-filled cloud which will burst any minute.

Waiting, listening. Turning overheard words this way and that till they grow emaciated from constant handling. Nothing substantial remains, only the odd teasing whiff of smoke. It is a climate Dunyazad has lived in before, that she has lived through before. Why does she feel so weighed down then, why does her skin burn as if it will never be cool or tranquil again? Dunyazad longs for a change of air. Nothing ambitious or impossible, just a brief escape into the city. Even for an hour, even if it means turning round and recognizing those dogged footsteps that trail her at a respectable distance. Dilshad, she is aware, has many unlikely friends and allies in the palace. She at any rate will know how to smuggle her out somewhere – to the crowded, anonymous marketplace perhaps, or to the hammam in the old quarter where she can be just another body being cleansed. The hammam, Dunyazad recalls, which she and Shahrzad last visited as innocent children.

*

In the hammam, a naked Dunyazad, surrounded by unknown bodies. Swathed in steam, water, assorted fragrances, the insistent voice of the self and its distinctly outlined body are subdued into a blur. She feels – not just protected, but held; with a closeness that need not be feared or examined because nothing is expected in return. Eyes closed, mind drifting, she submits herself to the embrace of this anonymous ghost. With this yielding comes something via memory, an image as diffuse as the clouds of warmth engulfing her. Again an embrace, but this one is inhabited by three naked bodies, one old, two young; held fast by the perfect ring of protection that absolute trust throws around them. The older figure, the mother, dries the smaller of her two daughters. The child Dunyazad feels the brisk, competent movement of cotton against her skin, then a quick but whole-hearted hug. The three of them leave the hammam together, hands linked, one gleaming daughter on either side of the proud mother. Dunyazad opens her eyes and moves like an automaton from the lukewarm steam room to the hot room.

There Dunyazad is thrust forward from one newly recovered memory to another, equally fragile, but which she approaches with reluctance. Her mother's death: it began when Raziya, mother of Shahrzad and Dunyazad, stood at the threshold of the women's wing, watching her daughters leave for the sultan's palace. She had no last-minute advice to offer the bride-to-be or her attendant. True to her name – Raziya, the woman who is agreeable – if she had reservations about her children being offered up for the sacrifice, no one heard about it. Except the wazir perhaps, and he was adept at reducing voices, especially those raised in protest, to a complicitous silence.

Raziya, however, was no accomplice. Though silent (or cowed? bitter? despairing?) Dunyazad, on turning around a last time, saw her mother's face. The look on her face: as if the muscles had lost their elasticity all at once; the bones disconnected and knocking about, meaningless, in a shrivelled-up, airless bag. A look, Dunyazad knew instantly (though she had never yet looked the ultimate terror in the face), not just of grief, anger or hopelessness; but a look which belonged on the face of death.

Later in the palace, preoccupied with word, sword and desire, they had not gone back to this look, considered its implications. And they had no news from the wazir's mansion, nothing out of the ordinary. What was happening to Raziya was so subdued and imperceptible that they hardly knew she was dying till she actually collapsed. A broken heart, people whispered, when she was wrapped in Shahrzad's unused shroud on the five hundredth night. But Dunyazad, grieving for her mother in her ante-room in the palace (the sultan and Shahrzad in the royal bed), saw an image different from what was described to her, and from what she herself had seen earlier. She saw her mother's heart for a moment before it was shrouded from sight and buried for ever. And what she saw was not a broken spring, but a chamber where outrage swelled the air; stretched it to grotesque dimensions till the tightly packed, thin-skinned balloon of a place exploded: the aftermath of an enraged heart.

Even before this heart and its exposed contents can be rewrapped, dispatched to distant and safer resting ground, Dunyazad feels an insistent arm against hers. She turns, catches the odour of fresh sweat. She hears a theatrical whisper: 'Time to go but the palace can wait. There's someone who wants to meet you. Come, follow me.'

Two women, the young one leading her older companion, emerge from the steamy belly of the hammam, say a quick prayer using the purest of waters. The pair, shrouded in their humble robes and veils, then make their way along the narrow, winding lanes, heads down, eyes on the street. They move across the city in swift, inconspicuous silence.

*

Later Dunyazad will ask herself why she followed Dilshad so meekly. Did she suspect that it was all arranged, almost predestined? Did she recognize fur-faced Dilshad as the catalyst who would prod her to action? But for now, Dunyazad is in a windowless chamber in a rambling house on the edge of the city. For some reason, the dilapidated mansion calls to memory her father's house – though his was obviously as rich and well-kept as his dignity. The room she now sits in, for all its dust and cobwebs, could have been the wazir's solemn room with its burden of books, its floor paved with prayer rugs. In her memory of that room, there is a narrow, empty space with a touch of something missing. Though it was the room in which Shahrzad accepted the challenge and gave her word, the promise would have to be proved elsewhere. And this place, a temporary hideout for a purposeful young man – there is something incomplete about this room too, reminiscent of the other one.

Dilshad seems at home. She leaves the room briefly and returns with bread, dates, fruit and sharbat. Dunyazad considers the young man, Umar, her unremembered nephew, and now a challenge to the sultan. Umar looks nothing like Shahryar. The wazir's bearing hovers round his straight back and well-defined chin; sweet Raziya shines out of his earnest eyes and warm-coloured skin. (And where were her parents when Dunyazad's poor son was born? Why was he marked, destined to be all Zaman, a half-formed creature of the night?)

The solemn young man before her says, 'I know my duty – I have to respond to the call of God. God calls me now to protect and consolidate values of the spirit.' Umar, like many young men learning to be stern, pretends that he has no time for feelings. There is still a boy in Umar, and he is visible to Dunyazad despite his beard and haughty air. But all the boy's ardour and newly awakened passion are being used up as the man spins yet another design of a well-behaved, orderly world.

'I see a circle,' Umar is telling her. 'A perfect, whole garden. The ruler is its fence. Behind the ruler stand great walls of soldiers, built and maintained by his money. The money comes from the subjects – but they are protected by justice, and it is justice that the ruler guards like his crown.'

Dunyazad follows Umar silently as he guides her across a landscape which she was part of, but which *he* now describes like an eyewitness with a mission. Shahryar's reign of blood, the decimated families, the refugees from Shahabad to other lands. The offence against God and his city.

Umar: though he is her beloved Shahrzad's son, there is something fundamentally austere about him. He is more the wazir's child than Shahrzad's. She can see that he is, like Shahryar, a builder; but he would prefer a canal to Shahryar's garden, or a well to his father's death-conquering tomb. And where is Shahrzad in this boy? As if he has heard her question, Umar mentions Shahrzad at last: 'I loved my mother, but another love directs me now and pushes me forward. Our city, her people, their well-being . . .'

Umar's eyes glow with rational fervour. It is impossible to disagree with him. His high ideas of reform and morality move her even if she has heard them or their ancestors before. But Dunyazad notices (as she takes in his regal bearing, his slips into the self-inflating *we*) that he too talks of Shahrzad as if she is dead and gone. Can someone you love ever die? When your back is bent with memory, when love still plays its drumbeat of desire and drinks your heart's blood? The young man before her is a prince. He is next in line, he is adult, he is impatient for the throne. (Dunyazad remembers another life fleetingly, a life she has left behind in Samarkand; and the throne on which her stepson sits, self-sufficient and out of reach.)

It is clear that she has been brought here to play a role in Umar's scenario of redemption. Dunyazad makes no promises; but she is aware that she has not displayed indignation or revulsion. Her silence has already made her part-accomplice. Still, it is a long time since she has felt the tingling anticipation of discovery. Could it be that well-matched pair again, signalling from where they used to, just round the corner? Love and power. Love or power. If it is not love it must be power. But this time she must chase this faithless shadow and trip it up. Throw herself bodily on it, pin it down, hold it till it is hers, till it is part of her.

9

Dunyazad is in bed, wide-awake and fresh from her trip to the hammam. Despite its stingy size, the picture-window in her room makes a tantalizing promise. It frames a glowing corner of a moon-blessed night, as if there is a whole world outside waiting to reveal itself. But where is Dunyazad to go, who to invite to an assignation? In this place all rooms lead inexorably to the royal quarters, the sultan's bed the only natural destination.

Still she sits up waiting. Perhaps she knows that the day with its cache of forbidden gifts is not yet over. Perhaps she is confident that Dilshad, adept in palace intrigue, will not leave her alone yet. Soon there will be a discreet knock on the door, announcing the arrival of her wily companion in adventure. She has already seen several Dilshads today. The free spirit who comes and goes from the palace as if walls and guards mean nothing to her; the naked, excited girl in the hammam; the conspirator who delights in mysteries, disorder, anything underhand. Now – in this night with its familiar promise of tale and marvel – will Dilshad shed her numerous disguises? Strip herself of all those flimsy, hint-woven veils to reveal something closer to the skin?

*

Dilshad is seated by Dunyazad's low bed, her legs tucked comfortably under herself. Uninvited, she leans forward. Her clever fingers bury themselves deep in Dunyazad's hair. They stroke and part the hair, strand by strand, grey and black. Dunyazad's scalp tingles. She looks up into the face bending over hers. She is no stranger to the caresses of women, but this girl is so full of strange, unspoken challenges. Why does she find her comforting then, tender, so unlike the sister she loved?

Dunyazad's arm lifts itself off the bed as if it has a life of its own. Her hand approaches Dilshad's face, hovers there for a fluttering moment, then comes to rest, gingerly, on the date-shaped patch of fur near the full, sulky lips. Though her eyes still tell her the unsightly mark diminishes Dilshad as a woman, her fingers thrill at the seductive touch of velvet. Even before she can stop herself, Dunyazad whispers, 'Is it a birthmark? Have you always had it?'

'It was a gift,' says Dilshad, smiling. Dunyazad traces the smiling mouth with a finger, searching for irony. But there is only sadness in the smile, the sadness of a clown who has forgotten she is wearing her happy painted mouth. A smile weighed down by intimacy with the harem, bedchamber, dungeon, and who knows what else?

Dilshad knows the ways of the palace – its private bodily functions, its best-kept secrets – better than Shahrzad or Dunyazad, the chief wazir's talented daughters. And in a palace under siege, vulnerable to every stray virus including conspiracy, the inmates can find themselves in the wrong places, playing the wrong role. In the Shahabad palace tonight, it is the slavegirl Dilshad who is the purveyor of knowledge, the teacher; Dunyazad the humble pupil. The day has revelled in the smoky intimacy of the hammam, in a stealthy visit to a rebellious prince. It has ventured into dangerous territory that brings together past and future in clandestine coupling. Now all this seems only a many-stranded prelude to the real story. For the first time Dunyazad hears from Dilshad about a freakish half-woman, half-poet. Whoever heard her whispered accounts of strange journeys never travelled alone again. Whoever she kissed – and she kissed Dilshad once, to say goodbye – was left with an indelible memento.

*

All kings are collectors. All of them, whether sultan or raja or chosen leader turned supreme. Their whims and preferences may vary, but most are partial to filling up their treasure vaults – with gems and coins, books copied out by scribes in letters of gold, or stallions, slaves and subjects. But the prize collection is not stowed away in the same vault. It is hidden in the harem, or zenana, or a special palace, or bedchamber. These valuable items are women of all shapes, colours and sizes.

The citizens of Shahabad need not hang their heads in shame – their king does not lag behind his counterparts elsewhere in the civilized world. There is a prize collection of jawari, a private collection of slavegirls, in Shahryar's palace too. Talking women, dreaming women, acrobatically fornicating women, mute women, freaks who are only half-women. Shahryar's palace, after Shahrzad's triumph, once again swarms with women – slaves, singers, dancers, concubines, poets, philosophers, contortionists, but all women. There are Persians, Kurds, Romans, Armenians, Ethiopians, Sudanese,

Berbers, Hindus. In this world walled with the soft folds of women's flesh, the jawari play sister, rival, mother, nurse or lover to each other.

Once a slave-buyer brought a rare and entertaining catch to the palace. The woman was obviously a foreigner. She knew so little Shahabadi that her answers to the sultan's questions were laughably childish. Her voice was hoarse, reminiscent of the cawing of the crows in the land she came from. And her appearance did not disappoint either. She had lustrous black tresses hanging heavily down to her knees, but she also had a sheath of hair all over her body, too dark to be called down. It was more like a sleek, lightweight fur. The crowning touch was that this woman, according to the slave-buyer, was a wandering poet in her own country. She was called Satya, and apparently made the mistake of taking her name seriously. Her verse, a little too truthful for some tastes, offended the ruler of her city. He summoned his hangman and the noose was slipped round her neck and tightened. But at the last minute the hangman felt an unreasonable compassion and loosened the rope. Her neck was ringed with angry red bands and her voice was changed for always. But she was still alive, and he smuggled her into a merchant's boat that was to travel the high seas the next day.

Shahryar and his cup-companions were struck by the story. They tried to coax Satya into reciting one of her poems, but she stood there silent, stupid and hairy. Just as they were beginning to lose interest, she caught sight of a girl with a goblet, standing by an open window. She rushed to the place (the girl moved aside in alarm) and stared at the patch of sky visible from the window, her mouth hanging open. She shuddered, then turned around, her eyes bloodshot and unfocused. She said, to no one in particular, 'Fire – flames in a palace mean fire. There are swords unsheathed, meat is being carried away. Three women and a palace, then a monkey and donkey marry.' Her words made no sense to her listeners. But there was an eerie sense of remoteness in her eyes, as if they were travelling to different places and times though she stood there, safely trapped. Her manner was portentous; she was in the throes of a fit; and when her words filled the room, they immediately took on the shape and weight of an oracle.

Once she had sweated her way back to earthbound normalcy, her usual mute self, one of Shahryar's advisers spoke up. (He was the author of the edifying treatise *A Guide to Slave-Buying*.) 'The Hindu jawari are faithful and tender, but unfortunately they tend to die young. Now this one – her eyes are not deep-set, so she can't be an envious sort. She doesn't blink too often either, so that's malice taken care of. Her hair is thick and wiry; obviously has courage. And though she sounds mad, I think I can clear that doubt – the black part in her eyes is not larger than the white, so there's nothing to worry about.'

A trembling, exhausted Satya was paid for and taken away to the freaks' wing of Shahryar's harem. At first she was given the new name Bilqis, in honour of the woman with hairy legs who spoke to butterflies. But Satya refused to respond to it. Shahryar's adviser on slaves pointed out that the woman must have a Shahabadi name tagged on to her old life since she was palace property. But he suggested a compromise since this was a special case. Considering the number of hours Satya spent gaping obsessively at the sky, he suggested Satya-sama.

Truth-sky, a double-barrelled name apposite for someone torn between two places. Satyasama, a faithful description of a woman who sought all manner of truth in the infinite lap of the skies.

For a while Satyasama was a court favourite, at least as long as her strange visions and pronouncements continued to awe or entertain everyone. But a palace is a restless, fickle lover. Besides, a large contingent of Roman women (the most reliable slaves for looking after their masters' valuable possessions) had just arrived in Shahabad. Satyasama, relegated to obscurity in the women's wing, found time between visions and sky-gaping to fall in love with one of the eunuchs guarding the harem. There was nothing much he could do about it, but the eyes of the palace were on them as they were on everybody else. Who knows when someone will break or bend a rule simply because of being alone and forgotten?

Satya's face at this time brought together as never before the excited wonder of the child or the poet, and the torment and pain of understanding. But soon her eunuch was in the dungeon, waiting to meet the executioner. For a few days there was some speculation on what he had been caught doing. Perhaps he only smuggled Satyasama to the palace roof so she could see the sky in all its wide-open glory. Perhaps his hand reached forward, tenderly wiped the racked, sweaty face after a fit. But these details were irrelevant; the executioner's busy axe had already gone to work.

And Satyasama? There were whispers that she had a human father and a jinni for a mother. It was best to leave her alone. It was best to leave her in peace in a windowless room, such peace as she could have without her half-lover and without the sky, even a ragged little patch of it. No one seemed to notice that Satyasama was fading away day by day. Her fur dulled and fell out in tufts; she was a half-empty bag of bones. Her young friend and admirer, the slavegirl Dilshad, was a devoted nurse; but Satyasama knew she was doomed. She would never master her new language completely, and her sudden fits and visions would never leave her. The scars round her neck would never heal, her voice never regain its original pitch and clarity.

But before she died in Dilshad's arms, she mustered the strength to give the girl a parting kiss, a kiss that had nowhere else to go. It hooked itself on to Dilshad's skin, a blessing or a curse. The poet was gone; she became memory; memory turned into legend. But as long as a slavegirl carries her kiss around like a tattoo on her face, the poet's soul – Satyasama's hardy beast of a soul – will manage to stay alive.

10

Dunyazad sits in the stomach of the palace – very few tenants have survived its heart – firmly anchored to the present. Only a few hours back, Dilshad crouched monkey-like by the window and chuckled, 'Have you heard? The old man has found consolation. A new bride will soon make her way down to the dungeon.'

She paused, but Dunyazad did not question her. Dilshad waited a little, then shrugged. She picked up her lantern and moved to the door. 'It's nothing serious,' she added, speaking, it appeared, to herself. 'He is a sultan, and sultans, as we know, must marry now and then.'

The last lamp has spluttered itself out of breath. There is a lull, all too brief, of silence. But the darkened room, a hungry empty bag, cries out to be filled. And it is; gently, insidiously it begins to fill, in distant corners first, then closer, closer still to the satin-slippery nest tethered to the window. Tonight of all nights, when she wrestles alone with what must be her doing – or undoing – Dunyazad cannot be allowed to falter. And listen, there are messengers enough, numberless voices to confirm that the self is never really alone, or single, or impossible to patch and mend when violated. A frayed old ribbon still boasting a glimmer or two of colour has wound its way from the restless burial grounds to the palace. There, there at the foot of her bed stands the wazir on a posthumous mission for his law-loving grandson. Her father's face, through

95

prolonged intimacy with earth and worm, does not look fit for paradise. But he, for once, is indifferent to appearances. 'Daughter,' the death's head before her is trying to say. But the last sliver of shrivelled, hanging flesh fell off too many years ago. His teeth went with the gums that dissolved to rot. Though bone meets bone in a well-aimed bite, the word is muffled by a sharp, loud click. He is able to say no more.

Then from the murmur that surrounds him like an aura, a voice grows distinct. It is left to her mother, Raziya of the copious, milky breasts, to sing a low, twisted lullaby. She halts Dunyazad's wandering thought that Dilshad may be lying; that Shahryar, no longer the man or fountainhead of power she knew, is pitiable. 'Does remorse always absolve? Is there no such thing as a permanently brutalized man?' Raziya's words have all the certainty they did not in life. 'This man,' mouths her potent whisper, 'thought he was God and every night and morning proved this pitiful delusion. Do you have so much compassion to spare?' Her breath expires over a long-drawn minute. 'You can be the woman I wanted to be,' hears Dunyazad, and a blessing lands on her head like a net with a feathery touch. It slips delicately down the length of her body so that she barely registers its caress. It contains her. Then it tightens. Sighs and moans fold into the anonymous darkness, thickening it.

Tonight, for the second night in a row, Dunyazad comes face to face with a past she does not know. Is there no end to the surprises it will spring on her? Will it ever make way for the future?

Dunyazad wills herself to focus on the presence she has sensed all along, waiting behind her head. There is some story waiting to be born here, a story she must deliver though she has not been part of it. Dunyazad puzzles over the images that surface – fragments, splinters of a broken mirror. Her sister is behind her, silent, a mere attendant for once. She waits patiently for Dunyazad to piece the plot together bit by bit, gloss over cracks with an ingenuous plaster. A scene rises before Dunyazad, vapoury, trembling, but a complete entity, a poem born whole. Though newborn, its intricacies are clear and highly wrought.

There are two people in the ivory-bordered frame, a man and a woman. The man is telling the woman a story. Or wait, perhaps it should not be called that, shy as it is of fantasy and symbol and fiction. (Though how the listening woman would have plundered his reports, cast *her* net on all their possibilities, if only she had come across this bounty earlier!) The man is young, a stranger, and a commoner in the company of royals, but he is no plaything, no talking machine of marvels. The woman feels poverty-stricken as she listens, but she wants to hear more. She knows, oh she knows about ship, journey, camel, desert, danger, knowledge and freedom. But word and dream and language – when have they not craved the power, the real magic, of travel?

Dunyazad sees Shahrzad, a girl for the first time though she is a mother three times over, discovering what it is to love without terror. The girl Shahrzad is watching the young man talk to her children. Dunyazad hears her think, 'There are no demands or promises that bind us. It is all the same to the world whether we never see each other again or run away together. No old story – of a lustful slave mounting a faithless queen, or a martyr talking into existence the word-borne fragilities of love and redemption, or the public good – can contain us.' The man falls silent, turns his head towards Shahrzad. The children blur out of view. At that moment, all she has to do is, stop holding her breath. Let go of that iron-marrowed will to love Shahryar, save him, save the city. And it will all be gone: her eternal trial, the burden of the throbbing chastity between her thighs that only her king can judge as sickly or flourishing. The solid palace will burst like an ephemeral bubble and she will be free. Free not just for another day, or of the executioner's axe for ever, but free to breathe, to begin her own travels in the time that remains to her.

Dunyazad, eternal virgin, looks on steadily, never blinking. Long ago she eavesdropped on Shahrzad and her husband, but this time, she can see. What she sees: it is as if nature, who knows what it is to have her desires thwarted, seizes her one chance of fulfilment. She plays umpire while two, a man and a woman, play the game of love. The two, Shahrzad and her lover, fight a battle as it is meant to be fought, their only armour the frailty, the generosity of their nakedness. Their modes of narrative will never quite be one. Yet who wants a pale copy of her erect-nippled breasts, or of the sloping valley of his back curving firmly into twin arcs?

Dunyazad's face glows with pleasure. She can embrace sleep now, having come close, very close to the triumph of a willing caress. Tomorrow she will ask to meet Umar again. She will hear him out while he wastes her time with his morality and vision and a new order of things. He can talk of a holy war all he wants. But she – she will tell him of a simple, modest petition she plans to make. Before the impending royal marriage, the sultan and his two real brides will make a pilgrimage to Shahrzad's tomb. Away from the prying attentions of vassals, guards and harem, all the fawning apparatus of courtly existence, they will pay one last tribute to the saviour.

11

Dunyazad, Dilshad and Shahryar are in the garden of paradise; or almost. In heaven, even death is beautiful, its aftermath artistically preserved. The only language time speaks is the language of eternity. The horror of death and separation, the pain of grief, all are distilled and purified into a poem. Dunyazad and Dilshad are in Shahryar's paradise. His elegy for a woman loved, *his* poem, stands before them, claiming immortality.

Shahrzad's tomb. The pearly tear of a redeemed lover; or a mammoth, milky ghost with a perfect breast for a head. A great splash of light-reflecting white. White, the colour of death; pure white, dazzling white, omniscient death.

The mausoleum, head-on: it is a square, domed structure, weightless, of unlimited space. Walls, doors and vaults appear insubstantial; the mundane pillars of reality have been banished. And it is tranquil, as if the city does not exist. All the workers have been ordered to stay away for the day to evoke the peaceful aura the tomb will have when completed. The few wooden scaffoldings left outside serve as foil to the tomb's peerless, marble façade.

But if the outside is stunningly simple, a lyrical contrast waits inside. Flowers, leaves, birds, borders, sanctified words in cool green jade, symbols and shapes – the infinite echoes of abstraction – embedded with blood-red gems reminiscent of the royal bed. Shahryar kneels before the marble-lined pit in the centre. 'This is where she will wait for me,' he says softly. 'In a few weeks, her beloved body will be removed from the temporary tomb in the garden and brought here – to her own eternal bed.' Dunyazad's eyes meet Dilshad's. To her surprise, the young woman does not look scornful, but grief-stricken.

Outside again, Dunyazad finds a stone seat that is ideal for a full-frontal view. She sits down and looks; Dilshad joins her, then Shahryar. Confronted with the evidence of his vision, the sultan has the tact not to describe it. Dunyazad gazes at her sister's new, ethereal palace, trying to resist its alluring magic. Shahrzad could not live in a world of unrelieved beauty and symmetry! If she did, she would not be happy; so much perfection would have suffocated her. But the magic will not let Dunyazad go; the spell is working on all three of them so that words, any words, are superfluous.

There is a surfeit of quiet. The white-laden world is still, too still, the calm it proclaims almost unnatural. As they sit there gazing at the tomb, it seems to change shades. The glare softens, the pristine white mellows. A breeze wafts in, stealthy messenger of stormy tidings. The air thickens. Dust, so fine-grained it could be silk, rises, spreads. Now the tomb of love is visible only through this winged rain of sand. Before them they see the shifting faces of purity assaulted by mud and grit. Then suddenly, with the quick thrusts of a practised sword, the dust parts briefly to allow a persistent band of ghosts to pass. Umar and his fellow rebels have surrounded them. The sand no longer strokes their skin with a silken touch. In the clutches of the storm, they can feel its rage in the cruel mote in the eye, the choking nose, the parched throat, the teeth crunching muddy impurities. Dunyazad registers a welter of confused impressions: Shahryar calling for help; running feet, curses, shouts; Shahryar and his unsheathed sword, Umar with a glinting wave of steel before his face, intense and exalted as if at prayer; a raised shield, then a lance led by a broad glittering head; and lurching towards Dunyazad, an enraged woman, everything wrong with her face: veil torn aside, an oily film of sweat, mouth stretched open in an ugly silent shout, a patch of sandy fur where it should not be, blood streaming from a grotesque eye. Bodies charge, pounce, seize. They strike and break. They fall. Head bent against the fierce onslaught of the wind, Dunyazad feels herself being moved, carried along with the bodies relentlessly pushing their way into the building.

Shahryar is a captive in the tomb he has conceived. The guards who appeared from nowhere to protect their sultan lie outside, dead. Those in the tomb, alive, are also spattered with grime and blood. But the rebel prince is cool, as if he is not dripping filth on to his mother's last marital gift. He stands on the edge of the pit looking down on the bound figure of his father. When he speaks, his bitterness is not entirely hidden by his immaculate poise. 'Your time is past, father. Now you should – if it is not too late – turn your thoughts to the all-merciful and plead forgiveness for your sins.' He sees Shahryar's wet eyes, the lips struggling to compose themselves and say something momentous. For a minute it appears that Umar is willing to wait and hear him out. Then he turns his back on the old tyrant; it is time for his triumphant march to the palace. Shahryar, the all-powerful sultan of Shahabad, is left behind in the tomb meant for Shahrzad, a prisoner of his memories.

The city, Shahabad of Shahrzad's redeeming stories, has been delivered to safety once more. There are crowds, vast crowds, as if every harem and market and dungeon has been emptied out on to the streets for a brief spell of celebratory airing. The crowd is not silent. Several homegrown epitaphs to Shahryar's reign are composed and tried out. 'Did he think redemption was so easy? A single man's affair?' demands a disgruntled citizen. Another voice chimes in: 'I hear his queen forgave him. But do you think she forgave herself? Why would she have died so young otherwise?'

But they become obedient subjects again when Umar's new wazir addresses the faithful. 'What happens when a city weakens? The kingdom it holds on its ramparts, a whole empire, an entire civilization, can wane and die . . .' He does not mention Shahryar. The name is rapidly turning into a legend, or an incurable disease. But who knows when a legendary disease will strike again?

*

It is Dunyazad's last day in the palace. Though she has helped to bring about the end of its old life, the palace spirit, that old villain who thrives in secure enclosures, does not seem unduly disturbed. It is she who feels ill at ease, her thoughts racing nervously, as hemmed in by these bloodthirsty walls as she was the very first night. She does not have the heart to stay on. Even with a new sultan, a new regime, there can be only one palace for her, at its head one tyrannical god.

Her task is done, Dunyazad tells herself. But if it is, why does she feel so unfulfilled? In time she will learn to resign herself to her sister's death, to her afterlife only in memory. Why should this search for Shahrzad continue?

Dunyazad watches the small arched frame of sunset visible from her window. Her male disguise, the desert traveller who brought her on this futile mission, lies on the sofa like an inevitable shroud. Her farewell audience with Umar was brief and to the point. Though willing to show his gratitude and generosity, she senses that her presence carries some of the taint of Shahryar; of the inglorious, barbaric past. Dunyazad has not seen Dilshad since that day's work at the tomb. She seems to have gone underground, nursing her wounds of rebellion and betrayal. Dunyazad carefully pushes aside the image of that pain-racked face. There are no other farewells left to be said.

But just as she prepares to go to sleep, there is a furtive knock on the door. A slave, trembling with the daring of her first secret assignment, hands Dunyazad a letter.

'Two royal heads,' writes Shahryar, 'may sleep on the same pillow, but two rulers cannot live in the same kingdom.' It is not clear at first whether the second head belongs to Umar or Shahrzad. But Shahryar seems to have almost forgotten about Umar, so muted are his complaints about his imprisonment. It is the past that is vulnerable to a string of shrill questions. 'How could I not rule over her? How could I not rule? How could I not join myself to her if it meant my salvation?'

'The tomb is hers because it holds my memories of her; my grief; and now my wasting body. The mausoleum, the paradise around it, my obsession, all are my tribute to Shahrzad. But she escapes me.' The body, the beloved body, finds no mention.

Dunyazad reads the rest in one great gulp. She wants to cry out 'Liar!' and sink to her knees with gratitude, all at the same time. Now that he has hinted that the monument and Shahrzad are separate entities, Dunyazad is not sure whether to believe Shahryar's fantastic tale. Does he really not know where Shahrzad is? Or is it all a metaphor, this talk of their rivalry, their tussle for power and her subsequent escape?

There is, at the end of it all, a kind of poetic justice in the old tyrant's imprisonment in a tomb of his own making. Dunyazad considers this, and concludes with sadness that her judgement is wanting. It is, in fact, almost as crude as Shahryar's belief that love, love born and nurtured in the living, beating heart, can be preserved in stone. She and Shahryar will never meet at a common point; their courses run parallel because both played supporting roles. Looking back on the thousand and one nights, and the days and nights that followed, she sees that it was always Shahrzad who was its central magnetic figure. Both their journeys, Dunyazad's and Shahryar's, and their different perspectives, led to her. (And can she forget that minor but shattering cameo-role player, Shahzaman?) When the storyteller's voice fell silent, when her later creations miscarried, it was they who felt the pain of being wrenched apart and orphaned.

The mistake, of course, is to imagine that a happy ending is possible when you have survived a shipwreck in a sea of blood. Shahryar should have killed himself in remorse, or at least renounced the city and the world, become a mad hermit in the desert. And Shahrzad? Can life continue, static, peopled with little events, commonplace milestones, after martyrdom?

*

Dunyazad, worn out with her travels and the prospect of the journey that still remains, is fast asleep on that last night in the palace. A gift comes to her mid-sleep. She is on her way back home, though it is not clear whether that is Samarkand, Shahabad or a place as yet unknown. But such uncertainties do not seem to matter in this caravanserai in the middle of nowhere where she awaits the refreshment she has ordered. She can smell something burning. Somewhere in the distance, in the bowels of the earth, in a dungeon perhaps, someone has lit a fire. The serving girl who finally comes to wait on her reeks of smoke. Even more astonishing, she looks like Dilshad. But the mark of fur is dulled; in the dark room it seems it is not there.

A spark of awareness sets her alight. Pleasure mingles with pain. Dunyazad knows, that instant, that she is in a dream; and in the midst of the dreaming comes the knowledge that this is as important as – no, even more important than – life.

'Who are you?' Dunyazad demands as her heart hammers in her chest its one unreasonable demand.

'You know me, sister,' the girl says, 'as well as I know myself.'

Dunyazad gapes at her, but allows herself to be led by the hand to the window. In the fading light of the spent day, Dunyazad sees the girl, young, young as Shahrzad was when Dunyazad followed her to Shahryar's palace. The resemblance ends there. Shahrzad too sparkled; but like a burgeoning wave she had more, much more than the dazzle of cleverness – and this, this monkey-girl with her enticing lies?

The girl waits for Dunyazad to finish examining her face. Then she says, in the low-pitched, alluring voice Dunyazad has never forgotten, 'And it is tightened, and it is cut.' These words, the satisfying formula of the storyteller weaving her way to a finishing point, tying it all up, Dunyazad has heard a thousand and one times before. Now, spoken again without warning or preamble, they flow over her in a blessed, redeeming wave. Her despair flies away from her, back to that closed tomb for a nameless body. If the sister she seeks waits for her in a tomb, it must be wide open, its crypt agape, destined never to be enclosed again.

'Come, Dunyazad,' says the girl, her words chasing Dilshad's mischievous grin off her one-eyed monkey-face. 'You and I have a script of our own – a story or two waiting to be told, *our* texts of gold to be written, every page remembering us to posterity. Dunyazad, will you travel with me?'

PART TWO

VIRGINS, MARTYRS
AND OTHERS

A DREAM,
A MIRROR

'I thought of a labyrinth of labyrinths, of one
sinuous spreading labyrinth that would encompass
the past and the future . . .'

Jorge Luis Borges

NIGHT FALLS AGAIN. It is a soft night, willing to nurse a wounded soul with memories, fingers, words.

There are four figures in this night's embrace, two women and their two goading jinn. One of the jinn, a fleshy, majestic woman, sits apart from the other three, behind a screen or a door. She holds a mirror in her hand, an ancient, ivory-framed mirror. She is too self-possessed to reveal her impatience; while she waits for the others to begin, she looks at the sorcerer's weapon in her hand. It glints obediently, reassuring her that there is nothing in the world – real or imagined – which it cannot reflect in its glassy depths; or which it cannot stretch, enlarge or distort. Who knows where exactly the truth lies, how many dreams and faces you must befriend or learn to love on the way?

This is Shahrzad, once Virgin Daughter of the wazir. Once the bride of Sultan Shahryar, the saviour of the city, then the wise sultana, then the wily sultana. Now she is the late queen, or simply a missing storyteller. Reduced to invisibility, she is waiting for Dunyazad, her follower and accomplice, to catch up with her and restore her to life.

Of the remaining trio, two are on a low bed. One of them is the lady Dunyazad. She too has a mirror, but this one is cracked and spotty, its carved ivory frame yellowing with neglect. It lies hidden under the pillow where she has banished it. Not far from this pillow, her clever hands unravelling the knots on Dunyazad's spine, is the woman Dilshad, till recently a slavegirl.

Dunyazad's mission in Shahabad is apparently accomplished. There is nothing to keep her there, or to keep her from going home. But she has sent her fellow travellers ahead to Samarkand. For the present she has chosen to remain behind in this house full of strangers, alone with Dilshad. And Dilshad, who has won freedom from Shahabad for her part in wresting power from one sultan, vesting it in another: she is free now to start life afresh, more or less; put as many miles between the Shahabad palace and her present as the growing distance to her lost childhood home. But first there is that small matter of an exorcism, of a murdered woman whose disembodied wandering spirit goes where she goes. A halved creature with two names, Satya and Sama, more than she needs, so compressed into one. A wayward, lie-spinning spirit, though all that is left of her is a scrap of fur, date-sized, cockroach-shaped.

This is the fourth figure in the room, the poet Satyasama who became a freak in a harem who became a jinni. She crouches by the window like a monkey, looking at the sky with the same rapt absorption with which her regal jinni-sister Shahrzad is looking at her mirror.

Night falls again. This time the room that holds the talking woman and her three companions is not buried in the stony heart of a palace. In a caravanserai midway between Shahabad and Samarkand, there is a small room, a well-lit, solitary nest perched high up on a whitewashed terrace. Though there is nothing between the room and the sky but a mere roof, the room also boasts a cheerful picture-window that frames an arch-shaped, sequinned sky. In the day it yields to sunlight like a permeable mirror.

This is Dilshad's room. Looking at it, it is difficult to believe that its occupant lived in a palace for years, even as a slave. It is a small room, quite empty. But it sits like a single eye on the terrace with its untrammelled view. Perhaps it is this view, perhaps it is the promised company of a shape-shifting, name-shifting woman; but Dilshad and her visitor Dunyazad are never lonely in this room.

The room is ready. The lamp is lit. Outside, the view waits patiently to be unveiled.

Halfway from somewhere, halfway to somewhere, Dunyazad and Dilshad nurse each other with memories, fingers, words. Two women, one possessed by a missing storyteller, the other by a muted poet. Two women and their goading jinn wander through the infinite wilderness of stories. Though their travelling dreams run parallel, destined never quite to run on the same track, there is always that one story hanging over both wherever they go. It is a familiar, ragged story, a porous umbrella of a story that barely shades its heirs and bastards, the narrative fragments it has given birth to. Whatever the incarnation of Shahrzad's story, wherever its location in time and space, the two women, Dunyazad and Dilshad, recognize its shop-worn soul.

Dunyazad knows there are storytellers and storyseekers. Her vocation is to *search* the story – to light up all its remote corners, not let a single detail escape. She cannot shake off a lifetime of caution. Even in these games of imagination, she thinks, it pays to impose a little order. Her object is predetermined: it is what she has already lived out. It is the furry familiar of night that has to be lived with, lived through, over and over again, afresh. In the womb of this woolly darkness she will always see two brothers and two sisters. She stalks the old Shahrzad story with wary devotion, drawing obsessive rings round it like a predatory lover. She sees all memories and visions through this one prism.

Unlike her younger companion, Dunyazad has been trained in the art of storytelling by the most prodigious performer of all. But still she shuns the variety of possibilities that so dazzle her young friend, the exhibitionist risk of the first person narrative, or the glittering tinsel of shifting times, locales and fantasies. (She can almost hear Dilshad say to her indignantly: 'Can you ask a coiled snake to stretch itself from one end to the other, lie frozen in a straight line?') But Dunyazad's talent is her sheer doggedness. Shahrzad's story (and so hers) she will examine minutely, zealously, from every point of view that occurs to her – a pregnant Shahrzad, a dying Shahryar, a wazir in anguish, a young Prince Umar, a fiend-possessed Zaman, even the outsider Dilshad. She will never doubt the pre-eminence of this story, the nucleus of her existence. Though it has already been lived out, it still waits to be fathomed. She cannot let go of it (nor will it let go of her) till she has made some sense of it.

*

Two women, Dunyazad and Dilshad, are midway between Shahabad and Samarkand. What next? Two women, having escaped a palace, roam free for seven days and nights. Or wait – these measures of storytime, seven days, a thousand nights, are pretty conveniences but their rule must be wily rather than absolute. For an hour or two these women are to be our heroines. Now that they have been uprooted – however briefly or tenuously – surely they can learn the trick of drifting down the wondrous deserts of centuries?

Change a feature or two, loosen a chafing garment, shrink veils, even bare a midriff, the exposed navel like a curled-up, sleeping berry. To make the business thorough, dye the language so that its unique gloss, its hints of particular shades, makes a subtle shift in geography. And their names, those marks that define them so distinctively? Remember, the desert has its lessons – those names engraved so clearly on our memories are only sand patterns, discernible for the moment but unfailingly mortal. They too are subject to the shape-shifting force of the wind. The skin of those old names – Dunyazad, child of the world, Happy-Heart Dilshad – can be moulted in the middle of nowhere, discarded once they have been used up.

What is left in our view: two women between cities, cities with palaces in their capacious, rapacious hearts. The two travel across time, across myth and legend. The family, the extended family of Shahrzad's story, its ancestors and descend-ants, seems inescapable. Part of an endless chain of refractions of the same story, as if it were eternal, its soul unchanging. They collect these like the woman who collected lovers under the nose of her jinni-husband. They collect virgins, martyrs, others who are not quite either. If their voices really replicate others of the past, only a fresh intimacy with these sisters across time will help them give voice to Shahrzad's route to salvation. And there is perhaps still another motive – to gain for themselves a view, however obscure, of a different future.

For seven nights and days, Dunyazad and Dilshad hear each other's stories. Dilshad has promised to play the scribe as well. There is no sultan in the room to listen to them or to chop off their heads, so they can dispense with the grand-scale infinity of a thousand nights. For a week, Dunyazad lives through the route she took to reach this room with a view, this room of talking and writing women. Dilshad responds (her understudy, the hairy jinni Satyasama, prompting her), with tales of travels half-remembered and half-imagined.

For seven nights and days there are dreams in mirrors, mirrors in their dreams. There is a festering memory in Dunyazad's story of the night. Dilshad or Satyasama take this pulpy, oozing memory and transform it in the hard and relentless light of day.

What is it like to talk for your life? For seven nights and days three women play a grown-up version – minus swords – of a dangerous but exciting game, The Martyr's Walk. If you were talking (or writing) for your life, what would you say? Dunyazad, Dilshad and Satyasama take turns playing the woman who saves herself and others through her fiction.

Will these storytellers be able to resurrect Shahrzad? Persuade the fourth player in the room to put down that mirror, come back to life, open her mouth and answer their question?

SEVEN NIGHTS
AND DAYS

'. . . she threw her arms round her sister's neck, and
seated herself by her side. Then Dunyazad said to Shahrazad:
"Tell us, my sister, a tale of marvel, so that the night may
pass pleasantly."'

1

Dunyazad:

Rowing a Floating Island

Shahrzad sits by the window in the empty harem, propped up with dozens of soft cushions. She has pulled her robe way up to her breasts so that her damp, bloated stomach is exposed to the air. It is a still morning, the kind that will grow into a stifling, airless afternoon. Shahrzad is tempted to call for her attendants to fan her, or cool her with a sponge bath and a large pitcher of refreshing sharbat. But she is reluctant to let go of this rare and all too brief time of complete privacy. She has sought out these ravaged, deserted rooms, the ones which housed her predecessor, Shahryar's licentious queen, precisely because she knows no one visits this part of the harem any more. In these rooms that once throbbed with the queen's secret pleasures, her sensual hunger a shining example to all her ladies-in-waiting, Shahrzad finds the solitude she needs to prepare for the twin tasks ahead. Dunyazad, whom she has sent to bed to catch up on sleep and store up her strength, will soon be with her. By then she must conjure a plan: how to deliver, with safety and speed, this baby that swims so purposefully in her; and how to recover in time for the night's storytelling performance in the sultan's ravenous bed.

Shahrzad considers the melon-shaped hill on her midriff, what used, nine months back, to be an ordinary, girlish stomach. Now her stomach has taken in some homeless soul, pickled it in her own portable, living ocean. Her skin is stretched so tight round this ocean that it is translucent; she can see a nascent life moving, sluggish but tenacious, already intent on its own survival.

This creature that has chosen her body as the vessel for its dangerous voyage: she, though she is mid-voyage herself, must somehow bring it to shore. She sighs a little at the thought. It is so very still and oppressive in the palace today. If only she could claim an earned holiday, take a day off in the gawky, untouched girl's body she used to wear, and visit her old home, see those innocent, familiar streets again!

Alone in the room with its mouldy cautionary tales about women who fall, Shahrzad lets herself droop. Her own pleasure in this room is the secret indulgence of melancholy. It is hard work to be a saviour. But to be a saviour rooted to earth by so much solid flesh, slowed down by prosaic pregnancy! Shahrzad is breathless and tired; both feelings, suicidal on-stage, must pass when this hour is at an end. She is also drowsy, so deprived of sleep that she can sense an empty space behind her eyes. But the unknown excitement that lies ahead, as well as the banal fact of her sticky, itchy skin, make rest impossible.

She does not fear the night ahead though she knows this will be the hardest one yet of all her palace nights. There is, of course, the brain-bending rehearsal to be got through before nightfall. But that she has been doing every single day the last nine months. It is the thought of the two very different

sorts of persons she must play today that drains her. Her
body, which has so recently declared itself a medium of
unpredictable pleasures, now demands its own private
redemption. It has, like Shahryar's unreliable desire, to be
coaxed and manipulated into a successful performance. She
has never paid as much attention to bodies as she has in the
past few months. Her own has been, with the greatest care
and deliberation, bathed, scented, ornamented; kissed and
caressed; licked, pierced, penetrated. The nights of tale-telling
have not in any way diminished the rights of bodily matters.
If anything, the body has been supreme. It has literally been
the object of the enterprise – to keep bodies whole and alive,
just as it was the subject of the original transgression, the body
as a vessel of the unchaste.

But this demand for undivided attention, this obsession
with its own capacity for fruition, has grown far too insistent.
Her body has declared its intention like a free citizen, or a
mutinous subject. It is another, more obedient body she needs
for her present purpose, the light and pliable one of a
contortionist, capable of response to all the gymnastics of
desire. Only this supple, shape-twisting woman can rise to the
need of the moment: to relate all she has heard, but also to
unleash and wield the power of an invention-embellished
memory.

*

It is no use changing your mind on delivery day. The body,
programmed to fulfil its relentless functions, is impervious to
second thoughts, deaf to frightened entreaties for a reprieve.
This is how a cornered animal feels – not knowing what will

happen next, but suspecting that fate is a harsh and ungentle master. Shahrzad tries to remember the terror that walked with her to Shahryar's bedchamber that first night; surely this should be less frightening? She calls out in panic, but to her surprise, her voice sounds normal and controlled. This is encouraging; her voice, which she hopes will save on a larger scale, is practising charity at home. As she pulls her robe down over her stomach, shuts her eyes and forces herself to breathe evenly, she hears hurried footsteps, and minutes later, she feels the soothing comfort of the slavegirls' light and anonymous hands on her, stroking and massaging. She yields to their rhythmic, hypnotic movement as to a lullaby.

Some time later – a phrase which holds luxurious uncertainty for her, a slave to the passing of time – she sees Dunyazad's taut, ready face bent over hers, and she remembers. She must get up, she has work to do. But she feels heavy, heavy, everything is pulling down earthward as if gravity is the only law of the land. Then a quick flash of pain hits her left thigh. She gasps.

'What is it?' She hears Dunyazad's urgent voice, then she is sinking again, there is a great big stone or a lump of lead tied to her, but she has not drowned yet. She drifts half-asleep, dreaming of water, of herself as a spongy, porous island that floats forever in the primeval waters of the imagination. There is no danger of drying up here, there is enough water to be soaked in day after day after day. But can you breathe underwater? She wakes up in alarm; a new pain thrills her entire body as an arrow shoots its way from her shoulders down her back and legs. She knows she must stay alert now, it is frightening to be woken with a shock every half hour. She turns to speak to Dunyazad and sees behind her bright sunlight streaming in through the window.

Dunyazad sees where her eyes travel. 'Yes, it is past noon,' she whispers as if the time of day could be a carefully guarded secret.

The pain subsides but Shahrzad looks grim and determined. The critical thing is to gain time, to hurry with these slowing, messy bodily processes. She has to resist being weighed down, she has to stay afloat. 'It's too slow,' she tells Dunyazad. 'We can't wait. Come, give me a hand.' Dunyazad and Shahrzad walk from one end of the harem to the other and back again. Now there is no pain at all, and with movement, Shahrzad is recovering her powers of concentration, and her usual look, her eyes shrewdly focused on the escape and glory to be won. The sisters, alive to the prerequisites of collaboration, take note of each other's posture, face and gesture. The two partners walk in step as they begin their preparation in earnest.

They begin, like good travellers, with a checklist of their equipment. 'Jinn,' Dunyazad calls out, and Shahrzad responds with a long chant of names and descriptions of those shape-shifting, flame-bodied creatures so essential to the fabric of her stories. The virtuous and beautiful female peri; the ghoul in deserted places and cemeteries; the qutrub, transformed into a beast at night, feeding greedily on corpses; Kabikaj, the jinni who commands insects; and the half-hearted but agile jinni, the nasnas, that makes do with half a head, half a body, one arm and one leg.

Shahrzad pauses. The pain has begun again. It informs her that her body, at any rate, is undeniably whole and full.

Dunyazad takes her arm, they turn, walk at a steady pace. The pain dulls; their study goes on. By the time they have exhausted all the lists that will thicken the undergrowth of the night's scenarios, Shahrzad is panting and dripping with sweat. They are almost on the run now, their concentration fiercely fixed, completely oblivious of Sabiha and the slavegirls waiting by the prepared couch.

Shahrzad's knees wobble. There is such a weight bearing her down that she walks, or waddles, with legs held awkwardly apart. Her stomach is a boulder balanced precariously on the narrow ledge where her legs are joined together. Her thighs have let go of their binding muscles as they are pushed out of shape to make way. She can feel them melting. A trickle makes its slow and reluctant way between them. She looks at Sabiha who darts across, lifts the queen's robe and probes gently with a finger. The finger comes away sticky with a little clot of blood.

'The journey has begun,' Shahrzad says lightly to her sister, though as she is led to the couch, she feels anything but light-hearted. She has traced the story of many a voyage, but never one which takes the traveller so dangerously close to the afterlife. Tonight's story must of course be the record of a long and difficult journey. She lies curled up on one side and whispers, 'Travels and obstacles, wonder upon wonder.'

Dunyazad smiles at her reassuringly. 'Bulukiya?' she asks. 'Do we tell him the adventures of Bulukiya tonight?'

'Yes,' Shahrzad says, 'we'll stretch it out into an endless chain of marvels. That should take us through to dawn. You can make' – and she licks her dry lips impatiently – 'appreciative noises and exclamations, as many as we can get away with – if I am this breathless.'

'Don't worry about it now,' she hears her sister say, but how can she not worry? Her existence depends on her remembering, and what she cannot recall, she must invent, or plunder from any other narrative that comes to mind. She lies there helpless, feeling the blood leak out of her every now and then. This worries her as much as the horrible constricting pain that makes her want to push and push, expel the ruthless parasite devouring everything inside her.

Shahrzad has got used to being on-stage. Though there is a sultan she must please, the omniscient narrator hovering over all scenarios and lives is herself. Her body too is now familiar with soaring, with grand scenes in which passion, danger and excitement can be flaunted. The rest of her waking life, large chunks of background scenes, are mere links and joints. In these moments submerged in darkness, she realizes how alone she or any martyr is. She then sees everything from her powerless perspective, a body spreadeagled, the mind glowing dully like the embers of the kitchen fire put out for the night.

But today, lying trapped off-stage, Shahrzad follows the soul in its journey to the afterlife. She weaves and wends her way in a world as remote as possible from this airless harem, through Bulukiya's adventures, her breathing altering as the pain spurs her to travel faster, move from one high-pitched marvel to another. She sees Bulukiya through his search for the herb of immortality; confronts serpents as big as camels; sees strange islands, hears trees laugh, discovers others heavy with clusters of human heads and birds on their branches. On Bulukiya's shoulders, she has an audience with the king of the jinn and hears about the innumerable hells of Allah. In Jahannam, only the least of these, there are a thousand mountains of fire. On each mountain there are seventy thousand cities of fire, in each city, seventy thousand castles of fire, in each castle, seventy thousand houses of fire, in each house seventy thousand couches of fire, and on each couch seventy thousand manners of torment.

On this couch, the one in the gloomy chamber of mundane, domesticated torment, Shahrzad the storyteller, caught between working hours, is crouched on all fours, moaning. Darkness rears, a hungry wave preparing to enfold her. If she submits to its embrace, she can go numb. All pain will be at an end, nothing but rest stretching in an endless desert before her. Martyrdom will be her oasis in this desert of silence. Though she has not yet triumphed, she has kept the murderous sword of the sultan at bay for nine long months, and she will die the death of a fighter who has fought to her last breath – but stop, she does not want to die, even if it means eternal rest or paradise or even martyrdom. She believes in an afterlife, she who was the wazir's star pupil in matters of faith and devotion. But it is life she wants now, the child's too, but her own first, even this life with its harems, dungeons, palaces, its forbidding walls and shrouds. She is young, she wants to see it all through, just scale one of those gates and look at the other side and oh – too late, the pain has torn her open and killed her. But wait, she can feel part of her slipping out forever, she can hear a smack and the baby's enraged cry. It's over; she has not yet been dispatched to paradise; and Sabiha will take care of the baby. Her part is done. Her body is her own again, to risk or to save. She lets herself sag completely. Her body meets the couch in a swift slap, and she falls asleep instantly.

*

Shahrzad wakes up feeling stiff and dirty but with a wonderful sense of well-being. Her stomach is sore and empty, she wants to eat and eat, she wants a leisurely, fragrant bath, she wants – and she struggles to sit up. She has just noticed that the window frames a piece of darkness.

'It's night,' she begins accusingly and then sees a stiff, glittering figure moving towards her. Dunyazad, swathed in gold brocade, a virgin bride who knows a little too much, comes closer, sits by her bedside, waiting for her blessing.

'Where are you going,' Shahrzad asks, though she knows of course, why else has Dunyazad come here dressed in those ridiculous clothes that don't suit her? Dunyazad will take her place. Her enigmatic sister knows how to wait, poised like a feline hunter stalking her prey. And her sister's motive is simpler than her own; she wants to save Shahrzad as much as Shahrzad wants to save the city. But will her sister, taciturn, quick to anger, be able to talk all night?

She gives Dunyazad's face a searching look and receives a tender smile in response. Dunyazad is not one to take foolish risks. Shahrzad recalls how on the one or two occasions she planned to explore the city dressed in boys' clothes, it took her hours to convince Dunyazad that it was perfectly safe. She looks around to see if any spying slave lurks nearby, then gestures to Dunyazad to bend towards her.

'Where is it?' Shahrzad whispers. 'In your robe?'

Dunyazad blushes but she immediately shows Shahrzad what she wants to see. There are very few secrets between them. The small, sharpened dagger is just where Shahrzad expected it to be, hanging snug and hidden between the waist-folds of the rich, voluminous skirts.

'We have to get rid of him while he is still prepared to listen to your stories,' Dunyazad says calmly. 'I can't bear to see you go on and on like this night after night. Tonight is the perfect one to silence him; Shahabad's new king sleeps safely in Sabiha's arms. This sultan is completely dispensable, having finished that little task. There is a kind of poetic justice in the timing, don't you see?'

Shahrzad sits up, shaking her head decidedly when Dunyazad tries to help. They sit face to face, considering each other thoughtfully. Shahrzad could talk of love and piety, abstractions which enthrall both of them, daughters of the same stern and loving father. Then the image of two figures on a bed flashes before her. In the stories she has told Shahryar she has included both chaste and unchaste wives, perhaps to show him that all kinds of men could be cuckolds. But often, in recent nights, she has felt a secret delight when revealing the adventures of a licentious woman, as if she would like to push the sultan a little further into the confusion of reality, and his own deluded expectations of it. There is a saying she has sometimes heard her mother use: 'If a serpent loves you, wear him as a necklace.' Though Shahrzad has never been sure what exactly this means, the proverb has recently installed itself in her head like a guiding light.

There is always salvation, the ultimate goal, that she can

unveil enticingly to dazzle Dunyazad and all other doubters. Salvation, a journey flagged off by the wazir, lights up and sanctifies a more worldly but equally interminable quest. Righteous power waits at the end, and a good name in all men's ears. Today of all days there is a strong sense in Shahrzad of several worlds in precarious coexistence, a sense of walking and talking through any number of sticky, intersecting bubbles. If Shahryar suffers from the sight of that hellish, self-duplicating image of infidelity, this is her jahannam, a palace of mismatching days and nights. A wonderful setting for a story, but the palace also holds the storyteller captive. Perhaps it senses her plan; sees her straining to stretch time, *her* time, into a number as close as possible to infinity.

For a minute Shahrzad sees, as if Dunyazad's face is a mirror, the sword sheathed in the heart of the palace and unsheathed every dawn. It can get her any day, it can get her tomorrow morning. But is she to be defeated by swords and hearts, whimsical notions of holder and held? The real antagonist is only old time, that banal creature who does not know that several lifetimes can be lived in an instant. In the stone palace with its drab-skinned exterior, its secret enclosures of rich nests, their nuanced intricacies, she now faces Dunyazad squarely. Her tone she has learnt from her justice-loving teacher, though not the words: 'Here I am, talking for my life and yours, and you talk of more bloodshed? Look at this empty harem. Can't you hear its walls weep?'

Dunyazad knows that if she is allowed to put the dagger to good use, Shahrzad would still be a saviour, ridding Shahabad of a head gone askew. But she is a good accomplice. She gives in, though from her unrelenting face it is not clear if she is convinced. Can danger be addictive? Are there women who come alive only when there is danger at their heels and their blood races with terror? Dunyazad knows she must postpone these questions. For now, in this women's chamber, on this day of double hurdles, Shahryar, the all-powerful antagonist, must be brought to his knees without resorting to his own brand of weapons. Shahrzad must rest a little, then dress for her role as the night's perennial bride.

*

Dunyazad has refused her maid's offers of help and shut herself in her room. The girl means well but for now, for just an hour or two, she must be alone. She sees the clothes already laid out for her. Like everyone else in the palace, like the wazir, the servant girl expects her to get into her uniform for the night. She frowns at the quiet, girlish dress, sits down, begins to undo necklaces and bracelets.

Yes, it is time to recover her old self, the waiting, willing accomplice. The dagger is gone; the eternal spectator, insufferably meek, is back. Shahrzad, having produced an heir of martyr stock, is ready for her reward. It is she who will see Shahryar uncrowned again. Together they will play out their nightly torments, couple with delicious, dangerous truth-telling.

Dunyazad stands, peels off the stiff bridal clothes that encase and protect her languishing virginity. She would like to throw them aside carelessly, but finds she is smoothing out, folding and carefully putting away in a chest a costume she may now never need. Waiting behind her thin screen in the bedchamber, Dunyazad has heard Shahryar's nakedness. His moans have reached her; so have his teasing moments of silence. An occasional mindless cry has touched her, drawing out an echoing wail in the pit of her stomach. But now she has put away lovers, husbands, crowns, Shahryar. All treacherous thoughts of supplanting Shahrzad. From her corner of their triangle she will never quite see or learn the secretive rites practised between lover and beloved, or sinner and redeemer.

But there is something that is her own, something that she is just beginning to see. Shahrzad and her tyrannical husband are closer than the obvious links of man and wife, ruler and subject. The womanly fabricator, the builder who strips others' creations of what takes his fancy to build monuments for his own times – there is a parallel here. Dunyazad recalls a useful proverb her mother taught her two growing girls: 'If the dishes increase in number, it's likely they are from the houses of neighbours.' Shahrzad must remember this too, especially when she slips someone else's passing idea into her narrative, or when she cribs a phrase or two, sometimes an entire frame. But she is safe – no one looks at a nose or an eye out of the context of a face; or at a solitary balcony or pillar on an entire edifice. The synthesis will be hers, and in that sense, the authorship. *His* reconstructions will make him a great builder. But wait, Shahryar. What happens to a builder when he is reduced to simple, penurious easel and ink? His new creations, though built in mind with the most solid of granite, would be mere phantoms. And the woman – what will happen to you, Shahrzad, when the urgent need for storytelling, the demand for prolix invention, is withdrawn? Will you be satisfied with bedtime tales to your children?

Dilshad:

Nine Jewels for a Rani

Once, in the land called Eternal City, a one-eyed monkey-woman was chopped, limb by limb, till all that was left of her was a misshapen trunk. This thing of matted fur and blood refused to die. It lay in the shade of the treetop that had been its home, moaning eerily at passers-by. Once in a while, a compassionate inhabitant of the land would stop and consider the thing: What act of mercy would heal and revive it? Or let it die at last into a blessed silence?

One midday, when the sundazed city slept away the heat, a few Eternals secretly made their way to the tree. They stretched their ears open all the way and listened carefully to the thing's moans. They stood there, risking sunstroke and worse, waving away pesky flies, till the sun slid down the sky into late afternoon. Then they shook their heads sadly in admission of defeat. Today too they could not decipher a thing, not a single intelligible word, in the monkey-woman's moans. They crept away, silently promising to be back. They left just in time; because a few minutes later, a large, noisy group of Eternals drifted towards the tree. Several of them brandished sticks, glinting blades of steel or rusty old iron chains. A few carried prayer beads.

There were all kinds of people in this group: different colours, sizes and shapes, men and women, even a few children. But it was hard to tell them apart once they surrounded the thing. They could have been members of the same happy family, so much in accord were they as they jeered at the thing and poked at it with sticks, boots, long-nailed naked feet – all to see if they could make it moan louder.

The thing twitched like a truncated lizard's tail. Sweat streamed down its bruised breasts, changed course at its navel, and dripped to the ground from its hips, or the stumps where its legs should have begun. It did not stop moaning. No matter what they did, it kept to the same volume; the same pitch; and it remained a stranger to silence. As they heard the moan go on and on, a few Eternals mumbled that they had never heard anything so steady and rhythmic before – except the breathing of a living thing.

Meanwhile the crowd was growing restive. Were they simple idiots to be satisfied with just poking and prodding? One of them threw away his stick and turned to the others. 'What a laugh,' he said. (He had a bushy grey beard and a nose like a hungry vulture's beak.) 'This thing actually thought she could sing! She gave up everything for it – and listen to her now!'

His words were met by an enthusiastic chorus of wolf-whistles, kicks and prods. A precocious child, anxious for attention, gathered all the spittle in his little mouth, and sent it flying at the thing in a bull's-eye jet of venom. 'That's enough,' boomed a firm voice. (*This* one had thin lips and a belly so swollen you'd think he had swallowed half the city in a gulp.) 'We've done our duty. Let this thing be an example to all Eternals!'

The thing that used to be a one-eyed monkey-woman lay there – whether they came and went, whether it was day or night. The woman, or what was left of her, moaned.

Once a stranger from distant places, a woman called Dilshad, visited Eternal City. Wherever she went (and the land was full of sights to see), she heard this lingering, keening wind; a message of foreboding that permeated the air as no spoken word can. Dilshad found it unbearable. 'What is that thing,' she asked her hosts. 'And why does it lie there wailing?'

The Eternals probably had many eloquent theories to present to their visitor, and in their usual inimitable style. But this is what actually happened.

*

The little girl Satyasama was an orphan. Or so we must assume, though there have been rumours that her parents, a thriving Eternal couple, deserted her. These rumour-mongers insist that the parents are to be pitied, not blamed. When Satyasama's downy baby face grew a mask of fur, the parents were sad and frightened. But when her forehead widened and receded, and the sharp family nose was blunted so that her features grew suspiciously simian, they were furious; they just had to throw her out.

But a few Eternal elders scoff at this story. They claim Satyasama was from the very beginning an orphan of the city streets. One of them, a reliable and perceptive witness, describes her as a little foolish, the sort who would suddenly steal away from a riotous game with other children to climb the tallest tree she could find. She would swing her way up, all her muscles straining with concentration, a little hammer beating time to the blood racing to her head: up, up, up!

The other girls in the city would never have been allowed to run loose as Satyasama was, roaming about in search of taller trees, her legs entwining their rough-barked trunks with familiarity any time of the day or night. But Satyasama was an orphan; no one kept track of what she did. And she looked like a monkey, so not one elder in the city cared that her blood stirred strangely at the prospect of climbing. Not one of them knew that as she climbed higher, this nameless stirring grew till it threatened to overflow the small hidden place it was locked within.

Separated from girls her age (and indeed all ground-loving Eternals), Monkey-Face indulged her overwhelming passion for solitary aerial views. Once she had reached the treetop, she would crouch on a branch reverently, waiting for her heart to stop its clamour. Then she looked and looked; worshipped the land at large.

Satyasama (or Monkey-Face) stared at the city below and the sky above till she had committed to memory their visible and not-so-visible features. This childish desire to fill herself up with looking did not weaken as the years went by. Instead the girl's appetite grew; her clandestine career was firmly established. There wasn't a single treetop in the city that Monkey-Face had not visited.

There was one particular tree, a lush peepal, that she went back to again and again. Of course she didn't know that many wise men had chosen the peepal as the perfect backdrop for meditation and enlightenment. Nor did she know that they usually chose to sit in the shade of the tree, eyes shut. Monkey-Face's interest in the peepal tree was a little different. She found that its highest branch, curved into the shape of a swinging seat, fit her back and rump perfectly. Settled in place, her eyes travelling where they pleased, what she saw leading her to all kinds of strange thoughts and dreams, Monkey-Face grew into a young woman.

It was on this tree that she had the accident that was to change her life. (Later, many would claim that it was an accident in the conventional sense of the term – an unfortunate event; a few dissenters whispered that it was fortunate; or a happy accident.)

One night, when simple, yearning Monkey-Face sat high up in the peepal, gazing at the moon, lightning struck. It struck, without warning, the very tree Monkey-Face sat on. She did not move an inch. She was held in place by the silver branch that grew arrow-twigs all over the sky, then set it ablaze. It was a sight to culminate a lifetime's search. And Monkey-Face, unaware of her good fortune, was seeing it already, from a seat with a ringside view.

Slowly, when the sky folded its magic kit of moon and stars and lightning into a cloudy waterless sea, Monkey-Face woke up. She blinked. The spectacular private show was over but it had left her with a tangible souvenir or two. One: the entire world seemed to have shifted over to the left side. The right was out of business. Monkey-Face, now one-eyed, bent cautiously and examined her body. All there, but the tree – what had happened to her watching post? Like her eye, the peepal was marked for ever; no wise man would ever choose *this* freakish tree for his enlightenment-seeking umbrella. But

Monkey-Face, whose loyalty was unswerving, swore to herself that the peepal would be her home always.

Now that One-eyed Monkey-Face had found herself a home, she was fully grown-up. With just one eye (and that one trained to focus long-distance) she had even more trouble keeping up appearances. Her fur was entirely ungroomed on the right side. Her rump was a matted mess of flattened hair and a torn tuft or two. More important, she suspected it didn't matter. In her bones she felt her beauty had nothing to do with fur or face. All she knew was that it was the moon-gazing, the tree she had chosen which lightning would then choose, and the subsequent one-eyedness which had something to do with it.

Slowly she got used to herself. She got used to the lopsided but acute vision, the obsession with detail yoked to the partiality to panoramic views. But no one felt sorry for this dweller on tangled branches. Perhaps this was because Monkey-Face was never pathetic. There was, remarked observant Eternals, something about that one eye. It didn't gloat or wink or anything crude like that. But that one eye which had survived lightning had a way of seizing an object or a person or a view and fixing itself. It could even train its avid gaze for more than an hour on the empty distance.

Once Monkey-Face had learnt confidence, begun to revel in her one-eyed self, she was ready for the second phase of her career: she took to singing. At first her singing attracted only a few stray monkeys. Though they were not human like her, they were tame and docile. They sat around her branch, listening, their posture telling her they were her devoted slaves. Once a passer-by left a tin below the tree. After that, every time she sang, the other monkeys would silently materialize out of nowhere, swing down the trees, and dance round the peepal. When her song was over, they would give her the few coins in the tin and slink away.

We have seen that very few in the city considered Satyasama a woman. It was not just her gender that was in danger of being lost. Living high up on the city's fringes, she was also liable to have her name suddenly taken away from her; to be given another in its place; lose that in turn. Satyasama, who had grown into Monkey-Face, was transformed in an instant to One-eyed Monkey-Face. When she began to sing her early songs – the ones that summoned a simian audience – she became One-eyed monkey-woman. This name was to stick for many years, even after the dancing monkeys vanished for ever. But the coins in the tin kept coming; the Eternals had got used to her singing. (Many came to hear her because they thought it was a freak show, but there were others who enjoyed her simple, lyrical rhymes.) So the singing One-eyed monkey-woman, One-Eye for short, became in time a singular but genuine citizen of Eternal City. Her days of orphanhood seemed over at last.

One-Eye lived in a land of two-eyes. The citizens of Eternal City went about with their 20/20 vision firmly lighting what was in front of their noses. They rarely knew what happened behind their backs or below their feet, but these deficiencies they considered minor sacrifices for clear-sightedness.

Unfortunately Eternal City, like so many other lands, was divided. Not by flowing rivers, or craggy mountains that invite you to cross the barriers they put up; but by the innocent, baby-blue sky. The sky divided Eternal City into the eastwallas and the westwallas. The easties felt their pupils dilate, gain sharpness and power and peace from the ascending light at sunrise. They worshipped that piece of eastern sky; chanted ten thousand and one names in its praise. They invariably greeted each other with the pious wish: 'May the light rise in the east tomorrow!'

The westies found this early morning devotion a bizarre and alien thing. Surely anyone with an iota of sense or piety or love for motherland would see that it was the west he should turn to? Here, each evening, was the grand spectacle that humbled every doubting soul: that glowing orb, sinking lower and lower in the sky; star-sewn night, its solemn disciple, inching forward to bring rest and sleep to the most heartsore of creatures.

Luckily there was enough sunlight – and a good number of risings and settings – to go around. Everybody got a piece of the sky, so to speak. At least this was the centuries-old arrangement. You couldn't reach up and divide that blue expanse neatly with a piece of chalk, could you? So the eastwallas and westwallas muddled along somehow. Occasionally they even managed a few memorable celebrations together: there were some easties and westies who actually got together at midday or midnight. They made laws and music and paintings and buildings and babies and business. Would the sun, they reasoned, rise every morning if it didn't set the night before?

All this was in the good old days when One-Eye had just begun her post-lightning singing career. She had begun with simple rhymes that she chanted in a sing-song voice. She sat on her split treetop, describing the world before her, its simple

joys and sorrows, much as a child names things in a landscape
she has just discovered. One-Eye sang of herself, of her tree,
of the wind and the rain. She even sang of the sky – that
cherished theme of Eternal existence. And the Eternals – those
who stopped at the foot of the tree and listened – quite
enjoyed it all. All the world loves a simple fool, especially a
performing simple fool. One-Eye's singing (at least to date)
seemed as pretty and innocuous as the twittering of birds. And
the Eternals were aware of the power of sound effects; they
had heard, both easties and westies, how birdsong enhances
the moods of sunrise and sunset. So One-Eye sang on unmo-
lested as long as a childish voice sang her music.

Then One-Eye discovered a friend. She found her, her
very own rani, in an unlikely place.

It happened on one of those harshly lit, dusty afternoons.
All the sane people in the city were fast asleep – those who
could in cool beds, others at their work or on their feet. One-
Eye could not sing or sleep; she felt a terrible restlessness.
There was not a single dark cloud in the sky. But she felt as
excited as a bird that has sensed the oncoming of a thunder-
shower. Before you and I can begin to wonder how a woman
can feel like a bird, One-Eye had leapt off a tree and made
for the heart of Eternal City.

She clambered up drainpipes and slid down awnings,
jumped from one roof to another, peeking, prying, doing what
came naturally to her. Then in the dilapidated, dimly lit
interiors of a building earmarked for demolishing, One-Eye
found her. Her restlessness melted away as the rani took her
hand as if she had been waiting for her.

At this point of my story, I usually hear a voice or two hiss from the wings: 'Wait a minute! What does this derelict rani look like? Come on, describe this queen of yours!'

Sorry: our heroine may have only one eye, and she may be a performing monkey, but a stubborn secretiveness cloaks her like a tight-fitting coat of fur. Later, during those long hours of cross-examination and lie-detector tests, One-Eye would mumble incoherently about her rani. The sunstruck eternals would try to pin her down with a volley of questions. 'Who is she? What are her aliases? Is she anti-city? Anti-sky?' Not one arrow would find its place. They said One-Eye's replies were evasive or incomprehensible. Later, when they were finished with her, she could only moan.

The moral of this digression into the future: if even the sunstruck Eternals (with their brains blazing fires of madness) could not beat a description out of One-Eye, who am I, a mere storyteller, to try? A few publicity-seeking Eternals have spoken of a smelly old crone who lurks in the decrepit building, but when pressed they have admitted that they could have imagined her into existence.

What I do know though: it was after One-Eye had this close encounter with her rani that she discovered the powers of her blind eye. The first time One-Eye felt her semi-blindness lift like a flimsy curtain and dissolve into vapour, her music changed for ever. At that blessed moment she saw the world before her no longer leaning to the left. Instead she saw a huge circular wonder with a million strands and textures and grand designs. In these fits of double-sightedness One-Eye saw the city afresh. She took in what she saw, the riddles and clues, the number and complexity, and condensed them in inspired haste, almost afraid the curtain would come down on her eye before she was finished.

Slowly, with painful sessions of practice, One-Eye learnt to summon these fits at will. She sang of storms; of changes in the sky; of the eternal marriage between east and west. She offered these songs to anyone walking past below. But in her heart of hearts, they were all for her – she who had given her those moments, however brief, of sight. ('Make a song like a diamond,' the rani had told her. 'When it glitters so hard that it lights up a mind, I will receive your message of love.')

One-Eye was never sure when the sky that lit her heightened vision became a rag for two quarrelsome dogs to tear to bits between them. I suspect it was around the time the newly set-up Departments of Shame, Fear and Loneliness became powerful in the city.

I have to say a few words about these departments. It would seem (from their very names) that these departments would be the last to receive official sanction. But Eternal City, for the last few years, had suffered one heatwave after another. The winter sky, always a phenomenon in these climes, had all but disappeared. Though very few tears were shed for this cool grey sky that was never really at home in Eternal City, the new sunlit era had another source of trouble – heatwaves that engulfed its sky-worshipping natives and gave them sunstroke. The most severely sunstruck ones felt their brains melt like wax. When the sky grew cloudy and their brains cooled, the wax dried in all kinds of strange, contorted shapes. To all appearances they seemed ordinary Eternal City dwellers. But inside, their grotesque, sunstroked brains were working away on a crusade to spread madness.

One of the symptoms of this madness was the growing belief (first secret, then not-so-secret) that the sky was not big enough for both sunrise and sunset. Once the sunstruck ones took to proselytizing, and more and more Eternals glared up at the sky, jealously keeping their half free of clouds from the other side – it was only a question of time before large, mobile masses of shame, fear and loneliness began to float around, aggressive orphans demanding a permanent home. They found it in the new departments located in the hallowed precincts of Eternal City's Council.

From her treetop, One-Eye sniffed the air anxiously. She could sense a violent storm coming, smell the unnatural, irreversible changes it was bringing to Eternal City. She sang as loud as she could. Sometimes, in the depths of night, she whispered like a restless ghost. She sang of clouds that drifted and rained whether they were in the east or west; of the dangers of the sun's course being tampered with; and most of all, over and over again, in a hundred different words and ways, of the cycle of day and night.

In her head she travelled to the rani's derelict room; waited outside the closed and cobwebbed door as a humble suppliant. She sang to the door in deep silence till it opened and so did her blind eye. The rani stood before her, tired and older but still the mistress of One-Eye's dreams. The rani saw her need at once. She consulted her memory which went back ten centuries, pulled out a song and wore it on her forehead so that One-Eye could memorize its shape, colour and cut.

Back on her treetop, bottom-sore with the long hours of tense perching as she had summoned the rani, One-Eye broke into song:

> 'A few clues I give to you, my friends,
> that you may seek the treasure:
>
> Nine precious stones the colour of blood
> pierce the skin of darkness.
> In the sparkling heart of day
> a lump of pure gold.
>
> Mine the gems; beat the blaze to a fine streak.
> Nine jewels quicken
> when strung on daylight's band.'

Some of those who heard this song wafting down to them from the lightning-struck treetop stopped to listen. Naturally many were puzzled. It *sounded* lovely, but what was it all about? A few gave up: what did that One-Eye think, the stupid beggar, taxing their brains like that? Didn't they have better things to do? But there were others (many many more than One-Eye or the sunstruck ones knew) who took away the song with them. They took the lines away carefully, word by word, to put together on their own.

Then there were others who heard only snatches of One-Eye's song; only those parts they wanted to hear, the parts they could twist for their own ends. 'Day? Night?' they thought. 'Is she pro-westwalla? Anti-eastwalla? Or the other way around?' (Either way – they shook their heads grimly in the dreaded departments of SFL – it won't do.)

Soon after, One-Eye was summoned for her first interrogation. She had been on the treetop for so long that she felt quite giddy on the ground below. It was in this somewhat confused state of mind that she arrived at headquarters. The sunstruck Eternals were waiting for her there. They pounced on her right away.

'Who is this rani you sing to?' they demanded. 'You are inciting people to violence. How dare you talk about blood and beating when you are looking at the sky? And most of all, how can night and day come together? (Even our babies know the sun divides day and night into opposites.)'

One-Eye was bewildered. She was lonely, afraid, even ashamed. She shut her good eye (right there in front of them) and beseeched her rani: was she going mad? Or could all of them be mad?

When she opened her eye again, she told them:

> 'The day is the sun's heart, the night its soul.
> Will you mock this peerless design,
> a necklace fit for a rani's neck?'

This, many Eternals swear, is when One-Eye's fate began to assume its ugly features. First they forbade her to sing her new songs as they were. (The Department songwriters had sweated all night working out acceptable versions.) One-Eye refused. Goaded by her unreasonable refusal, her tormentors locked her up in an underground chamber with just enough air to keep her alive. What she did there and thought there (and what they did to her) no one knew. A year later the Department heads, in a merciful mood, reconsidered her case and she was brought up into the glare of day again. One-Eye now looked like a subterranean creature. Her good eye was misty; fungus hung like trails of old lace from her fur.

They held their noses and told her the time for compromise was past. She could go back to her beloved tree, consort with whichever mysterious rani she pleased. But: she was to give up singing for ever. In fact, to make sure they didn't run the risk of trusting her again, she was to fulfil one more condition. She was to open her mouth only to eat. Only complete silence would earn her the right to be a free citizen of Eternal City. One-Eye asked for twenty-four hours to make up her mind.

That night there were all kinds of shifting, stealthy noises in the Council hall. Some said a group of admiring Eternals had stolen there in the dead of night. Others said it was the fabled rani, come at last to rescue her friend. What we know is that someone helped One-Eye escape that night to the blighted old peepal. Huddled precariously on her old branch, at midnight – that hour of freedom in Eternal City when it was neither day nor night – One-Eye sang. It was a full-fledged concert, a rendition of the Collected Works of One-Eye. It was a performance which would not be easily forgotten; which was just as well, because when the first shades of dawn rose, they were waiting for her.

They hacked at the tree so that she had to clamber down before it was all gone. Then first they chopped her limbs: one, two, three, four. Next the left eye, the blind and gifted one, was gouged out; then the right, so that blindness would be perfect and complete. The tongue, that word-dripping treacherous tongue, was pulled out and thrown into a purifying fire. It seemed a pity to leave the head. After all that was the ultimate traitor, the ringleader who had thought and imagined all those lying fantasies into existence. So off went One-Eye's head.

By the time they left her, her pile of offerings had mounted. Below the wreck of a tree lay disjointed limbs, four in number; a pair of meaningless, staring eyes; a burnt-out tongue; a picture-less head. The trunk that remained behind, the filthy bloody remains of One-Eye, writhed like a mad thing, then lay still.

Later they came back to dispose of One-Eye's mutilated parts and clean up. They threw all the bits and pieces – now stiff and rotting – into a cart. But when they touched the trunk, it began moaning. It was a hair-raising, heart-breaking moan, the kind that made many Eternals wish they were deaf, or that they could go into exile somewhere to hide their fear and self-loathing.

So Satyasama, then Monkey-Face, later One-eyed monkey-woman, acquired a new name at this late stage of her chequered life. She became the thing; the unrelenting moaning voice of the city. Very few in the city know the secret of the thing's incredible survival. But a mad old crone whispered in my ear once: 'She will refuse death though she is bereft of her friend the rani. She will resist succumbing to the relief of silence, its escape from pain and hatred, as long as that moan continues. As long as it is there, that ninth and last little jewel of life, Satyasama will still be alive. But only just, I think, only just.'

2

Dunyazad:

A Lover, a Tomb

The shell of his last chamber is a pristine beauty. But since he is inside, will now always be enclosed in its safe womb, all exteriors are irrelevant. Inside, then. A vast, high-ceilinged room, curved at its summit in a dome. The walls – and they are significant, because he has been forced to acknowledge their indisputable power for the first time – the walls are as solid as any he has ever envisioned, not just brick and mortar, but plated with sheets of stone, marble, and anchored to the deep-rooted foundation with hidden iron pillars.

The light here is never direct or fresh enough. Two intricately worked lanterns stand on either side of the room, one on a paper-littered table, one by a low sofa. Their glow is caught and dispersed in patterns, a complex, prismatic play of light and shade. Chips of precious and semi-precious stones on the walls pick up the light, wink in response, and occasionally flare into a quick flash of a signal. There is only one window, obviously not part of the building plans. It is a crude childish cut-out of a rectangle, made in a hurry; for a finishing touch, it has iron bars. The window is high up on one side of a wall, too high to reach without the help of a ladder.

Below this window stands an easel on the floor, ready and fitted with mounted paper. Sketches, dozens of them in various stages of completion, lie on the lantern-lit table nearby; so do ink pots, brushes, quills, pens, colours.

There is a man in this cluttered and unusual workroom, a man with an elegant grey beard. He is simply but expensively dressed in plain silk, both his robe and turban in muted colours. A long, solitary strand of pearls hangs round his neck, the only treasure still unequivocally his.

The man, ex-sultan Shahryar, is drawing – a little clumsily, since his untrained fingers cannot keep up with the task of translating the image in his head on to paper. His intensity, however, makes up for his lack of expertise. He must persist. Though he is not allowed to consult his team of architects and engineers, he owes it to posterity to sum up his career, clarify the position he claims in history, in real, concrete terms. It is as if the task at hand, the design he struggles with day after day, will be the solitary tale he leaves behind. He knows the building in his head is not just another tomb, though he hopes to be buried there, where his soul can fly as high as its soaring tower.

The most ambitious monument of all, in its unashamed paean to the human heritage, casts itself against the unapproachable heavens; thrusts itself head first into the vastness of time. Shahryar's tower, his plans for a lofty celebration of brotherhood, must be enduring testimony to the triumph of his life and its grand design. It is also, for now, his plea for freedom. Even if it means forgiving his upstart son and saving face for the loss of his throne, he must regain his freedom long enough to build that one, last heroic poem.

Shahryar, deposed sultan of Shahabad, plans and shapes though he can no longer execute. Shahryar drafts endless blueprints in his prison, the half-finished monument to his beloved Shahrzad. The tomb still holds out its promise of immortality, but its chaste dream is already part of the glorious past. It has taken on the appearance of a ruin, its beauty offset by the unfinished patches, poignant blank space. It is also, now, palpably a chamber of grief. Sorrow, futility have seeped into the very architecture of the place. The floors are covered with carpets not large enough in size or number to conceal the incomplete tiling and polishing, or the stray spots of damage – a dirty bloodstain, a chipped or broken tile where a spear has fallen. The window, introduced as a special concession to the royal prisoner, frames the only bit of unadulterated sky Shahryar can see. But its crudity, flaunted in this building of all buildings, is a festering sore. What can you expect of a son who is more excited by a granary or an aqueduct than a triumphal arch?

*

Like the tomb, the man has the appearance of a relic from the fabled past. He looks well enough, though his flesh hangs somewhat loosely round the jaw and stomach. And he is occupied, an important requisite to well-being in a life of confinement. He could easily fill his remaining years with the distractions convention allots to the noble and infirm – writing and drawing tools to keep his mind supple; rationed music and wine; and a slavegirl or two, young and alluring but loyal to the present palace regime. There is also the prayer rug, waiting patiently in long-suffering silence; and the small, austere mosque adjoining the chamber, his son's retirement gift to a father's starving soul. The sultan's prison is, after all, a cushioned one, nothing like the dungeons in which his own prisoners were tortured with hunger, thirst and irons.

But despite all this, Shahryar's days are numbered. Sultan Shahryar, once the pride, once the terror of Shahabad, is slipping, sinking imperceptibly into death. It is time, it could be said in Sultan Umar's ringing voice, for the old sinner to take stock. But poetic convenience – of a whole life, however long and chequered, marching past in solemn parade – turns out to be a kind lie. Shahryar has been a lifelong collector, a male counterpart of the seductress he and Shahzaman once encountered, the one who tricked her jinni-husband and strung a ring for each lover taken on a score-keeping string. Shahryar, however, has been more versatile. He has not only collected women, but gems, arches, kingdoms, calligraphers, stallions, automatons, wise words and many other curiosities. But what happens when a collector is separated from his collection? The foundation of his edifice totters; his system – to define, order and classify reality – grows shaky. Shahryar's head is in chaos, choked with a million sharp fragments. It is in this splintered state of disarray that he will have to meet his maker, face the terrors of judgement day.

But it is profitless to speculate on this imminent interview, even less fathomable to an outsider than an encounter between a pair of secretive lovers. The earthbound, cut off from discourse with divinity, are unlikely to understand the inscrutable twists of supreme judgement. What Shahryar takes with him, or his abject nakedness before that awful seat, is of little concern to stubbornly human eyes. The case, as it stands here, has to do with more modest questions. How does Shahryar die? How *should* he die? And is he absolved or punished?

Let it be said right away: Shahryar does not meet a bloody, gory end. He who put so many innocents to death, closed up his ears to good advice, conscience and the threat of dissidence, to all the anguished wails of Shahabad, will have a swift, laughably easy death. Though he is drifting loose of his moorings so that the end is inevitable, the actual moment is a swift fall off the precipice. He will choke; quickly, in a few minutes, a slavegirl's hand on his body, the clean, astringent taste of the killer-grape in his mouth. The city will not produce a righteous or misguided assassin for him. Nor will nature, with all her justice and wisdom, summon a flood or a wave or a stroke of lightning to bring him to book.

It is a death that could shake many a heart's faith in justice. Its narrative is an exasperating one, ending on a purely imaginative note; compensation in visible, satisfying terms is never paid. All thirst for revenge, any desire for penalty in the light of human justice, will have to make do with a disappointingly tame scenario. The son relieves him of the throne. But this is practically routine in the annals of history, or for that matter, in the transfer of power from father to son in the humblest household. Shahryar, in the days of mourning for a beloved wife, made a well-judged choice of a refuge – the mercurial slavegirl Dilshad. She betrays and deserts him. This hurts, especially when a man is too jaded to seize a virgin and alter her status for ever. But he has, after all, been a widower hundreds of times before, and he has always managed to find consolation. The slavegirl's treachery is not entirely unexpected; near as it is to inevitability, it has, almost, a touch of the banal. Only one strand remains, promising because of its ambiguity. Shahrzad's sister – so close to her, to his and her naked bodies in play and battle – slips out of the ancient four-cornered, bewitched entanglement of two men, two women. But in all, Shahryar's sentence and penalty make a self-contained family affair, in this case, a palace business. The city, always semi-mythical once in the palace grounds, recedes even further from the vantage point of the ex-sultan's impro-vised prison.

Weigh against all this the evidence condemning the accused. First, and central, the old flesh-and-blood memory impossible to bury: the procession of virgins led into the palace in their bridal finery, carried out in their shrouds, taking in a detour via a soiled marriage bed. This Shahryar will never really live down. It is as if he has willed it to his people, his descendants, this monstrous collective memory, an heirloom more vulnerable to shape-shifting legend than his brick and stone memorials, but part, and a dark, brooding part, of his legacy.

His heirs in the palace and city may in time learn to say: the king went mad for a few years. Or that he was a tyrant, and tyrants are susceptible to both cruelty and whim. Centur-ies later, a man turned thoughtful by psychological platitudes may say, Shahryar was a sensitive, imbalanced fellow, and the perennial battle between the sexes made him cynical. The man's wife, a woman with a mind of her own, may add, Shahrzad cured him. Or at least she lived long enough to see him recover and regain balance. He could go back to nor-malcy in the palace, such as this normalcy might have been.

But the sacrificial victims were tangible enough. They bled, their bodies were buried in two pieces per shroud. Are they to remain an anonymous huddle of spoilt meat forever? Then, the city, though it groaned and simmered, did not act. It waited without success for the rise of a saviour from among the oppressed. But now, with the city's discontent effectively harnessed by Umar, now, before Shahryar can slip away where he cannot be reached, it is time – though there are no witnesses to speak of – for Shahryar to make reparation.

*

Sometimes, locked up in his thick-skinned marble wonder, it is almost possible for Shahryar to pretend it is another time. This chamber is none other than that blessed bedchamber in the dungeon, sanctified all those years ago by his mind-bending sorrow and redemption. But there, when dawn arrived and the trials of night were once more – though temporarily – held at bay, time was still in charge; and he of it. Now the little window lightens and darkens. He sees only whether it is night or day. And in any case, what use is it to him to say it is two in the afternoon or six in the morning? Crownless, throneless, he does not have to seize time and set out – to hunt; to ride; to confer with the wazir; to test the new concubine; or to mount the horse for battle. He who has been safely tethered all his life to the palace routine has, when he has only a few months left to live, all the time in the world. Time to dream, to imagine; time to remember.

But wait; the tricks of memory are for children and old women. Shahryar is holed up in a luxury-lined tomb and he is safe. But if he is safe, safe as he was in the bedchamber in the dungeon, where is the quick-tongued woman? And who allowed entry to these obsolete visitors in her place?

No, Shahryar does not tremble with fear that a long and ghastly queue of brides dressed in shrouds, or necklaces of sticky red gems round their necks, will taunt him now with their visit. Instead, what happens is this. In those wakeful hours of the night, familiar to old age and imprisonment, Shahryar feels a sense of disorder spread in a smelly fog around him. He has learnt to recognize the first indications of this change of weather. He quickly shuts his eyes, concentrates; with the manly force that has stood by him in the past, he summons a city. A beloved city so well planned that it is perfectly moulded and cast. Constant, enduring. Shahryar is free to sleep in the staunch embrace of this vision, safe as in the arms of a stout-hearted brother.

But sometimes – and if truth be told, more and more often – his guardian image of an orderly universe is in danger. The threat is whispered by a gloating traitor in his head who recounts the cautionary tales of other great builders. The mocking voice describes in excruciating detail: the Black Castle built by Kush, wasted; many-pillared Iram, built by Shaddad over five hundred years, empty except for blood and air; the City of Brass, its inhabitants petrified and their queen mummified; the sacked city of Labtayt. Shahryar's dream-city darkens in the gloomy shadows cast by these unending illustrations of plunder. That hateful, potent image – a city (and its palace) in the grip of desertion and death – bores its way through his eyelids and settles with all its mass of decay in his own body. By this time, Shahryar, trained by nightmares, knows what will come next. He sniffs in anticipation; he is not disappointed. The tomb fills with a stench. It is silent, there is no one there with him – no sorcerer, ghoul or thief. But the marble and red gems have melted and turned into an indistinguishable heap of rotting bodies.

*

Shahryar suffers. Not from a belated repentance, but from a sense of unease that his testimonials to greatness, the crowning achievements of his life, will be stained and polluted by these messy knots of unravelled flesh and blood. He was raised to feel the correct degree of manly, then kingly pride. He never sought forgiveness for those three years of murder to prove a pointless point. At the end of the thousand and one nights, it was he who granted a magnanimous pardon to Shahrzad, allowed her to live, to love and be loved, to be fêted as the saviour of the city. The trial of his reign was over, the chapter closed. Shahabad limped back to its mundane old pursuits. And to be fair (like the wazir, who no doubt sits in paradise now, with a ringside view of divine law), Shahryar's life was a long one. He ruled before and after those three bloody years. His kingdom did not collapse. His people lived, some prospered. The palace carried on with its accepted twin businesses of conquest and splendour. If Shahryar were to think of composing an epitaph for his reign, he might say, 'His breadth of vision was royal. His battles and buildings were on an epic scale; so was his anger.'

Perhaps history too would find more than the epitaph 'killer of virgins' for him. His architectural creations spoke of union and symmetry, brought out the eloquence of marble, stone and rock. For ages to come, people would gaze at these visions of grandeur and try to describe them, though all description was doomed to fail. Perhaps a latter-day Shahrzad would find the means to describe them in the plot of a marvellous tale: Once there was a marble wonder . . . But how, meanwhile, to reconcile this evidence of refined taste – the man described by his relics – with the one who took a sword to not one but hundreds of innocent necks? Did this question infect the palace once the hours of killing and storytelling were officially at an end?

But all was well, the future glittered like a golden age to come as long as the wazir was still alive. Shahryar saw what a heroine Shahrzad was to their people. She could bask in her redeemer's glow for a lifetime. And Shahryar, out of his own admiration, and seeing the crowds and adulation she could draw, had conferred the title of sultana on her. Coins were minted with her name, frequent edicts from the harem issued. Surely he of all people should know the worth of a good, modest woman? But around the time of the old wazir's death, some subtle shift of power took place. Orphaned, Shahrzad the saviour seemed to learn to fend for herself all over again. She slowly changed; or her real, usurping nature came to the surface. Though she called it her empathy for the people's needs, her ambitions were visible once too often for the comfort of royal advisers. The thought came to Shahryar one day that this most chaste of women, Wise Shahrzad, was turning into Wily Shahrzad. One of them had to win. Shahrzad disappeared; he mourned her deeply.

Shahrzad disappeared. Shahryar does not know if she lives, but if she is dead, he hopes it was swift and painless. This is his sincere wish. Otherwise, though he is in the tomb meant for her, he does not think of her for days on end. Sometimes, when he tries to reconstruct her face, it is a complex, composite picture that looks at him gravely. He can place a feature or two as belonging to his wife, or her sister, or a resourceful slavegirl of recent years, or even some strange and hairy female beast languishing in his harem. He pushes this unrealistic image away and turns to his design board. But the tussle between the harem leaking out of its safe walls, and the king's secure chamber, is not yet over. This is clear on the day Shahryar dies.

*

The design for the tower of freedom is almost done. Shahryar reclines on a couch, fruit and wine by his side, a young woman's hands on his half-naked body. Nothing she can do will stir him to life, this old devourer of virgins, but suddenly, in a rush of pleasure, he sees a flash of the tower's pinnacle, what remains to complete it. He bends, reaches forward to seize it, but now there is only an inscription at its tip, then its author, a woman poised for flight. Is this the angel of death who greeted Shaddad at the gates of Iram, the city that took him five hundred years to build? Any second now, the angel will open her awful red mouth and cry destruction.

Shahryar shivers – but wait, he hears the woman say huskily, teasingly, 'What happened then was . . .' But this is Shahrzad! She is calling him to attention, her countermove as always a spur, egging him on to reach higher and higher. The girl's groping hands between his thighs; the tart, refreshing taste in his mouth; and ahead of him, astride the tower that will never be completed, his old lover and enemy. He tries to gulp. The tomb he has built with such passion encloses him. It is completely airless.

Then past that tunnel of blank greyness, he is out in the light again, in the midst of it, in that old manoeuvring game that is never played out. The old warhorse remembers, just in time, to roar out his order with all the pride and dignity he can muster: 'Let the battle commence!'

Dilshad:

The Well-Constructed Lie

The other day Dilshad heard someone in the market describing the fifth wonder of the world. 'A marble ladder to heaven,' the rapturous man was saying, his eyes squinting as he looked up at the sky and stretched his arm as far as it would go. 'A testament to the nobility of man and the heights he can reach.'

The man was talking about the bhai minar, a wondrous tribute to brotherhood that once loomed on Dilshad's horizon. The tower tunnelled its way up through the open air in the distance like an ambition within reach of fulfilment. But the fifth wonder of the world escaped her; this is how it happened.

Dilshad had often heard that the night is dangerous for the traveller, particularly for a woman. Her own experience was that it is the afternoon which is treacherous, that hour after the midday meal when the sun's glare deceives the footsore traveller in a myriad ways.

Dilshad had been on the road for months, marvelling at the evidence she found of man's ingenuity. In the midst of an arid stretch she saw a huge stepped well, its depths cool in the earth's embrace. Miles away in an equally dry-brown terrain rose a staunch fort. Its steep, rough walls and its forbidding ramparts towered above her. Looking at this desolate stone-faced city, Dilshad felt awestruck, not because of its size or the stern encounters it called to mind – the clash of sword on shield, naked skin scraping itself raw against rough rope. It was the central theme of the place that overwhelmed and repulsed her. Not a single door or crevice had been left to its own devices by the planner; everything was in full view of the sentry's post. The outside world was an enemy, an advancing, dangerous army, and it was critical not to be taken by surprise. Then Dilshad was also told time and again: if what she wanted was daring, if she wanted to see a monument which ventured unashamedly into the unknown, she should see the wonder built by the brothers Azhar and Mazhar.

So Dilshad trudged on till she was within sight of her destination one afternoon. She saw a tapering column of flashing white far in the distance. It grew, this slim beautiful torso, as far as the eye could see till it disappeared into the clouds. Dilshad felt a sharp pang of disappointment. The flashing marble was as dazzling as she had been promised, even from this distance. But where did it end? Where was its head, its object?

Since then she has heard from many veterans that this is a hazard travellers often face. The romance of a monument is a practised rumour-monger. But its reality can be a let-down, whether you come face to face with the time-weathered beauty of stone and marble, or the forgotten bloodstains on each parapet. Then, Dilshad didn't know any of this. All she knew was that the minar she had wanted to see for years was within view, and that she couldn't bring herself to go a step further. Instead she caught sight of a tree whose shady arms invited her into its embrace. She lay down and considered the horizon.

There it was, smooth, rounded, glinting, the marble phallus that thrust its way into the sky. It invited her to come forward and be dwarfed by its audacious size and its celebration of flawless, manly beauty. What held her back then, dawdling under a plebeian everyday tree?

Dilshad grappled half-heartedly with this question, and when she heard voices behind the tree, she let it go with relief. A high-pitched, excitable voice said from somewhere among the branches above her: 'Donkey bhai, you've grazed enough. Let's while away the warm hours with tales of heroic men and their feats.'

A low, gravelly voice answered him from the ground: 'Yes, Monkey bhai, come down and join me. Let's recall how the marble triumph came to be, step by step, stone by stone.'

With the air of two people negotiating a route they have travelled a hundred times before, Brother Monkey and Brother Donkey launched into a long and somewhat repetitive story: Azhar and Mazhar were brave and wise men. Azhar was particularly good with his sword; Mazhar rode his ink-dripping pen like a winged horse. Together the brothers made a formidable team. Though they didn't have royal blood, they soon proved they were fit to rule. But before Azhar and Mazhar earned their exalted position, they had to conquer one enemy after the other – bandits, plague, hunger, warfare. When all these were overcome, when the dead were buried and mourned, the brothers built a short, stout column as a thanksgiving. Azhar designed it; Mazhar supervised the inscription, in exquisite calligraphy, 'God is very good.'

In times of peace, even the enemy is beloved; so Azhar and Mazhar fell in love. As expected, the brothers, who had never been known to fail, got the girls they wanted, a pair of big-boned sisters who would provide hours of rest from their worldly cares. The second storey of the column was now built. The inscription, flowery this time, read 'Love is very good.'

Inevitably, children were born to them. Obedient daughters, and even more important, obedient sons. Azhar and Mazhar added to their marble wonder. The new storey was a long, tapering one, and it bestowed the ultimate praise: 'Life is very good.'

They were running out of reasons, but the minar, they knew, was unfinished. If they didn't build and build, who would remember their numerous victories over life and all living things? Their heroic vision told them that a stone or a manly arm or an inscribed couplet could soar so high that the sky was no limit.

When the minar seemed to be within touching distance of a low, dark cloud, the brothers – ageing but still virile – admitted to each other that their time was up. They went up the minar to see if it was finally finished. On the way they paused at each storey, remembering how it had come about, and admiring their design and the view. From the top they could see all of their kingdom and more. They told each other: Brother, we have grown old and our sons will rule after us. But this will remain. As long as this minar stands, our story (a story of triumph) will live!

The beastly eulogists were silent for a minute. Then the donkey said casually, 'Azhar, the elder brother and designer, has always been my hero.'

Monkey spluttered a little before he got out the words, 'Mine is the inscription-walla! Is there any doubt that he was the more heroic of the two?'

There was a grim silence before the two came to blows.

This sudden change of mood was so unexpected that Dilshad peeped around the tree trunk to see if she could help. But they had already found a mediator. She heard them ask a smooth, round pebble on the ground to judge between them.

The pebble lay in the sun-soaked quiet for a while, then said decisively: 'My brothers, I who have been lying close to the earth for so many years know a few details that may have escaped you. Listen: when Azhar and Mazhar went up to the tip of their minar, they found it was not as close to the clouds as they had hoped. This is the tricky thing about all towers. The higher you go, the more the damn things need building. Azhar, brooding on this truism, looked down; was seized with an attack of vertigo, and fell to his death. Left alone, Mazhar stayed up there turning a deaf ear to all pleas to come down and go about what remained of his royal business. He had become obsessed with the idea of a perfect epitaph for Azhar: two lines, twenty-four syllables that he would inscribe on the pinnacle of the minar himself, words which would gloss over the distance between marble invader and sky-blue territory. We know he was a clever man, and perhaps he would have found those potent, conjuring words. But in a few weeks he was reduced to a starving, ragged madman, reciting long streams of gibberish into the silent, deaf ear of his heavenly audience.'

One look at the faces of the donkey and monkey was enough for Dilshad to see that the pebble was in trouble. They were so enraged by this irreverent postscript to their story that they began to kick around the heretical pebble. This was more than Dilshad could tolerate. Unlike the pebble, she had no new information or insight to offer. But she found their fanatical devotion to their story, and by extension the minar, so objectionable that she left the refuge of her tree and stepped forward.

They stopped, surprised, and in that moment Dilshad dashed forward, picked up the pebble and put it in her blouse. The monkey and donkey, having recovered from their surprise, were unimpressed. They advanced on her threateningly.

'Give it up,' they jabbered and brayed in chorus, 'or we'll take it from you.'

Dilshad was not sure she could outrun them. So she managed a ladylike squeal: 'Turn around!'

The sycophants of heroes gallantly turned their backs to her. She fished out the pebble from between her breasts and swallowed it in one great hard gulp, just as her tormentors turned around and charged her.

They chased her down the road for a while, then lost interest. 'Keep the stone,' they called after her spitefully.

Dilshad ran on, ignoring the hard fist that unclenched and stretched its fingers in her stomach. But hours later, as she went on towards that receding wonder which moved further away from her with every step, she thought she heard a faint chattering voice call, 'May your lovers be donkeys who betray you!' And then a mocking bray chime in: 'There goes the eternal wanderer, a homeless monkey-woman!'

3

Dunyazad:

Three Scenes and a Father

The wazir sits alone in his garden. All the servants have been dismissed. The house is still; so is the night air. It should be a time of peace – an hour or two of tranquillity between two long gruelling days in the palace. But in the lush garden designed to mirror the paradise to come, the wazir does not wait for an assignation with peace.

His sharp ears pick up a faint wail in the distance. It is midnight then, time for the sultan to retire to his marriage bed. Time for the hopeless nightly clamour of virgins' families. A few minutes, and the bride will be stripped to the skin that will be on display just once, its trembling freshness fingered, handled and penetrated so that a few drops of blood may be shed; foreplay for the more definitive act of conquest that dawn will bring.

For the high-principled wazir, virginity holds the city's real treasury in its tight grip. Mock virginity, spend it recklessly, and you plunder invaluable coffers. You tear apart the fine silk of a people's moral well-being, both here in the royal city and in the paradise hereafter.

The wazir's back stiffens as he turns towards the east, waiting.

The still air, virginal, expectant, has been pierced and overwhelmed. A sharp wind blows now, harbinger of restless, shifting clouds of sand. But it will not rain. In place of pelting rain beats the hard heart of the rising wind, a heart drowning in a downpour of mud and filth.

Then suddenly, though his garden holds a mirror to paradise, the wazir is trudging across the desert. He does not know how long the journey has lasted – hours perhaps, or days. All he knows is that he is alone in the face of an impending storm. He does not see a single path before him. Occasionally the wind lies low, gathering its strength for its malevolent purposes. The spongy ground is then sleek, having swiftly obliterated all footsteps. A thousand travellers may tread this lonely floor and leave no mark.

The wazir is adrift in the desert, at his age, in spite of his position, minus servant, camel, or even a small pitcher of water. Will the journey never end? The thirst snakes up his tongue and settles, an invincible devil in his sandy, gritty throat.

He bends his head, almost humble, shuts his eyes and walks on doggedly. His legs and the back of his neck throb with this monotonous exertion. The fitful, gusty wind is on the rampage once more, rising all the way to his unprotected ears. It wails in the meaningless way a powerless, dumb creature laments an irrevocable grief.

He resists this thought. Even in his state of extremity, he disbelieves this vision of total and abject surrender. His eyes open wide. He has sensed right; now when he has repulsed hopelessness, hope swims into view. At a distance he sees the edge of the featureless stretch of sand; it is defined by a gleaming, opal-hued pool.

He stumbles towards it. He is closer, almost there; and a heavy arm falls on his shoulder, holding him back. He hears the stern voice as if a clear bell rings, slicing neatly through the clamorous wind: 'No, you haven't finished.'

He has heard the voice before; in his father's rooms, thirty, forty years ago; or in his teacher's spare cell, embellished only by the holy words he explains. The wazir twists his neck painfully to see. He looks for one or the other – the venerable figure with the flowing beard, or the strong, craggy face framed by the whitest hair he has ever seen. There is nothing. He turns back to the pool, raises a foot, moves forward. He is firmly pinioned again. The weather-beaten voice is back, this time its hardness shaded with mocking. 'Did you think that was all? A whiff of morality, a pinch of justice, and the task is done? Is salvation to be bought so cheaply?'

The wazir wants to deny this with every fibre of his being. He has suffered that tightrope walk all his life – the acrobatics of power in the palace, balanced on the torturously arrow-straight path of righteousness – and is he to be taunted like this? He is desperate to speak but his tongue refuses to come unstuck from the floor of his mouth. He hears a sympathetic laugh. The words that follow are not entirely unkind. 'The journey, dear wazir, begins here. Be patient; you will have your fill of the pool.' And in that instant a pair of strong, capable hands clasp round his neck, choking him.

There is less and less air. He feels his world darken, his body gets heavier as he suffocates. He is under a thick quilt of sand, drowning. The hands twist his neck in one sharp movement; his breath goes; and the same instant he is on the wing, drifting lightly towards the pool like a small unsteady flame.

The pool glints, a single round eye. Its surface is transparent but its depths remain unrevealed. As he realizes this, the eye blinks. Then he is in it, up to his shoulders, in the cool water he has thirsted for. He flounders, finds a foothold, recovers. He dips his face in the water, then shakes the reviving moisture out of his hair and eyes. He feels something, a piece of flotsam, cleave itself to his newly slaked tongue. He spits but it remains stubbornly in place. The taste of stale vinegar fills his mouth. He opens it, peels the tiny strip off his tongue and examines it. It seems to be a piece of shrunken dead skin; he winces fastidiously, holds it away from himself before throwing it into the water. In that moment when it leaves his hand he suddenly gasps as if he has been hit. He has just looked about himself, and seen the pool for what it is – a wardrobe of exclusively female discards. A whole population of dismembered bodily parts, pickled in a viscous fluid, are floating around the wazir; a long snake-haired, purple-throated head, a hairless thigh, a lone breast with a hideously engorged nipple. All of female Shahabad seems to be represented in this hellish oasis. He feels the pain of every severed head, every slit throat, every torn, shrivelling limb.

He is brutal in his haste to push and clear a way for himself out of the pool. His hands claw at a hyacinth-face, minus eyes and nose, floating towards him; his legs thrash at slimy tendrils that wrap themselves lovingly around him. In that cruelly elongated series of minutes, he seems – and this is the worst of the horrors – to recognize some of the mutilated spoils. A breast, a stomach, a pear-shaped buttock, greet him with familiarity as if he has met them before on their rightful flesh-and-blood owners.

He pulls himself out, collapses on the sand. The vinegar in his mouth flies out as he retches. Slowly, deliberately, he hardens himself to flint. Has this really happened? And why? There must be an explanation; he will discover it; till then it must all be borne. His hand unclenches as he masters his revulsion and outrage, and he realizes he is holding something, something soft though not very pliant. He sits up, looks. He is no longer vulnerable to shock. It is almost as if he expects the carefully selected memento he is holding: a human hand, small, well-born, beringed. It is an ordinary hand but it is unbearably evocative.

The wazir bends over it gracefully and strokes it, this way, then that, with his bearded cheeks. He kisses it tenderly, then slips it back into the pool where it bobs on the surface before sinking from sight. The wazir walks away without turning back as if he has not left behind him, in the pool of swelling encumbrances, the capable hand of his first-born.

*

He is back on the sands, though not so helpless or over-whelmed this time. He has been hardened; a part of his heart has been steeled for decisive action. When a mansion grows out of the ground, out of the thin gritty air, the wazir is ready and on his feet.

He is just in time to intercept the sultan's messenger. Before the eunuch can say a word, the wazir calls out, 'Is there a virgin in this house?' He has seen the question in his mind before it is spoken aloud, but still he shudders when the words echo in his ears.

He notices that the eunuch sneaks a look at a curtained window upstairs. There are two faces there, peeping cautiously. They duck when they see the wazir looking at them, but he is sure he has recognized one of them at least.

The wazir is about to enter the house but he hears a wail in the distant sky. Quickly the eunuch says: 'It is time for prayer. Let's come back later.'

One of them departs for prayer; the other slips into the house. The young woman at the window joins him. She sees him dig a pit feverishly in the courtyard. He looks at her and at the second spade lying idle. They don't seem to need words; already she is picking up the spade. He notices in the midst of his sweaty endeavour, in passing: she has only one hand. But the other hand seems to compensate; she is digging as fast as he is. When the pit is deep enough, she steps into it. He covers her up with mud, careful to leave tiny pores on the surface so that she can breathe.

The wazir is back. He finds the eunuch on his knees, on the floor of the courtyard, bent double in prayer. Upholder of the faith that he is, he waits in respectful silence till the slave is done. They look at each other; when their eyes lock, the eunuch calls out: 'O mansion of marble columns, do you house a female virgin?' The wazir is amazed at this superstitious idiocy, but the house replies in a muffled voice, 'No.' The eunuch shrugs as if a talking house is an everyday occurrence, and leaves.

The wazir looks at the freshly dug courtyard, deliberating. He feels a measure of shame, relief, disbelief; there is also a

dull pain in his chest like an omen of heartbreak. He sinks to
his knees and scoops up handfuls of mud till he has uncovered
the source of the voice, a plump white goat that looks at him
with limpid eyes. Their tears mingle; he scoops her up in his
arms, the beloved goat, with joy and regret.

*

The wazir is in a hurry. He is running across the desert,
looking for his daily place of assignation. It is time for him to
make his offering to his hungry god. He can feel the goat's
heart beating against his chest. It is a nervous erratic beat, but
the creature makes no attempt to escape. She is in fact
snuggling up to him lovingly; their bodies are pressed together
in a cocoon of trust.

Strange to say, it is not the goat he is thinking of as he
scales the sand dunes. It is his daughter, Shahrzad. What is at
stake, he tells himself, is not her life or death. It is the seed of
possibility in her. If this seed is watered, even with blood, it
may sprout knowledge and power. Does the child hold the
seed or not? She must, she seems to, yet – if he is mistaken, if
he is reading more than he should in those flashing eyes and
ready tongue – he may be guilty of filicide. In seeking the
redemption of the all-powerful sultan, in seeking the salvation
of his powerless subjects, he may be laying himself open to
damnation. If he fails, Shahryar may still be saved by someone
else. But who will save him then, the wazir with his first-born's
blood on his hands?

The wazir is panting as he reaches the heart of the desert.
The goat seems to have grown in weight and value though
she looks the same. Finally he sees the large, manly figure

materializing through the curtain of sand that hangs before him. It is late; though the stranger says nothing, it is clear from his face that he is a stern, demanding taskmaster. 'It is time for your meal, my lord,' whispers the wazir. 'You must be starving.' His voice is husky with the concern and desire of a mother face to face with her ravenous, waiting child.

The lord, a gigantic man with wild unwashed hair and red eyes, watches the wazir as he tenderly bathes the goat. 'Is she yours?' he asks. 'Remember, only something you love will fill my stomach with your devotion.' In reply, the wazir lets the goat go from his ministering hands. She stands docilely between them, dignified in a goatish way.

'I' – the wazir pauses, corrects himself – 'we will appease your hunger for all time. My heart is full; it overflows with tenderness,' and the wazir pulls out a long, glinting knife. He holds it up for them all to see. The goat looks up, its eyes momentarily blinded by the sunlight trapped in the blade of steel. To the lord's amazement and delight, she then turns back to the wazir and stretches her neck to make his task easier. 'We feed you with joy, master,' says the wazir as he embraces the goat's neck and the hand with the knife flies down, plunges deep. The goat bleats joyfully as her head falls to the ground. In the silence that follows, the wazir builds a fire, begins his task of cooking.

The goat, the wazir's daughter, is now cooked meat. The wazir is anxiously waiting for permission to serve the meal. But there is another detail; his god does not want to eat alone. 'Eat with me,' he commands. Honoured, weary, the wazir sits down by the lord, the goat before them. He waits for the lord to taste the first mouthful.

'Do you eat without your child?' asks the lord with a touch of indignation. 'Am I not good enough for your daughter to eat with?' The wazir begins to tremble with despair; it is too much, this new, irrational demand of this relentless god. But he gets up, goes to the remains of the cooking fire where the goat's head lies uncooked.

'Daughter,' he calls beseechingly. 'Come, sweet Shahrzad. There is just one more thing we must do together.'

He concentrates all his love, wisdom and sense of fair play to a spot on the ground; he wills her to appear; and to his astonishment, she does. The wazir seizes her hand and rushes back to the waiting meal. *He* cannot ask for anything more, he will *have* to eat at last!

Father and daughter race back to their tormenting guest. But he is gone; so is the meal. They feel a sharp moment of anguish, then see the paradisiacal oasis that has sprung up before them. The god has been fed, they realize, as they feel their limbs, their stomachs and hearts melting. They will never be separated from him again.

Dilshad:

Rupavati's Breasts

When Satyasama was a very young woman, she dreamt of fame and wisdom. Like many young people, she thought both lay in wait for her. All she had to do was seek them out and stake her claim. Now she wonders at the daring which sprang from her ignorance. Or perhaps it was only a kind of innocence which told her younger self that she was not being foolish or greedy. If she were either of these things, would she have set out from home as she did, a traveller who would pay her way with wit and courage?

When she had been on the road for a few years, she lost some of this baggage of confidence. But there was no question of giving up or turning back. She could only go on, her feet just a little heavier, her hands light and almost empty.

Then one morning, Satyasama fell into step with a woman hurrying along the road, carrying a huge bundle of firewood on her head. Satyasama could see the muscles on her stiff neck, taut with the strain of balancing her load. The woman's face dripped with sweat. She refused Satyasama's offers of help, but let her wipe her face with a piece of cloth and wet her lips with water.

By the time they reached the place where the road forked in two, Satyasama had told the woman her story. A little to Satyasama's surprise, the woman took it all quite seriously. She paused at the turning and told Satyasama: 'Look, I'm going to leave you here. You have to go on to the next crossing. Then walk away from the road till you reach a cluster of narrow, dirty streets. Go down the last of these streets and you'll find a yellow-green house – you must meet the couple who live there.'

'Why?' began Satyasama, but the woman cut her off impatiently.

'You have to begin your search somewhere,' she snapped. 'I have heard that these old ones have memories like oceans – full of salty titbits of wisdom. You might as well see what you can learn at their house.' And before Satyasama could ask any more questions, the woman was gone, hurrying down the muddy path that led into the fields.

Satyasama watched her back recede till it shrank to the size of a dot. Then she shrugged her shoulders and turned back to the road. She had nothing to lose; for the next sweaty hour or two, she walked in search of a yellow-green house.

Her first impression was that it was breathtaking – she had never seen such an ugly, ramshackle place before. Beyond the open, rusty gate she saw a narrow strip of what may have been a garden once, but was now a riot of weeds, slugs and decaying leaves. A faint smell of something overripe hung in the air.

She held her breath for a minute, then walked across, her feet sinking into the squelchy mess. Just beyond, there was a stone platform at the entrance of the house. It was protected by a tiled roof held up by four smooth pillars. Satyasama saw two people in this porch, a man and a woman, each leaning against a pillar. They sat facing away from each other.

She went up to them and told them her simple tale. She must have impressed them with her openness, or perhaps they were just bored with each other. Anyway, they agreed to tell Satyasama a little of what they knew, and invited her into the house to wash herself. Neither of them got up to accompany her, so she went into the house and looked for a bathroom. There she cleaned her face and hands, then peeled off her filthy slippers. She poured water very slowly over her feet, prolonging the pleasurable moment when dust and fatigue dissolved in the murky puddle on the floor.

The house was peculiar; it seemed to have been built without a plan. One room meandered without sense into another. Satyasama would like to have explored all the rooms on her own, but she heard her hosts call to her from the porch.

They waved her to a spot on the stone floor where both could see her. She sat down facing them, a ready and willing pupil.

Satyasama did not know their names. Though they seemed delighted to have someone new to talk to, they did not offer to tell her anything about themselves. The old man had a flat, almost featureless face, with a coarse wisp of straw for a beard. The rest of him was an inconspicuous stick. The old woman was like a dried-up berry; her small face was perfectly round and wrinkled. It was framed by a few inches of dry, stiff hair as if a broomstick had landed on her head and got stuck to it.

'Once you are through with staring at us, I can begin my

story,' she said sharply. Satyasama apologized and stared at
the floor instead.

'The best place for you to begin,' the old woman went on,
'is my memory of Rupavati. Or to be exact, Rupavati's
breasts.

'Perhaps you know' – though her face said she doubted it
– 'that the Buddha-to-be was once born as a young woman
called Rupavati. With such impeccable lineage, naturally
Rupavati was the best of womankind. She had a beautiful face
and body; and she wore that rare gem, a generous heart.

'One day, Rupavati saw a beggar woman so mad with
hunger that she was about to eat her newborn child. Rupavati
tore her breasts off her body and fed the woman, then went
on her way.

'When her husband heard about it, he was amazed, even
a little frightened. He said to the sky and wind and open fields:
"If no one has ever done something so heroic before, let
Rupavati's breasts come back to her."

'The breasts came flying through the air like two wide-
necked pitchers. With a resounding clap they attached themselves to Rupavati's bare chest.

'Meanwhile Indra was watching all this from the sky. He
slipped down, jealous god that he was, to question Rupavati.
He took a quick, suspicious look at her breasts. They were
well-shaped and just the right size; nothing there told him why
she had done such a wild, mindless thing. So – he asked her,
his narrowed eyes moving up to her face, did she want to be
a god? Assure herself of a place in heaven?

'Rupavati returned his look with her usual compassion. "If

I desired nothing for myself," she told him, "let me turn into a man." And her second-hand breasts disappeared; she became a man, Rupavata.

'Later Rupavata was reborn as a brahmin called Chandra-prabha. Heroism had by now become a habit. In this life, Chandraprabha offered himself once more to a hungry crea-ture. But since he didn't have any breasts to give away, he had to go all the way this time. He gave up every inch of his flesh, every drop of blood, to a hungry tigress about to devour her own cub.'

There was silence for a minute. Then in place of applause, the old man let out a quick, pointed hiss. 'Facts,' he snarled at the old woman. 'You have all your facts wrong. How dare you pollute this house with such unrealistic lies? Listen – and correct yourself before it's too late.

'To begin with, the Buddha, even a Buddha-to-be, would *never* choose to be a woman. Don't you know why Gotami walked those long dusty miles to plead with her enlightened son? The Buddha did not want women in the Sangha. Then, when his young disciple Ananda put in a word for the women who wanted to be nuns, the Buddha finally relented. But even as he laid down eight weighty laws for these theris, he sighed: "Look how we have whittled down our time to come. In my dreams I saw the doctrine grow and flourish for a thousand years. Now its lifespan has dwindled to a mere five hundred."'

The old man raised a trembling hand; the old woman and Satyasama looked at it, mesmerized.

'The memory you have mutilated and held up shamelessly for the world to see is actually a sparkling, unblemished jewel.

Look – here it is. A long time ago, the Buddha-to-be was born as a beautiful, virtuous man. Naturally he was called Rupavata.

'Rupavata owned a large farm which he cultivated with the help of many workers. He looked after them well, shared his produce with those who worked hard for him. In the protective shade of his umbrella they all grew and prospered.

'Once this noble farmer was walking along the boundaries of his lands, examining the hedges that protected them. Suddenly he heard a heartbreaking cry. There was no one where the noise came from. But there was a shapeless bundle – no, there were two lumpy bundles, one big, one small. The big bundle crouched malevolently over the small one. It seemed that the big bundle, which on closer observation turned out to be a peasant woman, was going to swallow up the small baby-bundle. Strangely enough, the baby was quiet; it was the woman who was wailing as if she had seen a terrifying monster face to face.

'"Woman!" called Rupavata. She let go of the baby and fell back in fright. "Has hunger torn away your human face?" She gaped at him like a deaf-mute, but he held out his hand. "Get up," he told her. "Pick up that filthy baby and follow me. I will keep both of you from hunger." She stumbled in her haste to obey him. She picked up the baby (who was still silent) and followed Rupavata as if she had been waiting for him all her life.

'The beggar woman and her child were fed; bathed; clothed. They had a clean, fresh bed in a corner of Rupavata's house. The woman came to Rupavata a few days later. Her eyes filled and she moved to fall at his feet but he stopped her.

"Wait," he said. "Are you willing to work?" She nodded. "I will give you a name," Rupavata told the woman who had been a homeless beggar. "Now you are Rupavati. Your hunger, my compassion, your gratitude – these links will bind us together for ever." And taking her hand in his, Rupavata married Rupavati. He adopted the child he had saved from being eaten.

'The years came and went so that no one on the farm remembered a time before Rupavati. She served Rupavata with unswerving devotion, working harder than all the farm workers put together. Nothing could ever come between this husband and wife, or so it seemed. But as always, there was a secret canker growing all this while – leaking out of that shrouded, bestial past of Rupavati. Her son (still nameless for some reason) grew. He grew into an ungrateful lout. He was happiest wasting time with the laziest and most discontented lot among the farm workers.

'Things came to a head when Son plotted with these rogues to rob Rupavata of his harvest. Luckily Rupavata had a terrible stomach-ache that night. (Rupavati had morning sickness and it was telling on her cooking.) Rupavata lay groaning near the bulging sacks of grain. Son sneaked up on him with an iron rod. Just as the rod came down on his head, Rupavata screamed, "Rupavati!" She was there in a trice. Silently she took in her husband's bleeding forehead, the evil iron rod, and her son's blazing eyes. Then she stood between them, the son of one life and the husband of another, and pushed aside her sari pallu. She plucked one breast and flung it at Son's feet. "Here," she said, "take the breast which milked an ungrateful son." She would have plucked the other breast too, but Rupavata stopped her. "Keep one," he pleaded. "One for our own son-to-be." So she kept the right breast, but she called up to Indra in the skies: "If no one has ever been such a grateful servant before, let Rupavati remain one-breasted." Her wish was granted. And what a pious, exemplary wish it was you will realize only if you understand this: that as long as she chose to remain single-breasted, Rupavata was safe from all enemies.'

To Satyasama's surprise, the old couple did not quarrel again over the details of the story. They seemed to think the job for the day was done. Stories were forgotten for the next hour when they showed her where they kept their rice and oil and salt. Satyasama listened to them meekly, found everything, and cooked their meal. After she had served them, she ate what was left over, cleaned the kitchen and put the cooking fire to sleep.

There were only two mats, so Satyasama curled herself up into a ball and slept at their feet. When they woke up, the sun was crawling towards its lair like a pent-up monster. Satyasama brought her hosts bowls of cool water to wash their faces, hands and feet. They leant against their usual pillars and looked at her, their eyes twinkling with pleasure and, she suspected, some amusement.

'So,' began the old woman conversationally, 'what do you have to say for yourself?'

'Yes,' chimed in the old man with enthusiasm. 'We shared our memories with you this morning. Give us something of yours now.'

Satyasama was overcome by temptation; she didn't see

why she shouldn't have a turn at this game of remoulding Rupavati's breasts.

'I don't know where the Buddha comes into it all,' she said. 'You should learn not to hide behind big names. I have taken your memories and sifted them with my own sieve. This is what passed through its hundred and one pores.

'There was a man called Rupavata married to a woman called Rupavati. They were ideally matched because both were virtuous. They had only a tiny piece of barren land, but they slaved at it day after day in all kinds of weather.

'Once a hungry brahmin called Chandraprabha passed by their home, weeping that his life of begging for alms was a very hard one. They called him in and fed him their watery noon-meal of kanji. All that was left was a swallow each. They wet their mouths with those few drops of gruel, glared firmly at their flat, growling stomachs, and invited Chandraprabha to lie down and rest.

'The couple had only one mat in their hut, but they willingly gave this to the tired brahmin. He fell asleep almost immediately, worn out with weeping and a full stomach. Rupavata and Rupavati dozed, sitting on the mud floor, their backs resting against each other.

'Suddenly a wail broke into their sleep. They jumped up and looked out. An emaciated woman in tatters stood outside their hut, clutching a sullen, dirt-crusted baby to her hip.

'"I am Chandraprabha's wife," she wept. "My child and I are starving."

'Meanwhile the brahmin had woken up and joined them out-side the hut. He looked at his wife, then turned to Rupavata, his face aghast. "She's going mad with hunger," he gasped. "She's so hungry she is going to eat up our child."

'Rupavata was stunned; his mouth fell open. Rupavati's mouth also opened, but only to snap at Chandraprabha, "Don't be silly. I've never seen a mother eat her child, and I've seen many hungry mothers. What kind of a mother did *you* have?"

'Chandraprabha looked abashed for a minute, but then he remembered that he was the guest; and a learned brahmin at that. And his hosts! They were only an ignorant pair who broke their backs tilling what was obviously a barren piece of dirt. An imprudent couple, yielding like obedient animals to the first generous impulse that came along.

'Chandraprabha drew his plump figure up to its full height. "The only way out," he announced solemnly to Rupavata, "is for your beautiful and outspoken wife to practise her virtue. Rule 3112 of the written law says that a woman is the source of life. What that means is that Rupavati should pluck out her breasts and feed one each to my wife and child." '

'It was all too much for Rupavata. Life was hard enough without having a breastless woman for a wife. Would she die without them? But perhaps Chandraprabha, like the others of his kind, knew what he was talking about?

'Rupavata hesitated. The poor man really did not know what to think or do. Then to his surprise (and relief) Rupavati strode forward, her hands on her breasts. Everyone – Rupavata, Chandraprabha, the hungry woman and child – waited in silence, their eyes fixed on those firm, fleshy globes.

'Suddenly Rupavati flung her hands away from her body, lunged forward and grabbed Chandraprabha's ears. Before any of them knew what was happening, she had twisted the ears off his head. Chandraprabha stood there like a ruined, crumbling statue, watching Rupavati planting his bloody ears in the soil she had hoed that morning. She watered the sown ears with her tears of rage. "If no one has done this thing before," she stormed, "a thing which should have been done long ago – let his ears come back twofold. Let my twin breasts remain on my chest."

'At that moment, Chandraprabha's ears popped out of his head. To their amazement they were not muddy or bloody at all, but wet as if freshly washed. Meanwhile, Rupavati's anger had watered the parched soil so well that the earth pushed up tender ears of corn – row after row. This corn Rupavati cut right away and fed the hungry woman and child. Once their stomachs were full, she sent them on their way. A frightened Chandraprabha followed them at a distance, muttering learned curses. Then Rupavati led Rupavata back to their hut for an uninterrupted snooze on their mat.'

As Satyasama sent her young couple back to their hut for a little peace and quiet, she noticed the faces of the old man and woman. They had grown angry and twisted; their features glowed ominously in the failing light. Then the old woman grabbed her broom; the man groped for his walking stick.

'Lying romantic!' spat the woman. The broom whisked and waved at Satyasama as if she was a cockroach.

'Dangerous!' spluttered the man, now that he had laid hands on his stick.

'Out, out,' they chanted in a shrill duet. The broom and the stick managed a few cuts and scratches on Satyasama's legs before her rump received a healthy parting kick.

Satyasama lay for a while on the dark, empty street where she was thrown out, tenderly stroking her bruises. She could smell a drain nearby, and she also noticed that she had left her slippers behind. But lying there, in that sore and smelly darkness, her heretical ear pressed to the ground, she heard the murmur of a river flowing past, its force held in control. She listened till she felt she could get to her feet and dust herself down.

Satyasama never saw that house again. Nor did she hear any more garbled stories of breasts flying back and forth. She knew, even that night as she went on her way, that nothing had been settled, except that the old ones stayed put in that stagnant house and she wandered where her bare feet took her. But by the time Satyasama reached the main road again, she was cheerful enough to whistle softly to herself. She walked ahead rapidly, her back upright, a pair of proud sentinels pushing their way out of her body.

4

Dunyazad:

The Adventures of a Sultan

The city is a mangy old dog that has survived a street fight. It lies licking its wounds in wary silence.

The city of Samarkand should be in mourning, but for the moment, the event to be mourned is uncertain; its nature as yet undefined. It is not able to bring itself to believe and say aloud: Shahzaman is dead and gone. Who knows what cave or desert he may be hiding in, simply for the pleasure of sweeping back into the city and taking them by surprise?

The sultan has disappeared. The city is headless. Such are the times that grief has not yet penetrated hearts and brains, nor drawn tears out of a single eye. In a few days, when they begin to suspect that this is not a madman's wilful vanishing act, the citizens will stir themselves. No, not in the throes of bereavement, but in the clutches of the real ruler of the day, that subtle dictator, rumour.

When did it begin, this recent chapter of the city's bruises? Many competing voices are raised to answer this question, but the chief wazir's barber, a man not easily silenced, has a particularly curious tale to tell.

*

Night has fallen, bringing with it a brief reprieve from the day's cares of ruling and being ruled. Sultan Shahzaman is at leisure, drinking with a favoured group of his cup-companions. Slaves fill cups to the brim with the heady brew that helps men to either forget or remember; and Farid, a brilliant young man new to the court, kisses the ground before Zaman. 'I heard a wonderful tale today, your majesty,' he says. 'Like all good stories, it is witty, and it celebrates ingenuity. Will you permit me to entertain you with this trifle?'

'You know I am no lover of lying fantasies,' says Zaman, then nods indulgently. 'But now that all serious work for the day is done – perhaps a quick, small one that will give this wine a biting edge . . .'

The others smile and exclaim in praise and admiration and relief, and turn towards Farid who begins: 'We all know something of the clever devices of women, don't we? Think of the first lesson we learn as men; or the lesson we need to relearn every single day.

'But to get to my story. There was a wealthy, respectable merchant in a distant land – India perhaps, or China. This worthy man was terribly unhappy because his mother had lost all modesty. Though her husband had died only a month ago, her thoughts had already turned to love. She took one lover, then two, then three, not caring about the shame and scorn she was bringing on her son and his family. The merchant was deeply disgusted. He felt tainted. If the source of the fountain is dirty, can the water be pure? If a mother could be so brazen, what could he hope of his wives and daughters? The merchant could not concentrate on matters of trade. He left his business in the hands of a friend and took to travel.

Then one day, as he was walking about in misery, he met a powerful brahmin who was also a magician.

'The magician heard the merchant's tale and burst into bitter laughter. "You, a mere trader, hope for a chaste woman in your house!" he scoffed. "Do you know what happened to me? When I chose my bride, a beautiful and tender virgin, I decided I would take no chances. On our wedding night, I shrank her down to the size of an ant and kept her in an empty date seed. I swallowed this seed and it remained safe and undigested in my stomach. Using magic that had taken me years to master, I would spit up the seed every night, release her, and take her to my bed in her normal size."

' "Then one afternoon, when it was raining and the whole world was green and ready to love, I felt I couldn't wait for nightfall. I brought up my seed-wife through my mouth as usual. Though I was half-mad with desire, I couldn't help noticing that she too was panting as if she had been running a race. A grain of rice hung on her ripe red lips. I was about to brush it away, but her darting tongue quickly took it into her mouth out of my sight. I became suspicious. All thoughts of lovemaking disappeared, and I forced the grain out of her mouth before she could swallow it. I looked into it with my magical eye and saw a lover hidden there. While she sat safe in my stomach, the wily woman had learnt my magic and used it to mock our love."

'The merchant listened to the magician's tale and—' but Farid never gets to the merchant's fate.

The sultan has stood up; and on cue, so do all the others. A few of the cup-companions look shocked. They are old-timers who have heard many strange and incomplete rumours about the last queen's death. But a callow Farid gapes at them in bewilderment; their faces stoke the fear he feels at the sight of Zaman pale and frozen, cup in hand.

'Your highness,' says Farid, his attempt at a light-hearted tone betrayed by his tremulous whisper, 'this was in China or India – a mere story in some place far far away.'

The shah slowly thaws and comes back to life. 'Get rid of him,' he roars, and Farid is dragged away by the guards. The others tremble as they watch this first casualty of a new era, an innocuous storyteller. But Zaman has already forgotten Farid and his childish lies. He is now muttering as if talking to himself, 'The bird screeches for me. There is something,' he begins, then shakes himself free. 'Leave me now – there is something I must do.'

*

That night Zaman does something he has forgotten is fraught with danger. For many years now, since his two visits to Shahabad and his marriage to Dunyazad, he has been lulled into complacency. He has not seen anything untoward when looking out of a window. But tonight, tonight after that relentless prodding of a grotesque memory – he rushes to the window in his bedchamber and looks out; and it all comes back more powerful than ever before.

Outside in the velvety darkness grows a palm tree, its sinuous trunk topped by a shock of quivering green. In this leafy heart hovers a descendant of the immortal simurgh, king of birds. This old friend, a feathery tree-spirit, has shown him so many sights before, truths not revealed by even his best spies – and God knows he has enough of them.

He can see the spirit is angry, very angry tonight. He leans into the night air awaiting orders; but it is a question that hisses its way across and strikes him full in the face. 'Where is your ring? Who have you given your royal-sealed ring to?'

In reluctant reply, Zaman sees that other tree by the turbulent sea, two frightened brothers crouching in the inadequate refuge of its branches; the huge, horned, sleeping form of the jinni below; and the woman. (Zaman knows the tree-spirit is looking on as well.)

The woman, the collector of skin, flesh, lovers and their tokens, stretches out a few inches from her master's nose. The jinni sleeps on a pillow she has made of her clothes on the ground. His mouth opens a fraction every other minute and sucks in the sea air; he whistles as he exhales it.

The naked woman looks up meaningfully. Two men, Shahryar and Zaman, slip clumsily down their tree. She gestures rudely at Shahryar, ordering him to mount her. He trembles but he manages to ride her obediently, a boy on his very first horse. Then the woman pushes him off her as if she is brushing away a fly. He springs to his feet, ready to run. His eyes never leave the sleeping jinni; on his face, mixed with fear, there is a hint of gloating – the joy of danger manfully met.

Then it is Zaman's turn. Standing there in limp fear, he feels naked and unprotected. Then anger stirs like a thickening worm. This is unheard of – is he a slave? Is he Black Masood, Shahryar's queen's plaything, to slip down a tree and do his mistress's bidding? But he thinks he can hear the woman hiss impatiently: 'Hurry up or I wake the jinni. Where is your sword, you eunuch?' The words harden his resolve and he flings himself on her with a dry, muffled sob. But the jinni-woman has other plans. She rolls over, holding on to him all the while. She is sitting on top of him now, her eyes empty black pools. They suck him in with their contempt. It is all over in a few seconds.

Then the woman pulls out a string from a silken purse. Holding the purse between her teeth, she adds Shahryar's glittering ring, proof of her conquest, to the other ninety-eight on her string. Zaman's ring is the hundredth.

This is an old story. Shahryar, poor fellow, took ill and tried to cure himself with virginal blood. But he, Shahzaman, did not need a thousand and one nights of womanish lies. If you have been hurt, wedged tight in a rotten pit, do you go back to it to become whole? Zaman, of course, has his queen, wives, mistresses and slavegirls; but for visionary sustenance, he looks to the likes of his keen-eyed tree-spirit.

It is at the spirit's instigation that Sultan Shahzaman now bans rings. His ring cannot be recovered; should not be found, on a lustful creature who weakened him with her filth. So: no rings in his city. Rings strung on a pretty string? The string hidden in a silken purse? No string then, no purses in the markets. The royal guards search every house and hand in the city. A few disobedient fingers are chopped off in broad daylight; in the dead of night, surprise attacks turn homes upside down.

Dunyazad sends word to Shahzaman. She is usually so cool and quiet, so self-possessed, that he is taken aback by the undercurrent of anger he can sense in her words. 'The palace guards are spreading terror in the city. There is enough intrigue already; do we want a revolt?'

These presumptuous words, intrigue and revolt, prick him. He looks at her coldly. 'Do you know the way to the harem?' he asks her. 'And if you do, why not stay there?' Zaman has heard about the men who wait on Dunyazad to talk official business. What business does she have but to care for the one imbecile son she has given him?

Dunyazad, her rage and mortification carefully controlled, retreats to the harem and sends for her own spies. The royal prohibitions escalate. Caskets, chests, boxes, all failed miserably in their task to keep evil pleasures locked up; why shouldn't they be banned?

The people of Samarkand no longer have a routine. The violence, the panic, the senselessness of it all ravage everyday life like an epidemic. Even rumour flounders; though it fattens itself on their terror and rage and impotence, it cannot anticipate the sultan's next battlefield.

The fount of wisdom, the spirit perched on the tree, knows. Shahzaman is out in the moonless night, practising being invisible in a plain grey robe. He sees, at a distance, a black slave going about his work in one of the palace rooms. The slave's back is bent; Zaman watches him intensely. When the man straightens his back, the outline of his broad shoulders and full, firm buttocks is discernible even at this distance. The man leaves the room, emerges from the palace into the darkness. Shahzaman feels a thrill of recognition; leans against the tree trunk; and the knowledge of it – of the riddle, of the whole perplexing morass – flows into him. The enemy is black in colour. Zaman looks deeper into the darkness, into the skein of skin that holds it. And he sees a smooth-skinned creature, a woman who covets darkness above all.

But how to ban darkness, night? The sultan's powers are legion, and he can light up the palace, the city, turn night into day, banish sleep and secrecy. But the carriers of those mysterious twin evils? The tree-spirit summons two interconnected scenes in an unending play of lustful betrayal: a black slave slips down a tree and mounts the queen; now the queen is in a royal garden in Shahryar's Shahabad, now she is on a couch in Shahzaman's Samarkand. The scene dissolves into the open air and the slaves disappear; two kings who despair of womanly fidelity take their place on the tree. They are safe there only for the moment, only till they come to the notice of the woman below – the naked one dressed only in her cunning desires, cheating her jinni-warden again and again to collect a string of humiliated lovers.

*

In Samarkand, the sultan's adventures are filling up prisons. More and more people turn into shadows as they slip into hidden chambers in terror-stricken households. Spies are the heroes of the palace, spies and those skilful in disguises. The sultans have always had spies, both in times of war and peace, to keep in touch – it is said – with their subjects. But with Shahzaman's battle-cry urging them on, the network grows till this web of hardy weeds chokes the city. Spies infiltrate neighbourhoods, families, friendships; all ties are broken in two. And just when the people have learnt to be mistrustful of everyone, the sultan himself takes to disguises – to spy, it is believed, on his own spies.

While the sultan and his spies play hide and seek, the streets are being cleaned up of people. Dungeons groan with their newfound weight. There are some, though black or female, who prefer death to being locked up; the executioner is training laymen, so many limbs and necks does he have waiting to be chopped. Decapitated heads stare down at the city from where they are immured in cement turrets. Their strained grins would edify the people, but half the city is underground. To match the sultan's spies and disguises, the city has learnt to dissemble: that it does not know black men, slave or free; or any women. Though purged of these evils, the city, strangely enough, remains as unmanageable as a recalcitrant child. There is a severe shortage of bread, and a heavy silence hangs over its brightly lit homes and streets, all frozen at midday.

All eyes and thoughts are fixed on the palace with an equal measure of dread and anticipation. Rumour, leaking out of the enclosed splendours of the palace through slaves, artisans and servants, alerts the citizens to every move. But when what they await comes to pass, its swiftness, its ease, takes their breath away. For several days there is a rumour about a bitter scene, an irrevocable breach between Dunyazad and Shahzaman. Then the sultan, out in the night in search of his paradise, or in communion perhaps with his tree-spirit, is lost. Dunyazad, his queen, directs the search parties. The throne is empty, though not for long. For the time being, the blood has stopped flowing; the dust settles on the ravaged city as if the storm has passed. The city elders know from experience that it is too soon to lift a head and say with confidence, 'Yes, a tyrant has got what he deserved. A new king will be found, the throne will be filled, life will go on.'

*

Yet it does go on. A new king, his forehead bound with the gem-studded royal turban, is led to the throne. He is a very young man, almost a child. But though he appears to be dazed, he conducts himself with dignity. There is a woman who is watching him from a window, a quiet, ingenious woman who can rule, though her power will always be circumscribed by her invisibility. But she seems content with her unofficial status; she does not claim the title of sultana. She remains sayyida, the lady Dunyazad, briefly holding the reins for her predecessor's child, who she sees is more fit to rule than her son. The throne has passed under her able eyes to the son of the queen who died, it is said, in the arms of a black slave.

While Dunyazad conducts the search for her missing husband, the city slowly fills up again with those who have been in hiding. Though no one believes – as yet – that Shahzaman is dead and gone for ever, wounds are being aired, the mutilated nursed, the dead mourned, night and order tentatively restored. For the first time in months, the palace, though still a source of anxious uncertainty, is no longer the sole focus of attention. In this brief reprieve from the public eye, in this time of disorder when conventions may be flouted, Dunyazad has acted swiftly, in league, it is said, with a powerful and discontented general in the royal retinue. A boy on the throne, a ruler in the harem, a silent, inhibited army; and the city, limping back to life, remains surprisingly calm. Though an occasional whisper links Dunyazad to the sultan's disappearance, not one voice is raised; nor is there any sign of the agitation that usually accompanies a sudden transfer of power. Though no one says it in so many words, the city seems to have turned, briefly, into the queen's ally.

Dunyazad rules discreetly, on the young king's behalf, for almost a year. She rules, but she is about as visible as Zaman's reigning tree-spirit. Samarkand heals. The new king is austere, but tolerant and God-fearing; he also learns the necessities of power at amazing speed. The discontented general of Shahzaman's army is found with a slit throat and a note confessing to the mad sultan's murder. The extraordinary circumstances that thrust the new king on the throne recede. He never mentions his mother, killed in her bedchamber many years ago, or his father who hated darkness. He is known to treat Dunyazad, stepmother and kingmaker, with great courtesy and respect. But eleven months after he ascends to the throne, Dunyazad is relieved of her onerous duties. As she retreats, an immovable screen settles between her and the rest of the world as if her existence is debatable. It is not clear what Dunyazad thinks or feels when she is relegated to this respectable background once more, this time for good. She leaves no records of her own behind, not even a story or two like her more famous sister.

But many years later, when Shahzaman's excesses and Samarkand's nightmares are reduced to memories, a historian known for his accuracy writes:

Three weeks into the new year, Shahzaman, Sultan of Samarkand, disappeared from the palace grounds at night. Since he often travelled the city in disguise to supervise the execution of his somewhat eccentric orders, several valuable days were lost waiting for him to return.

The first search parties sent out were unsuccessful, but a fortnight later, after the new king assumed power, there was a bizarre and gruesome spectacle under a tree a few miles beyond the city gates.

The milk-white stallion Zaman had loved was there, dead, stab wounds on its winged legs. Under the dead horse was a locked box, a plain wooden one. A dagger lay inside, covered with old and new bloodstains; and the missing sultan's clothes, torn to shreds. A small piece of jewellery nestled in these ragged folds. Later, a body filled the coffin that was given a quick, modest burial. No one in the city was sure if this body was the sultan's. But everyone agreed – though they could not support their belief with evidence – that in the coffin, on the body, was the hard, glittering heart of the whole mystery: a gold ring, a ring with a royal seal.

Dilshad:

The Woman Under the Deadly Skin

A thousand festive lanterns lit up the night outside. Satyasama lay in the bed by the window, trying to ignore the frivolous sparkle of the stars. She reminded herself that she was tired after the day's journey and longing for sleep. But the room she had rented in the traveller's lodge across from the famous ruins was small, airless and hospitable to mosquitoes. She sighed, shut the window and dressed herself. She went out into the waiting night.

Satyasama had heard that there was a bustling village near this road, but she could see nothing of it. All she could see was a series of heavy, brooding shadows, the ruins of what was once a wonder-city. The following day would reveal the faces of these enigmatic creatures. She expected to find heroes and heroines in stony embrace, and mythical monsters, hunters, dancing girls. But like all travellers, she too wanted to be a genuine explorer; do more than see what others had looked at and described. She wanted to discover some fantastic secret waiting for her under fallen blocks of granite, rubble and fragments of sculpture.

Long before her journey to the ruined city, she had decided

what this discovery was to be. Once a man, a venerable old scholar, had told Satyasama: 'When I was younger, I came across a rare fragment of a traveller's tale. This account refers to an ancient structure called the Hall of Virgins. I have not been able to locate this ruin, but its inmates of stone – if we ever find them – should tell us many eloquent tales of their chastity. I remember, for instance, the special mention of a carving in a hidden nook of the hall, a lifelike portrait of a strange woman called Poison-Skin. And though this is hardly reliable information, I have also heard a story that helps us imagine Poison-Skin's exemplary beauty.'

'Here it is,' the scholar smiled at Satyasama across his book-strewn table, 'a small gift from me to you.'

*

Once, not far from the rich and dazzling city state of Vijaya, a poor goatherd called Nanni lay on a patch of muddy grass, watching the afternoon sky. She lay there, filthy but contented, as her flock grazed nearby and the clouds above glided past in graceful, hypnotic rhythm. Her mother was deep in the jungle gathering firewood. Nanni was all alone, except for the chewing goats and the warm, soundless sky. She shut her eyes and drifted into gentle sleep.

It could have been an idyllic setting for a romance: a mellow sky, a lazy day, and a young woman, pretty if dirt and matted hair are discounted, lying asleep like a happy animal in the sun. And there *was* a man on the edge of this scene, about to intrude into it, except he was no callow, handsome youth. He was an elderly man with a wide forehead, marked with wisdom lines like a dozen indelible caste marks. This man, for years a trusted minister of the great kingdom of Vijaya, was also the chief executive of the palace's network of spies.

The man moved warily to the sleeping girl and looked down at her. 'This is uncanny,' he thought. 'How can this creature look so much like our young princess?' A recruit like this did not turn up every day – imagine what he could do to the city's enemies with a girl he could pass off as his princess! He frowned, turning over a quick plan or two in his head. Just then a goat bleated. The girl jumped, startled and guilty.

Nanni gasped when she saw the stranger bending over her, but he spoke in the most soothing voice she had ever heard. 'What a beauty you are,' he told her. Then seeing that this only amazed her, he went on, 'If only' – and he wiped a tear – 'if only I had a daughter like you! I would give you a large mansion to live in, and rich clothes to wear, and many sweet things to eat and drink.'

He went on like this, describing a house with fountains and servants and flowering gardens till she felt weak with the strain of having to imagine it all. She could hardly believe her ears or her luck when he offered to adopt her and take her to the city.

'But what about the goats – what will my mother say?' she asked hesitantly.

He quickly solved this little problem.

'What if your mother does not let you leave the goats? Come back to her a rich princess and give her a surprise!'

Nanni agreed, delighted. Even her mother, a scolding, bad-tempered old thing, could not be angry then.

So the minister and the goatherd made their way to the

city of Vijaya, and stopped at an elegant house that stood all by itself in a large, enclosed park. 'You are now my daughter,' the minister told Nanni, 'but first you will have to learn to be a lady. Learn everything you can from these women. When I come back for you, you must be ready to live in a palace and marry a rich and handsome prince.'

The women in the house did not seem surprised to see Nanni; they bathed her and scrubbed her, clothed her and fed her so that her true beauty was revealed. Nanni learnt to speak like the highborn with surprising rapidity, and to be a pleasing lady, beautiful at all times. The kind women even gave her a rare potion to make her skin as fair and flawless as that of a real princess. They brought it to her first thing in the morning and last thing at night, and it tasted terrible, but being well fed and talking like a lady had made Nanni very obedient. After all, how was she to know there was an addictive poison in it? Or that she was in a training school for the city's vast and colourful range of spies?

Six months went by, and the minister came back to find Nanni transformed into a nymph any man would give up a kingdom for. He lifted her veil and feasted his eyes on the dark fish-shaped eyes and the fruity lips framed by a pale face. The women hovered around anxiously, waiting for his critical eye to notice something amiss. But he seemed pleased with Nanni, especially with her new milky skin, living marble as smooth and white as the pillars of the royal palace. He asked her to say goodbye to the women, now that she was a grown-up lady who would live in her own house. But first he was sending her on a short journey. There was a small bit of business: would she help him with a task set by the king? She did not see how she could help the king, but such were the minister's powers of persuasion that Nanni meekly agreed and got into the waiting palanquin.

She was taken to a garden resort outside the city, where the minister's servant was waiting for her behind a bush. He showed her a young man walking about in the garden. 'That,' he told her, 'is a prince, the son of our city's enemy. Now this is what you have to do. Remember you are supposed to be a beautiful princess. This is your chance to prove it. Go to him and make him fall in love with you. Tell him you are the princess of Vijaya. There is nothing like the sight of an enemy's daughter to fill a man with love; if you play your part well, he will take you to his bed. Remember: a single agent like you can do more than a full army to destroy the enemy. Once the enemy lies there, blue-skinned with your poison, you can escape into the darkness and come back to me.'

Nanni was terrified; she couldn't understand what was happening.

'But my father wants me to *marry* a prince,' she said. 'Are you sure you have understood your master's instructions?'

The man lost patience. He flung aside her veil and said in a furious whisper: 'Listen, you luscious little Poison-Skin, all these months of planning and you're going to play innocent now?'

'What poison?' she whispered back. 'And the name is Nanni.'

'Poison-Skin,' he said again, as if he was deaf. 'You drank those drops of poison day after day and thought you could remain the same old Nanni? You're going to love our city's enemies, little Poison-Skin,' he sniggered, 'you're going to love them to death.'

Some time later, Nanni slipped into the prince's chamber. She was struck dumb when she saw his dignified nose and his majestic shoulders. He, meanwhile, felt his skin burn; and he knew instantly that only this unknown apsara from heaven could put out the fire. They gazed at each other for a whole magical hour and then the prince broke the spell. 'Who are you?' he stammered as he groped towards Nanni like a blind man. 'Where do you come from?'

'From Vijaya,' she replied in a voice as silky as her lily-white skin. 'I am—' and she retreated a few steps before he could touch her. The prince was amazed that she seemed to have forgotten her name; but he had already guessed that she must be a princess, so what did a name matter? He reached for her, but she stopped him just in time.

'Wait,' she said. 'You are a man made to be loved, but I – my skin – there is an evil in me, a poison that will destroy you. No man should touch me till the day I die. Though I long for love as much as you do, I must take a vow of chastity for ever.'

Then she told the prince the minister's plot and how she was the bait. The young prince shivered but he also realized he was in the presence of a living saint. Grateful to Nanni for having spared his life, he asked what he could do for her.

'Nothing,' she said, 'but find me some ugly old clothes and an empty little house so I can hide myself.' She threw away her rich brocades and jewels, but no rags could dull the skin that still glowed like a full virginal moon. Then she parted from the man she had saved by not loving him, and went to the modest house he found for her. Nanni, though she was to remain Poison-Skin for ever, lived the pure life of a recluse, keeping her promise of chastity intact, a shining example to all women.

*

It was Poison-Skin Satyasama hoped to find in the ruins she was visiting, the ruins of the city that had held sway in this part of the world hundreds of years ago. Any evidence of Poison-Skin would do, just a little carving or a memorial stone – for some reason, Satyasama believed she would recognize her instantly. The next few days Satyasama walked from ruin to desolate ruin in search of her voluptuous and saintly goatherd, braving bats, snakes and the musty smell of neglect. Satyasama saw many things, all the stuff of the glorious, fabled past, but she didn't come across a single time-worn image of the woman she was looking for. Then late into an afternoon, wandering disheartened among the weedy shrubs that had sprung up among the ruins, Satyasama met a goatherd, a young man watching his grazing flock with a bored look on his face.

She sat down on a rock nearby and exchanged a friendly smile with him. When the goatherd heard Satyasama's story, he laughed; she was quick to take offence. 'I heard my story from a very learned man,' she told him sharply.

He grinned at her with suggestive charm. 'It's not a complete lie,' he assured her. 'Just a few weeds here and there, and once these are pulled out, you'll know what you are looking for.' He took a quick look at his goats to make sure they had not wandered too far; then he began *his* story of Nanni.

*

One day, Nanni the goatherd was so tired as she watched her grazing flock that she fell asleep. While she slept, a man passed by in his palanquin. This man was from the big and rich city nearby, and he was wily and powerful though you wouldn't have thought it from looking at him. He had the sharp, hungry look of a lean wolf. One of his arms was deformed and it hung uselessly to the side. His face was craggy and pitted, and he was toothless. People in the city whispered that he had been born with a full set of teeth, a sure sign that he would grow up to be a king. But his mother, afraid of what the real king would do if he heard about his babyish rival, had all her son's teeth pulled out. The toothless, one-armed fellow grew up and went to work at the palace; he did end up working pretty near the crown, because he rose to become a trusted minister.

The minister now considered the sleeping girl before him with interest. He took in her full, ruby-touched lips, parted as she snored gently, and the smooth, wave-like movement of her breasts as they rose and fell. She was, no doubt, young and ignorant; and also she was, he could see, in spite of the filth and tatters on her, very beautiful. 'A minister recruits cadre in the most unlikely places,' he thought to himself, and prepared his story with his usual swiftness. Before Nanni could scream or run away, he seized her. The girl woke with a start and stared at him, bewildered. Holding on to her, he said in an anguished tone, 'Where's your mother?'

'In the forest gathering wood,' stammered the frightened girl.

'Oh my child, be brave. It must have been your mother I saw in the jungle,' he said sorrowfully. 'I got down from my palanquin to see if I could help, but it was too late – the wild beast had already devoured most of her.'

He embraced the crying girl, promising not to leave her behind where she was in danger of tigers and God knows what else. The man took Nanni with him to the city, soothing away her tears and fears with kind words. He left her in a pleasant house in the care of two knowing old women, promising to come back for her in a few months.

The women bathed Nanni, combed the lice out of her hair and dressed her in a robe soft as clouds. 'Look at our young Fresh-Face,' they marvelled, and indeed that was a perfect new name for Nanni, shining with her newly revealed beauty. The women fed her a huge, delicious meal. The goats were forgotten; so was the mother, a tired, scolding thing after all. The girl was only a child, and there were so many new and good things to see and feel and taste here! She was moist putty in the kneading hands of her new guardians. They dressed her up, made her beautiful and a little vain. They also taught her all kinds of things which she found strange and tedious, but in time she learnt the art of disguising herself and the tricks of elegant conversation and manners. Another useful trick that was part of her lessons was the swift and soundless method of piercing a fleshy dummy with a knife hidden in her hip girdle. She did all this and they gave her what she liked best: heaped platefuls of food that they said would make her lose her hungry look. All the six months she stayed with these good women, they gave her a bittersweet brew to drink, a special beauty potion to make her as fair as a princess. Having learnt that beauty is hard and unpleasant work, she drank the sunset-coloured brew obediently day after day.

Fresh-Faced Nanni knew nothing of the royal army of spies that infested the city. All she knew was that she was pampered and well fed; being fattened in fact, her breasts and hips swelling by the day. Her skin, the innocent dirt-caked skin she never took notice of, was now a well-oiled glistening sheet, alive to fragrance and silk and caress. The women admired her, bringing sparkling mirrors to show her that she was no longer a mere Nanni or even a Fresh-Face but Pearl-Skin, a beauty fit to be a queen. They told her again and again that she was destined for a king. Didn't she have the graces of any rich and well-born lady, didn't she look and sigh and hunger like a queen? Pearl-Skin was inflamed with new desires; her skin felt taut with expectation as if it was waiting for a promised feast.

The body was ready, the skin hungry. The city made its move. The one-armed man came back as promised. He found his new professional assassin ready. The ripe and artful woman he saw before him was no longer Nanni the goatherd, or her successor Fresh-Face Nanni, or even the mellow Pearl-Skin. This woman was a curvaceous poison-skinned trap for the city's enemies.

Poison-Skin received her instructions and travelled to the first enemy's camp disguised as a rich widow. The enemy, who did not yet know he was an enemy, was filled with excitement when he set eyes on the minister's messenger. In the chamber lit by flickering lamps and incense, the enemy stripped Poison-Skin of gold, jewel and silk. He sucked her firm, hard-nippled breasts; his head swam in giddy circles, but this only spurred him on. Her hips swayed from side to side, a pair of open wings, while her legs held him in a clamp round his back. He could feel himself being sucked into a very tight, hot and dangerous place; it was too late to withdraw and step back from its fiery bliss. There was something about her touch, or her skin, that made him so numb and sleepy, he could feel himself beginning to drown. But she was waking him up now, he was almost awake, he was trying to raise a hand to say Enough! She pushed him off her belly, but only after a sharp thrust of fire plunged deep into his back like a naked, well-aimed dagger.

Poison-Skin, in the minister's employ, ensnared many victims, devouring each like a fly caught in the sweet and sticky motions of love. At first she quite enjoyed this heady power – having forgotten all about goatherds and princesses – but then she began to feel a terrible fatigue seep through skin to bone. Would there be no end to this loving and killing? She began to feel a loathing for beds and bare bodies. She had never felt pity for her lover-victims, and now too she did not feel anything as strong as aversion to them. It was her own pale, sheer skin that disgusted her, and the sick-sweet smell of crushed, rotten flowers that seemed to cling to her sweat.

In this unhappy, restless mood, she passed a goat shed on her travels far from her city. She was overcome with childish memories; she went in, looked her fill of the goats and the droppings and the hay and felt an unfamiliar sense of relief. She lay down on a mess of hay. The smell soothed her to sleep. When she woke, she heard a man stifling his sobs; it was a young goatherd, holding on to his thigh. He had been bitten by a snake and he knew that death was not too far away. Poison-Skin felt his sorrow merge with her own. She rolled over to him and took him wordlessly into her fleshy arms. For a day and night they loved each other, two soldiers in thrall of battle, skin and muscle, as if their lives depended on it; till finally, as their pungent, sweaty bodies fell apart, two streams of poisonous blood merged and turned into one wholesome, sparkling river.

The snake-bitten lover did not die. He went on his way, singing praises of Poison-Skin everywhere. She too had made a discovery: it was possible to love, to sing and dance and revel in the watering holes of the body, and emerge intact.

She took to spending most of her time in the goat shed. Its smell had become necessary to her. The longer she was there, the fainter the smell of her own poison-skin. Till one day, many passionate and rustic lovers later, she discovered that she no longer knew how to kill a lover; and that her skin smelt of goats, not sweet poison. It was as if every lover who emerged from her embrace to sing praise of her generous heart and earthy lovemaking cleaned Poison-Skin inch by inch. Her fame as a golden-hearted harlot travelled far and wide, and she acquired yet another name: Goat-Skin, lover of humble men.

Many months later, that crooked old jackal, the minister who set little Nanni's adventures rolling, managed to catch up with Goat-Skin. All he wanted to do, he said, was offer her a token reward for her services. He offered Goat-Skin a magic potion that would get rid of the goat smell for ever, and replace it with the fragrance of jasmine. Goat-Skin, who was holding court in a mess of dung and hay, glowered at him and threw him out. It was the only day in her new life that she felt sorry she could no longer poison an unwanted lover.

So Goat-Skin, in the course of her third career, wandered where she pleased with the companions of her childhood. After many a year, and many a lover, she too grew old. Names no longer mattered, and by the time she died, all her earlier disguises were long forgotten. Her army of friends, lovers and children had for long thought of her as Mother-Goat: a woman who fed their many hungers, keeping at bay the poison of sorrow clouding their hearts.

*

The goatherd was done. So was the day, the confident blaze of sunshine now dissolving into the muted, hesitant shadows of evening. Satyasama made her way to the mean room in the lodge. The next morning, she returned to the ruins one last time. She paid tribute, on its own terms, to the grand procession passing by her, figures and scenes from a bygone city. Years later, when an acquaintance questioned her about this dream of splendour, she found she had just a memory or two to offer, as inconsequential as small change. She felt for a moment the distress of an unexpected loss. But then she remembered her biographer-friends and that unseen hall of virgins, martyrs and poisonous women.

Perhaps the next time she was asked, she too would try her hand at peopling that hall of broken dreams and mirrors. In fact, she could almost feel herself there now, smell the hoary old thing reeking of bat piss, drawing her like a magnet to its stony heart. But who is this cracked and disfigured relic propped up there, a crumbling gatekeeper? And why does she have two heads – with twin faces that twist away from each other as if a single body can be torn in two?

5

Dunyazad:

The Palace Thief

The young prince had been especially good all day. He had prayed at the right times; not fallen off his surly stallion once; and his masters had promised to praise his memory and hard work to the sultan and sultana. 'Your words,' said one of his teachers, 'will someday be written in letters of gold, just like those manuscripts locked up in the sultan's treasury.' Now Prince Umar lay in bed, clean, freshly robed and blessed, waiting.

The child Umar had a nurse who put him to bed every day. She was fat, this nurse, and called, not unkindly, Sabiha of the giant globes. Sabiha's full, tightly packed breasts had fed him generously from the very first day of his life. She had in fact seen him through his infancy, years in which his own mother had bigger business at hand, though he, like the other two babies which did not survive, was weak and fretful. Sabiha was always there, large and comforting. She seemed to have been put on earth only to feed Umar, nourish him and protect him from the numerous evils royals are vulnerable to. Umar had not spent a day in his brief life when he had not seen her.

Though it was many years now since he had been weaned,

she still came to him every night, and left his chamber only when he was fast asleep. Many nights his searching little hands would slip into her robe and snuggle in the deep valley between her breasts. She would stroke his hair, sing a song or two in the thin, bird-like voice that lived, incongruously, in that padded body. But whether she was still or talkative, her presence trickled into him like that earlier steady drip from her nipples into his expectant mouth. Her presence, a comforting smell of milk, a whiff of garlic and sweat, sucked him into a safe place and lulled him to sleep.

Tonight, as a reward for his glowing face, the result of a day spent in the exercise of virtue, Sabiha was moved to go further than stroking or caressing his head, or singing one of her tremulous lullabies. In her placid, reliable way, she waddled up to him, took him in her arms, and told him a bedtime tale. She only knew one, this simple woman; and the tale she knew, and now told Umar, was a somewhat milky, bland tale. It was all about a great sultan whom the city had always loved and honoured, and who was always leaving his subjects to go fight wars and drive enemies away from his kingdom. But when his duty was done, he hastened back to his beautiful queen and palace. But alas – the queen only had a beautiful face; her heart was ugly with wicked wishes and desires. She had learnt to be secretive and love others when the sultan was not there. When the king found out, he was bowed down with grief.

Though the wicked queen died for her sins, the king was still so unhappy that it was as if she had not left him. She, or his memory of her, remained behind like an invisible ghoul. 'We are all like this, we women,' it whispered in his ear, and it was so cunning and persuasive that he began to believe it. So he called his wazir, a faithful adviser and friend, to tell him that he would marry every day, and the executioner could take away the bride the next morning. The wazir, his good jinni, cried out: 'But your people love you. If you do this, they will remember only this one cruel act.' But the ghoul was whispering in the king's ear and he would not listen to his wazir.

Luckily, before anybody could be turned over to the executioner, the wazir's clever daughter offered herself as the first bride. Again, the wazir tried his best to convince her of the danger she would face, but her goodness and her love for the sultan made her determined. As it turned out, the sultan and the wazir's daughter knew best what they were about, because over a thousand and one nights, she told him wise stories and proverbs, and he listened, and together they chased the ghoul away. Then the sultan was happy again, and he and his new queen lived in their splendid palace all their lives.

Though he had not heard this rubbishy trifle before, Umar felt, even as Sabiha's voice droned the monotonous, comforting words, that he was outgrowing his nursemaid's caresses. And this tale was really too childish for him; such a lying, girlish fantasy for *him*, a prince who was working so hard at growing up! Umar's hands flew out of their nest between Sabiha's breasts. Really, they were like old pillows, the cotton stuffing in them all bunched up and lumpy. He pushed her arm away firmly and pretended to be fast asleep.

The young prince lay in bed, waiting. Fat, generous Sabiha had left the room, believing him to be safe and asleep. She would not come again and play nursemaid, the boy thought angrily, and he could feel the story turn in his stomach like curdled milk. He could not understand why he was so irritable and discontented all of a sudden; why he lay there, sleepless and alone, feeling estranged from his babyish old life. Surely an insignificant story told by a stupid old woman could not change the palace, his home, for ever?

Umar lit the lamp by his side and his eyes wandered round the chamber till they came to rest on the wall before him. But the picture on this wall was not conducive to rest. Looking at the interminable patterns of vines and waves before him, Umar found himself aching for a simple, blank wall. The stylized images before him blended and moved into each other as he stared at them; so that what he saw was not a simple, rugged wall of stone and brick, but a hazy, shifting surface, as of an endless body of water. Umar shivered. The grey ocean before him swelled, rose into the air, and turned into a clammy, treacherous mist. He saw this veil hanging between him and the rest of the palace; like the fortressed secrets that distinguished the palace from the city outside; or that aura of mystery that kept the sultan and his wife apart from citizens, palace-dwellers, and even their own son and heir.

Umar had known no home, no world other than the palace. He knew that the palace was a refuge from the blazing day outside, and the herds of dirty urchins and vulgar crowds. But he also remembered another piece of knowledge that was fed to him along with Sabiha's milk: that it was at night – the time given to both fantasy and terror – that the palace shed its gilded mask and revealed itself. Then its hard corners could melt, its geometrical contours blur. Some guard or other may fall into a trance and at that instant, the heavy shutters would loosen. In this truant hour, if the iron-will vigil of the palace weakened, a shadow or two could slide in, each making its way to a different wing.

Umar remembered the uncrowned king of his earliest years. In these memories, the night's terrors were simplified and reduced to one figure. The unknown was personified in a creature who emerged out of the veil of darkness hiding the palace night, and stationed himself where Umar could not see him well, but was only too aware of his presence. Who was this elusive being who had hounded him as long as he could remember? He did not know why this unwelcome visitor came and went every night. At first, in his more credulous days, he had thought it was because the visitor knew that he, Umar, was lonely. But if the caller slipped into the palace through Umar's walls and slunk past his bed to the door, why did he never stop to talk or reveal himself? Why flaunt his visit if all he could do was cast a chill of fear on a boy before making for the sultan's wing?

Even at this distance of some years, Umar found it difficult to describe the man who had blighted his early, innocent years. His visitor had no recognizable features. Umar was not even sure he had been a man. All that was clear was that he – or it – had been a restless thing which never settled down to any visible, stable form. It shifted shapes, now a malevolent stain, now a wisp of smoke, as it twisted and turned in dark corners, behind screens, under Umar's bed. But if the crea-ture's appearance was elusive, its desire – to make its presence felt in the most graceless fashion – had never been in doubt. Its brief passage past Umar's room was enough to awaken peculiar, painful sensations that destroyed sleep for the rest of the night. Sometimes it directed Umar's tender eyes to some unsolvable or unsavoury question; sometimes it made him tremble with an unreasonable fear. But why did he tremble alone? Why didn't the prince call someone to save him from this housebreaker?

The prince, like most children, had a pair of parents, indeed a pair of very worthy, royal parents, the premier citizens of the city. In his early years Umar had seen little of them though. They were busy, as so many adults tend to be, with their own secret which they were reluctant to share with him. Their secret, whatever it was, seemed to be nocturnal; it raised its sleeping hood every night and bared its fangs. And it must be a clever and cunning thing because it had many names like different disguises; indigestible mouthfuls like martyrdom and repentance and salvation. As he grew up, he saw that his parents had loosened themselves from the tight grip of this mystery. At the same time, the palace creature's visits became less frequent; it was losing its power. Or it had got what it wanted and had been persuaded to leave the palace in peace.

Now his parents, the sultan and sultana, no longer went down to the dungeon every night, to the secret chamber where he was not allowed to go. Sabiha had told him this was because a jinni – that loved to eat little boys for a snack – lay hidden under the steps that slipped down to the dungeon. But as he grew up the dungeon had been robbed of some of its myths, and the jinni too seemed to have left.

Now the old executioner, Nadeem (who had a lovely booming voice and was also the town crier), lounged about flabbily, always ready to play a game with him. Once Nadeem showed Umar his set of implements: swords, daggers, an axe with a dazzling blade. They didn't talk much; but in their companionable silence, Umar learnt the power and undeniable reality of these instruments by running his fingers down their smooth bodies. Their sharp, ready edges glinted at him like rows of knowing eyes. There was no hint of sorcery here. Each tool had been sharpened and polished, the wielding arm trained to cut, chop, and draw real blood with brutal efficiency. These instruments kept truth and legend firmly apart.

*

Over the next few weeks, Umar stuck tenaciously to his resolution of keeping all companions, beginning with Sabiha, out of his chambers at night. Every night, the prince – the child Umar – willed himself to tear aside a miasmic veil. He willed himself to outstare the confusing, multiple images that emerged from the haze, daring them to frighten him. He was a boy who lived in luxury, this little prince, in the lap of plump cushions and rich carpets, and in chambers that could be dazzlingly lit with lamps and chandeliers. Yet this child – for he was one though his solemnity gave him the appearance of a miniature adult – was surprisingly straight-backed and clear-eyed. In the midst of monotonous splendour, there is a piquancy in self-imposed austerity, and it had been given to this child of riches to crave this sharp-edged pleasure and grope towards it. The boy forced himself to lie still in his bed, his serious, expectant face glowing in the steady light of the solitary lamp he preferred as a companion. Thus prepared, Umar was as ready as he would ever be to face and apprehend – alone – his freshly remembered dread of the night.

In the wake of Sabiha's tale and her departure, the night's dangers were coming back stronger for his reprieve from their power. He was too grown-up now to believe in palace jinn or palace thieves with magical powers. But in the thinning veil of the unknown about him, he spied a new challenge, a challenge that must be met if he was to be done with nursemaids, bedtime tales, the terrors of mystery and secrecy, all the crippling apparatus of childhood. In place of a wicked, thieving creature, Umar now saw something more difficult to name in the palace night that engulfed him. In the eye of the veil (or mist, or fog) was an empty space; the untouched heart of the palace; and here passed a puzzling parade of pictures and voices, condemned to endless replay. Umar stared at these fragments till his eyes smarted with tears. Or he tried stopping up his ears with his hands, denying the wails and cries that were repeated from time to time, with increasing and insistent indignation. But either way, they – the creatures of the night and the voice of their presiding genius – endured to play out their act for him.

Always there was an air of the forbidden that hung over these separate images that were mysteriously related to each other. The forbidden meant a separate world, secluded, rich, bafflingly complicated. Exciting, but never free of the taint of immorality. Umar saw two figures, a man and a woman, engaged in what appeared to be a secret ritual. Outside their chamber was a babble of voices, some wailing in hunger or despair, others storming at injustices piled up. The man and the woman seemed to hear nothing of it. They could have been sorcerers, so powerful was their concentration on what they were doing over and over again. He, the grey-haired one with the glittering robe, fiddled endlessly with a collection of little machines. These automata in various shapes – an exquisite miniature fort, an ingenious mechanical dagger, a box that dispenses wine – surrounded him, and he moved from one to the other, adjusting weights, mending springs. And she, the woman with the meeting eyebrows and the dissatisfied mouth, muttered softly to herself as she pored over the magical letters she was casting with a stick of gold on a basin of sand.

Every morning, Umar left his bed fatigued but undefeated. He hated all magic, and the more he suspected its existence in the palace, the more stubborn he grew. Already his decision to let go of his earliest companions, and the deity of make-believe that made childhood in the palace such a wonderland, was weakening the chaotic visitations of the night. Soon he would break entirely free of its hold. He yearned sometimes for a little help in his endeavour. He had long known there was something hidden in this palace, and not just a common thief, that malevolent creature of a childish imagination. But he could not approach his mother, question her. Shahrzad was not just his mother, but a saviour, a sultana. A queue of petition-bearing courtiers snaked outside her chamber. As for his father – he was the legendary and ever-receding sultan. But even in this vast, pitiless enclosure of royals, there was an unlikely accomplice or two. Umar, dizzy and drowsy from sleepless nights, began to spend more and more time with Nadeem, the executioner who had a soft spot for children.

Then one day, Umar asked him abruptly as if he had just thought of it: 'What is the city like? I mean, your city, the one in which people lead ordinary, humble lives?' (Umar did not know why he assumed a life outside the palace would be either ordinary or humble, but such are the benefits of a princely education.) Nadeem was so quiet that Umar was afraid he had offended him. But the lined and pitted face was deep in thought; and seeing the grave attention Nadeem gave his question, Umar felt a burst of joy. Here was somebody who dealt in facts. Nadeem had to pause and think carefully because he knew how important it was to find an answer that steered clear of magic and mystery.

'Come with me,' said Nadeem at last. He led the boy up to the palace roof. The height of their perch and the wide-angled view that lay before them increased Umar's dizziness, and he shut his eyes. He saw for an instant that old hated veil stir in the darkness behind his eyelids, and he took a deep breath as if preparing to dive. Then he opened his eyes, and gently shook off the restraining arm Nadeem had placed on his shoulder. He looked.

The city lay below them, a different world. It was enormous, varied. The city had grown and spilt over, well beyond its walls. The symmetrical perfection of its palatial centre had worn out even in the circles that enclosed it and protected it from its people. Umar was a little repelled by the city's disorderly look, and the apathy with which it bore its history of plunder. But he was also fascinated. He could feel, even at this distance, the regular beat of its enduring heart and the quiet strength of its mundane life. Its life had gone on for years, before he was conceived, and it would carry on after him. The secret was that though people lined up for parades, though they kissed the ground before the royals and lit up their streets to celebrate regal whims, the citizens' daily lives had a focus and logic and meaning independent of palatial marvels or fears. Umar, reared on the splendours of the palace, on its over-rich diet, came face to face with the scarred city and its banal, daily struggle for bread, and was moved to tears. The map before him held in its flabby old arms his future and salvation. It filled him with a sense of wonder. His manhood, when he would lead this city back to a time of healing, was just a quick plunge away.

Dilshad:

Four Lovers in the Wilderness

Once, in the days before Dilshad succumbed to the seductive ease of comfortable journeys, she reached the edge of a great forest. All along the way she had been fed the horror stories stay-at-homes conjure to justify their spinelessness. She heard, for instance, that the forest's lush vegetation covered heaps of bones, evidence of foolhardy passers-by. Or that among its rich variety of flora and fauna this wilderness boasted discarded jewels and limbs, all hidden in a tangle of jungly dreams. The few who survived had become strangers to their families and friends, so changed were they by their sojourn. 'Do you want to lose yourself among wild beasts and demons?' her well-wishers asked Dilshad. She listened to all the advice that came her way but she knew their concern was hopeless. She never could resist the lure of forbidden territory.

Later, trudging alone in the endless wilderness, Dilshad's desire to be an adventurer, to claim unmapped territory as her own, was somewhat tarnished. There were the predictable but unnerving sounds of the forest – her own footsteps echoing with every step, sudden shrieks, calls and trumpetings, a mystery lurking behind every bush. But what she had not bargained for was that those crazy stories she had heard before her journey now began humming in her head, as pesky as mosquitoes trapped in a room. These specks of fantasy were sneaky creatures; they had seen their chance and quickly turned bloodthirsty.

Dilshad managed to go on, but was increasingly lost and nervous, a feeling not helpful to solitary travellers. When she reached a stretch so overgrown with branches, roots and foliage that it made a dense wall without a chink, she gave up. She stayed there hoping to be rescued. And she was, though not quite in the way she expected.

The night was the longest Dilshad had ever lived through. She shivered on her tree perch, fear and imagination her sole companions. For the first time she wondered if there was something to be said for the tedious warnings of elders and betters. Then the sun finally rose, and even better, she heard footsteps. Tears of relief filled her eyes as she slipped down the tree to take a closer look at her saviour. He was a squat, well-built man with a few strands of grey hair waving like flags on his chin and scalp. His hand held a large axe in a confident, familiar grip.

Dilshad told him she was lost and pleaded for his help, or at least the use of his axe to clear a path. He looked at her, taking in every inch of her body from head to foot, in a measured, deliberate way. Though she certainly didn't look her best, what he saw brought a smile to his face. When he spoke, it was in a playful, teasing tone: 'You, a sweet delicate thing like you wield an ugly, rusty axe? Impossible!'

'But how do I get out of the forest then? And what about you – where are you going?'

'Not so many questions please,' he interrupted with a cold authority quite unlike the simple woodcutter Dilshad had decided he was. She was quiet, and he went on: 'I will use my axe to help you across the forest, but' – and a cunning look came into his eyes – 'there is the small matter of a price, or if you like, condition.'

'Of course,' Dilshad replied, feeling she was on familiar trading ground. It was as good as being out of the forest already.

He considered her again as if carefully assessing her value, then announced, 'I am here for a reason. I came to this jungle to be rejuvenated. Look: the minister of the Great City will be chosen in a few months. I have plenty of money, and I am a pretty tough fellow.' (He looked complacently at his axe.) 'But I need something special to gain a winning edge. That's why I'm here – all the wise old men I consulted told me I would find what I need in the forest.'

'And have you found it?' Dilshad asked, wondering where she had heard these words before.

'Not yet,' he snapped, 'but I will. I must find a pure child of the forest, unspoilt by the world of men outside.'

Dilshad began to see what her part of the bargain might be, and seeing this on her face, he moved confidently towards her. His eyes on her like an eagle, his hands on her arms, the axe between them like a reliable witness, he whispered, 'I will be powerful, very powerful; and you will be mine alone, my youngest and most beloved wife, and every wish of yours will be fulfilled.'

She did not resist. These four bald words now reek of cowardice, but remember they were already in the depths of the jungle. It was too late to turn back, and all the rules Dilshad had learnt outside withered instantly when put to the test in the wilderness. She had to get out of the forest; he had the axe; and besides, there was something appealing (or so she told herself at the time) in his gruff, decisive manner. It was wonderful to have someone else take charge.

Dilshad lost count of time; they seemed to have been there for a lifetime. One afternoon, when he was asleep, she looked at her face in a puddle. There she was on its shifting surface, her features quivering every time the breeze lifted a finger – but wait, that was not her face. The puddle was showing her someone she did not know, a watery woman whose knowing, restless face filled Dilshad with a strange hope. The axe, she suddenly thought, was not doing its job fast enough. She returned to the sleeping figure, sneaked up to the precious, well-worn axe lying by him and gently picked it up. She went to work on the trail. Her hands smarted and stung, her arms and shoulders stiffened with a dull pain. But in her excitement and fear she made so much progress that soon she was deep in the uninhabited woods.

But Dilshad was not alone; she could sense that she was being watched. She turned to the right, and through the foliage she saw a horn, then a quick flash of a graceful figure leaping deer-like to safety. At that moment she heard her axe-lover shouting and cursing somewhere behind her. She dropped the axe in fright and ran in the direction she had seen the deer disappear.

Much later, scratched, bleeding and panting, Dilshad found him. He was crouched in a small, well-hidden clearing, trying to pull out a thorny twig entangled on his horn. 'Let me do that,' she offered as gently as she could, and went to him before he could escape her. He gazed at her with a bewildered look (later she learnt he had never seen a woman before) but he allowed her to remove the twig and clean the bruise with a piece of her tattered shirt.

He was a strange and wondrous creature, this deer-man. Dilshad thought she would never tire of looking at him, at the single horn on his finely sculpted head, his thick tangle of blue-black hair, the virginal moss on his chin and cheeks, his muscular but sleek limbs. As her eyes moved down to the firm, flat belly above his piece of deerskin, she felt an ache begin between her legs; she also seemed to have forgotten how to breathe. She broke out in a sweat as she overheard the woman whose face she had seen in the puddle think, I will have this man whether he wants me or not – I will make him want me.

It was slow, but there was something exquisite in fulfilment deferred, and Dilshad learnt to savour the torturous inch-by-inch movement towards her object. They lived together, totally absorbed in skin, their only language sighs of longing and grunts of pleasure. As he grew more adept at appeasing his newfound hunger (and her overgrown appetite) his horn began to shrink. The skin thinned till it was almost transparent. The day Dilshad noticed that the horn was gone, leaving behind only a tell-tale bump on his head, she heard rough footsteps and a curse in a familiar voice. Her old master was stalking them. She grabbed her new lover's hand and whispered urgently, 'Do you know a way out of here?' (It is astonishing that she had never asked him this question before – but they were, remember, otherwise occupied.)

He pointed ahead, and they ran hand in hand. Axe-Man heard them and was on their trail. They ran, it seemed, forever. Dilshad's young man was so exhausted that he slumped to the ground. 'It's too much,' he gasped. 'I don't know why I can't run as I used to.' He lay there close to tears, more concerned about the waning of his powers than of the real danger at their heels. 'And,' he added with a touch of spite, 'I may have got the directions wrong – maybe we're lost.' She looked down at him impatiently – she could hear Axe-Man catching up with them.

'Follow me,' Dilshad snapped and ran ahead. For a while she heard him panting behind her, pleading with her to go slower. Then he grew silent but she refused to turn around. Suddenly she'd had enough of it all, mothering and seducing, taking orders and being seduced. 'I hope he bumps into Axe-Man and they hack each other to pieces,' she muttered nastily, and just then she tripped on some roots bulging out of the ground and fell at the foot of a raintree.

Dilshad had cut her lower lip; she could feel it throb. She lay there recovering her breath. The taste of blood on her tongue made her think: the king seizes a virgin girl, the courtesan seduces a virgin boy. She looked up at the tree's lavish canopy of leaves and demanded in disgust, 'Is there no way out of this old story?'

The wind stirred and the branches nodded gracefully in rhythm with her words. Then it dawned on her that she could no longer hear anyone; she couldn't hear footsteps or curses or appeals for help. More amazing, she looked before her and saw the way out of the forest.

Back on the road, Dilshad made her way to a market and

discovered that she had been away, trapped in the wilderness, only for a day. Here was a puzzle stranger than her adventures! Were her lovers mere phantoms? And the two-faced woman with her equally overwhelming terror and desire? Dilshad shrugged and walked on, tired of teasing riddles. Besides, she had several practical reminders that she must prepare for her onward journey. Her old clothes felt tight, her breasts sagged a little and her skin was dry and itchy. So she stuck to the familiar road before her, ignoring the suspicion that though she had crossed the feared forest and emerged intact, something was lost. Once she did that, the rest was easy. Dilshad looked the other way when a stubborn child in her wandered away, back to the dark and secretive place where a demon rules the undergrowth, a virgin and a whore on either side.

6

Dunyazad:

The Slavegirl's Palace

The turbid sky is in the grip of a silent nightmare. Clouds race past, jostling each other, unruly messengers burdened with bad news. The moon ignores their tumult. Her sickle-shaped mouth is stretched tight in a thin smile. It remains fixed even when the agitated clouds obscure her view; or when it is time, at long last, for the night's assignation.

The woman arrives first, dressed to blend with darkness. She is a slight thing, but she holds her body straight, a slender stick of bamboo. Her black hair is coiled into a fat sleeping serpent under her veil. She does not have to wait long before a man joins her. He is old, hoary, with gravelly skin of weather-beaten stone. His greying marble dome bulges with an all-seeing eye. He wears innumerable layers of clothing, bits and pieces of many costumes, fugitive scraps of different histories.

The woman, Dilshad, robed and veiled to escape notice, stands face to face with this palace-man. The city sleeps, oblivious, or indifferent, while two come together in its desolate heart, a woman and a palace. Or – in the spying gaze of a truculent night sky – a woman *versus* the palace.

'Come,' the old man whispers to Dilshad. 'Don't be afraid, I know the way.'

*

A cloud floats past. The moon blinks. Dilshad is now a green peasant again, a young slave eager to learn. The man with her, the palace-man, leads her to what appears to be a mountain of stone, marble, battlements, swollen domes, parapets, towers and gates. Her eyes travel up miles of impervious walls. Her head reels; she stumbles. Her companion steadies her and guides her to the iron gates. She looks at him. He has a lush beard, brown with hints of orange. He smells of henna, musk, a thousand unfathomable secrets. He sees her look, takes her hand in his. How curious, it looks so soft and well-cared for, this slave-buyer's hand, but it holds her so firmly!

She looks at the road one last time before the palace, holding her fast by the hand, demands all her attention. Then they are inside the palace grounds. The gates close; the wall obscures the road. The wall *becomes* the road, a seamless road to the sky. A huge hanging shadow moves into place over her, a protective umbrella. The central dome, benign, avuncular, will now guard her with his watchful eye, keep her safe always.

Now they are in the labyrinth of the palatial heart, in chambers within chambers, in the footsteps of craftily twisting and turning passages, in hidden niches and viewing galleries, in halls that replicate themselves, one leading into another. The hall of song and dance, the hall of justice, the hall of royal mercy – each hall is a small city; Dilshad catches her breath with awe. The glare, the dazzle, the scale of it all blinds her. She shuts her eyes to rest them for a moment.

She hears someone whisper in her ear, 'Look!' Her eyes fly open, afraid to miss something. They are past the halls now, at the entrance of one of the royal chambers. The arch above the doorway glows with necklaces of words, the letters inter-twining playfully with flowers, leaves and stalks made of jewels. Dilshad cranes her neck.

'Do you know what this says?' asks her companion. Her palace-man is now a nobleman in his prime, elegant in brocades, silks, pearls. Dilshad gapes at him, then at the line he is pointing at. She shakes her head.

'The world is here,' he reads aloud, 'all the world and its infinite secrets.' But from where she stands, Dilshad can see nothing in the room but a large lattice window. She turns to the man, bewildered. 'It overlooks the garden leading out from the royal harem,' the man says with a smooth, confiding smile. 'The view is excellent.'

They pass the room with the view. The passage before them stretches in an endless sheet of black marble. Though there are no real doors or windows, an abstract pattern reminiscent of a window repeats itself on the whitewashed walls. They are nearing the harem, now that they are in the stomach of the palace. The world outside the palace, or Dilshad's life up to this moment, is turning mythical.

It is getting darker. In the changing light, the passage is as long as the distance to the centre of the earth. Dilshad looks down at the floor, sees something snaking its way before her. It is a thin red line, a knife wound that is sharp and endless.

Is the world being split in two? But – the floor is paved with marble; underneath that stands solid brick and stone. She swings in alarm to the palace-man, but he is gone.

Alone, she hears a soft hiss. The knife wound stirs. It peels itself off the floor, a snake evolving into an erect species. Its pale, hairless skin has a raw look about it, a wound with its scab just pulled off, deprived of air. The footless creature hangs before Dilshad so that they are face to face. Its eyes are vertical, elongated, lidless. They brim with light like open windows. Dilshad's mouth opens in a soundless scream.

But its words are soft, even gentle. 'Follow me,' it hisses. 'I am the guardian of this threshold, the sacred frontier between the wings of the palace.' The creature guides her down the passage; suddenly, Dilshad is at the entrance to the harem. Then the bloody dividing line and its creature disappear, become the air the harem inmates breathe. Dilshad sees the palace-man again, this time a bald, oily eunuch in charge of Sultan Shahryar's harem.

What comfort – after those vast silences, those forbidding labyrinthine passages, to rest, to sleep a little in the harem's collective belly! What relief to curl up in a fleshy lap, sink to the bottom of a rocking, womanish sea!

But every time Dilshad shuts her eyes, drifts a mile into sleep, she hears a high-pitched wail. She can see a wall rising behind her closed eyelids, a wall that will outlast all dreams, callous to passion, agony, the dark cries embedded on its skin of flint.

She turns over; the wall recedes. The wailing and weeping are muffled by the sound of running water. Dilshad sees the petals of a marble flower open up, making a tub the size of a room. The melted wall is the unseen background for chips of mirrors and semi-precious stones. She can see a hundred frightened Dilshads wherever she turns.

The eunuch, her eunuch the palace-man, slips into his place by her side and takes her by the elbow. There is a proprietorial ring in his voice as he says, 'A bath fit for a royal bride. See – crowding the edge there – can you see those knots of sweet virgins, impatient for their turn?' Dilshad can see nothing. But when her companion inhales deeply, letting his eyelids droop in mock-ecstasy, a sharp fragrance bites into the air, eating up a chunk of it.

'But all this – and there is no one here really—' Dilshad stammers. The wailing is gone; she can try to sleep again.

'Yes, the harem was almost empty,' he says. 'But now, after Sultana Shahrzad's triumph, it is filling up again.'

Even as he speaks, Dilshad finds they have shifted to a balcony overlooking a large courtyard. It seems the hub of the palace, a marketplace of sorts, only this marketplace swarms with women. Dilshad can see a thousand and one of them. 'Who are they?' she whispers. 'Where have they come from?'

'Let me see—' says the palace-man, with an air of one compiling an inventory. 'There are Persians, Kurds, Romans, Armenians, Ethiopians, Sudanese, Hindus, Berbers.' He smirks. 'And they could be slaves, aristocrats, prisoners of war . . .'

It is a circus without animals, a play where several scenes are staged simultaneously. In one corner a group is practising strange contortions as if battling – or coupling with – air. Others pace alone, or recite to each other, cultivating the tools of wordplay, poetry, song and dance, pious quotations and historical allusions. Tutors raise their voices; Dilshad hears snatches of praise; a whole-hearted curse. A ring of women circles a fountain, meditating on the scenting of skin and hair. Their own skin and hair are caked with drying mud-like masks.

'This place *is* the world,' the words break into Dilshad's thoughts. 'You have to make yourself stand out, learn to hold the sultan's attention.'

The palace-man is considering Dilshad's thin, childish body with a knowing, assessing look. The old hand can see that she is almost part of the circus below. Already she is planning feverishly: will Sultan Shahryar think her velvety voice soothing, will he ask for her clever hands to nurse him?

The palace-man gives her a self-satisfied parting smile as he sends her into the crowd. 'Oh yes,' his smile seems to say. 'We will think of something between us, you and I – see if you too can be spoils fit for a sultan.'

*

The sky sheltering the palace roof is clear; pellucid. The stars wink roguishly as if they have no clue about the whereabouts of their rivals, the clouds. The swelling moon hangs apart, radiant, self-absorbed, brooding on her stomach as she nears full term. It is time, at long last, for promises to be kept, alliances – or conspiracies – to deliver their rewards.

The woman arrives first, dressed to blend with darkness. She limps a little, but there is an alertness about her, about the way she holds her body, poised like a sharp sword. Under the festive sky, under her hood, her face looks older than her years. One of her eyes is covered with a bandage; a date-sized patch of fur glistens near a corner of her mouth.

The woman, Dilshad, is early for the assignation, but that may be deliberate. The starlit roof is an old friend who has waited with her many times before, shared – or at least witnessed in mute sympathy – Dilshad's griefs, triumphs, her hot tears beyond human comfort.

How many hours she used to spend here, a fresh slave growing ambition like a second skin, dreaming and plotting! When the lonely saviour-sultana Shahrzad singled her out, taught her to read and write; when her sister from across the seas, Satyasama, shared her stories and the secrets of sky-gazing; what newfound pride young Dilshad lugged to the terrace, what an air of power and dignity! There was the night, for instance, when she had stolen up here from the courtyard in the harem, to commune with the dark horizon. She no longer remembers what triumph she was celebrating, but she recalls looking into the distance, too amazed to gloat. A thousand miles away lay the home she could barely remember. Her family must be somewhere in that inky darkness, grovelling in poverty. And she, oil-voiced, quick-fingered Dilshad, was in a palace, calculating the odds of conquering the sultan!

Then the other night, the cruel one, when Satyasama kissed her goodbye. The sky was slate grey; the moon asleep or sulking. The clouds, leaderless, drifted about pointlessly. But Dilshad's grief was not rudderless; or Satyasama's life ephemeral. If Satyasama had lived, perhaps she would have mastered Shahabadi, approached the world of readers and listeners directly? But why should *she* stand here, weeping helplessly, while oblivion circled Satyasama's corpse, ready to devour it? Dilshad would be Satyasama's biographer! She had, after all, been apprentice to a silver-tongued sultana. Shahrzad's saviour-stories lay in their vault of lonely splendour, trapped in letters of gold. These rare specimens were kept under lock and key, safely hidden from vulgar eyes like Dilshad's. She promised herself that night: one day she would lay her hands on those forbidden treasures, read them aloud, copy them out, add her own twists, possess them.

Dilshad hears a soft snigger behind her. She swings round but there is no one, just an ugly old bat hanging upside down on the side of a dome. Dilshad turns her back on it. She knows who it is though he is too tricky for her to catch him. It is that incorrigable rake, the palace-man, spying on her again. She no longer sees the world through his eyes. She knows the palace is not the world, but he won't give up, the sleazy pimp! She knows a thing or two he doesn't – she has sung a sultan to sleep, she has helped his son lock him up in a tomb of his own making. Now *she* can write an inscription of her own, confound those smooth-tongued couplets gracing the palace's walls and arches.

Then she hears a throat being cleared discreetly. This time it is no illusion. She turns away from the horizon, sees Sultan Umar's wazir looking at her. She cannot see his face clearly, but his head is inclined at a respectful angle. Without a word they move towards the stairs. The palace swallows them up. The moon, drifting out of cloudy slumber, is just in time to see them go, their shadows sliding after them. But there is a third shadow, though there is no one visible to cast it, a dour, ancient bat of a shadow. It stays close to the pair as they descend out of sight into the palace.

The three of them, the man, the woman and the shadow, are halfway down the palace, in one of the rooms of the treasury. It is in this room – a room with mirrors for walls so that its space appears infinite – that Dilshad is to receive her reward for taking on one sultan, helping to crown another. Umar's wazir and Dilshad walk past baskets of gems and a few marvellous machines, the old sultan's toys. Then they reach the pile they are looking for, neatly arranged in rows to face two walls of mirrors – stories told over a thousand and one nights, then recorded by the sultan's chronicler.

Umar's wazir bends, picks up two heavy volumes. He shows them to her and she nods. He indicates with a gallant gesture that he will carry them for her. He heads for the door. Dilshad loiters behind, reading titles. Then in a swift movement she pockets a few more tomes, tucks them out of sight in her voluminous robe. She looks behind one last time, moves to the door where Umar's wazir waits with two books, a lock and a key.

Dilshad goes on alone, free from slavery, blessed with books of gold. She is weighed down with rewards, but a shadow clings to her footsteps. There is one last encounter she must face before she lets the night go. She slips into the depths of the palace, all the way down to its guts, to a chamber with a hidden exit. This room, deep in the palace's insatiable belly, was singled out years ago by Shahryar's shrewd eye. To accommodate his secret nest of pleasure, the room – part of his dungeon – was ordered to cover its face. When its real nature was cloaked by the carpets and sofas and chandeliers of its owner, an entire history of pain was effectively veiled. What used to be a dungeon holding fast the wasted bodies of common prisoners became a hard-walled womb for a sultan. As part of his royal duties Shahryar had to protect himself from his beloved subjects. So the dungeon became a bedchamber, and it was hallowed by a thousand and one nights of redemptive stories.

Then as the victorious royals Shahryar and Shahrzad surfaced – not out of the palace into the open air but into the fragrant terraces and pavilions above, breathing an air purer than what nature could provide – the chamber in the bowels of the palace returned to its original function. Years later, the palace's hard-won aura of martyrdom wore off; the room that could play a clever imposter was in demand once more. The dungeon had come full circle. It was, once again, in Shahryar's last months in the palace, the sultan's impenetrable bedchamber.

But it was only a matter of time before this sultan's reign would meet the end he feared. Shahryar has survived it, but there is no danger left in him. It has been unmanned, leaving behind a greybeard with soft-skinned toys, building games and a patient, long-suffering prayer room – the only chamber of love he has not yet conquered. Now merely father of a sultan, he languishes in a tomb more secure than his hospitable dungeon. That face-shifting chamber, empty at last, is for the present nameless, no new function having been assigned to it. But it is too soon to throw out the remnants of Shahryar's long and powerful reign. The chamber has still not been stripped of its royal furnishings, or its veil cast aside to reveal the bleak prison underneath. But though jewel and glass and silver continue to hint of unimaginable opulence, the place looks a little unsure of itself, caught between acts in a moment of confusion.

This chamber, which became synonymous with the palace during Shahryar's reign, has been neglected in the last few weeks since its master's fall from power. But it now has a visitor, a woman who has stolen into the palace dungeon to confront the enemy face to face. She has only one eye to do it with, having lost the other in the skirmish at Shahrzad's tomb. When a mere slavegirl takes on a sultan, she can hardly expect to get away unscathed.

Dilshad puts down her collection of Shahrzad's works carefully. (Did the sultana ever read these, check them for falsehood? If she, Shahrzad, didn't, it's all up to her now.) Dilshad straightens her back, wipes the sweat off her forehead. She feels short of breath, encumbered by tons and tons of stone, all the brick and rubble and marble it took to make the palace. And the weight of souls – what about that? Dilshad senses stiffening bodies going heavy on her, thousands of them, prisoners of war, used-up brides, bricklayers, stonemasons, architects, calligraphers . . . Who is *she* to take on a palace? Her own story, a commonplace one after all, is only a scratch on its vast body, paved over and forgotten in a moment. Dilshad feels a sigh of fatigue escape her. It has been a very long night; she has never been alone in this dungeon before. She looks around, holding up her lantern, and sees the bed, the pile of silk and satin that Shahryar rested on so recently. She moves to it, sets down the lantern gingerly, climbs in and covers herself. Ah, its subtle embrace, a nest of clouds holding her as securely as skin! It is possible, with eyes shut, and alone in a sultan's bed, to forget many things, dungeons included. Then she hears a poignant-toned enquiry in her ear: Have you never yearned for the countless pleasures of my touch?

The musty bat, the musky palace-man, is at it again. Dilshad travels a few moments with him for old times' sake. But the feast of touch she remembers is a little different from what he is trying to summon. She sees Shahryar, a sultan in mourning. The sultana is dead and buried; the sultan's grief has struck him down. Dilshad and a few others are summoned to restore Shahryar. The girls go to work. But whatever they do, wherever they venture with their hot and eager tongues, all he can do is moan, or grunt, or weep like a drunken fool. Later all of them pretend it was an unforgettable, belly-filling orgy.

Now, in the dungeon, Dilshad admits to herself ruefully: she never succeeded, despite all her attempts, in waking Shahryar's jaded appetite. She looks at the imprisoned flame dancing impatiently in the lantern. What would have melted that stubborn sheath of wax, exposed the flesh inside to air, allowed the blood to course through its veins?

It is too late now to release old Shahryar. But his accomplice, the palace-man – slave-buyer, eunuch, pimp and veil of the sultan – stalks her, flaunting his claim of immortality. She can feel his will to live, shrouded in perpetual mystery, the dark secrets of the dungeon *his* eternal veil. She must do something so that this veil is pulled aside for ever; defile the dungeon in some fundamental way, brand it with her searing testimonial so that it is never used again, except as a home to wild beasts and marauding ghouls. It is not enough to escape like the wise sultana or her still-faced sister. They left, but did not leave a dent in the hard heart of the palace. All but the merest skeletons of their histories were swallowed by its yawning mouth once they turned their backs on its demands.

No, the battle is not yet over. This soiled dungeon, the bedrock of the palace's muscular immortality, is what she must tear apart. When its skin curls and peels away, its hidden nature, its bundled knots of fibre and tendon, will lie exposed in its ruins for all time to come. Dilshad takes a deep, calming breath. A ruin spreads itself around her. It is damaged, but it is also back to looking half-finished; waiting to be completed afresh.

Dilshad shakes off the soiled, comforting wrappings of the royal bed. She moves to the waiting lantern. She considers the appetite of fire, its insatiable hunger. She could feed the wide, gluttonous mouth of the dungeon a meal it does not expect, a potent and fiery banquet. Then armed with her newfound baggage of riches – freedom, the books she must insinuate herself into – she could set out after the ones who left, their stories in her keeping till she catches up with them.

Dilshad:

The Chameleon on the Wall

It was evening and Dilshad was hurrying along a rough, deserted path. She was so intent on getting ahead and finding a friendly shelter for the night that she ignored the arid landscape she was speeding across, rocky stretches broken only by an occasional stunted tree or bush. She thought she could hear a faint voice. It could have been a bird call or the wind ringing in her ears, but as she walked on, the voice grew louder and more distinct. There was no mistaking it; it was a high-pitched woman's voice, and it was singing.

There is something haunting about a lone voice at twilight. Whatever the song, it slows down the hastiest of feet. This voice, besides, was rich and sweet. It oozed into Dilshad's ear and filled her stomach with sharp hunger pangs for dates, figs and honey. The voice came from somewhere in the mellow glow of the western horizon. Dilshad squinted at the dusky glow and saw to her astonishment the silhouette of a mansion like a tall, noble skeleton. As she neared its spacious grounds, she could see it was no flimsy skeleton, but solid, smooth stone. She paused for a minute, considering the silent structure before her. Then it began again, the disembodied girlish voice, soaring above the walls to reach her on the other side. Dilshad didn't understand a word of the song, but its melody, and the piercing loneliness of the singing voice, seemed to be a desperate message from a prisoner pleading for help.

Dilshad made a quick decision. She jumped over the gate and went cautiously across the grounds in the direction of the voice. She saw a bland-faced wall with a barred window high up from the ground. She considered the wall, a slippery climb, then the tall, anaemic tree nearby, and went to work.

Balancing precariously on a branch leading to the window ledge, Dilshad peeped in and saw the owner of the caged voice. She was pacing the room, a frown on her face as she sang. She was no languishing princess, but an ordinary girl with a powerful carrying voice. Dilshad watched her, thinking that she would look more like the pleasing healthy young animal she was if her face were not so sulky. Then the girl turned and saw Dilshad, and both poignant singing and bored sullenness vanished instantly, to be replaced with a look of lively interest.

'Did you hear me on the road?' the girl asked. 'Is there anyone else with you?'

'No,' Dilshad said, answering her second question, and some of the girl's sulkiness returned.

'I was hoping a wandering young man would hear me and come to the rescue,' she pouted, 'but you will do, I suppose.'

Dilshad was quite ready to leave the way she had come, without waiting to hear what promised to be a curious story. She was hungry, she was late – and what was she supposed to be, some sort of travelling saviour of silly girls?

But Lonely Voice had conquered her disappointment and

was now coaxing Dilshad to stay, with a nicely judged mixture of charm and pathos.

'Don't go,' she begged. 'I live here with my brother, a perfect ogre of a man who is always angry or jealous. In a little while he will be here at his usual hiding post behind that screen, spying on me. That's all he does every day after sundown. I don't know what he expects to see when I am locked in here alone.'

'But why are you locked in?' Dilshad asked.

The girl tossed her head haughtily as if to say, What's it to you? But just then they heard a faint rustle of movement behind the screen. The girl's words faltered and her shoulders sagged. Dilshad strained to see the man who had arrived to spy on the girl just as she had said he would. Meanwhile Lonely Voice turned an appealing face to Dilshad. It was irresistible. Dilshad didn't know what Lonely Voice had in mind, but she nodded to let the girl know that she would help.

Lonely Voice sighed elaborately, then said aloud, 'It's such a cool, beautiful evening outside! If only – but I will have to amuse myself as best as I can. If there was someone with me, I could at least tell stories, but alone?' She turned to the little window and stood there, blocking Dilshad out of view of the screen. 'Oh, I see,' she said, 'I'll have to make do with that lizard on the window. Maybe it will do better than cluck its tongue when I talk to it.'

To Dilshad's amazement the grey chameleon hanging on to the wall near the window clucked, and there was nothing for her to do but say (in what she hoped was a lizard's voice), 'All right, tell me a story.'

Lonely Voice then told the lizard: 'A young woman ripe as

a luscious plum, with breasts like full pitchers turned upside down, was wooed by a virile young man. He came to her and said, "Come to me and I will satisfy all your desires." She didn't refuse, but was too frightened to let him touch her. "Listen carefully," he told her. "I know you will be in trouble if you take a lover and your people find out. So – I will use a bit of magic I know. The child you conceive will be born out of your pretty, shell-like ear. A virgin's life is a lonely one, isn't it? But you will have a child of love to dispel its gloom, and you will be blameless where it matters the most." The young woman agreed and moved towards him shyly. They made love all night long and, as he had said, she had a delightful little son out of her ear.

'Months went by and the woman had another admirer. This one enjoyed her eager but artless embraces so much that he gave her a slave, an obedient little slave who would be with her as long as she lived. The woman's life became free of all drudgery. The slave did all the boring housework, dressed her and combed her hair and saw to the feeding of the ear-born child.

'Her next lover was a poet. He sang complicated, image-laden praise to her elbow and the arch of her foot and her virtue. When he tenderly persuaded her to get rid of her clothes and come to bed, he promised her that she would turn into a sparkling star when she died; she would be immortal. He was so delighted with their night together that he added a more practical gift – a pot that would never be empty of food.

'Her fourth lover was a hermit who was passing by. She was the first woman he had slept with in a hundred and fifty years, and naturally it was a night he would remember for another hundred odd years. The morning after, he said to her, "I am going to give you a special parting gift: Be always what a man desires." His eyes caressed her from head to foot and the same instant she felt folds of her skin stretching and tightening, a pull here and a smoothening there, and an extra ounce or two attaching itself on to her breasts and hips.

'What is the best lover's gift the woman received?' Lonely Voice asked her audience.

'The pot,' Dilshad replied as her stomach growled its confirmation and the lizard clucked approvingly. 'Fill the stomach and see to the rest later.'

Just then they heard a yell from behind the screen: 'What! How can you be so stupid? It was the hermit who restored the woman's beauty *and* her chastity. She became what a man desires, and do you know a man who doesn't desire a chaste woman?'

At these words, half the screen collapsed; at the same time, the bars of the window fell to the ground with a terrific noise. The lizard fell into the room in fright. Dilshad's branch gave way when she jumped up in shock, and she managed to save herself just in time by crawling on to the ledge. She was frightened, but Lonely Voice didn't seem disturbed. She could hardly control her excitement as she waited for her brother to hide behind what was left of the screen.

Lonely Voice smiled at Dilshad's comic, crouching figure, then looked for the lizard. Once it was still again and listening, she went on: 'There was a king whose territories grew a hundredfold with every conquest. On one of his military campaigns his army was held up by a wide river. The king decided to ford the river but his men found it impossible.

Finally the king discovered that there was a chaste man who had turned himself into a rock and was sitting right in the middle of the river. The king, who was as cunning as he was brave, took stock of the obstacle and sent his men in search of a chaste woman in the neighbouring villages. Many women were brought there, and they tried, one by one, to overcome the rock by touching it. All of them failed and had to be slaughtered. But finally a potter's wife touched the rock and it turned over as easily as a piece of driftwood.'

'Tell me: who was more powerful – the chaste man or woman?'

Dilshad thought this was a pointless question. 'The woman broke the rock, didn't she?' she asked.

The lizard clucked agreeably and the man also said, 'The woman.'

They waited for something strange to happen like the last time, but there was only an eerie silence. Then the man shouted angrily; 'Of course it is the woman – what kind of a question is that? A chaste woman – that rarest of creatures – is naturally the most powerful woman.'

Dilshad was puzzled by the smile on Lonely Voice's face. But this bewilderment was only a one-breath wonder because the very next moment she heard a wheezing as if a stony old man was gasping for air. Then the entire wall facing Dilshad was covered with cracks like a spider's web. Open-mouthed, she watched the little window turning into a large, jagged door. There was a horrible crumbling sound and the air filled with brick and stone and dust as she fell.

Dilshad rubbed her bruised head as she picked herself off the ground from among the debris. There was only a tiny piece of wall before her now, and the story-loving chameleon was stuck to it like a carved relief. She heard footsteps running behind her and turned in time to see a woman, her robe lifted high, jumping over the gate. Dilshad saluted the lizard; then hanging on to her aching head, she ran to catch up with Lonely Voice.

7

Dunyazad:

The Dreams of Good Women

Dunyazad is alone in a tightly bound room, a room that is shrinking by the day. Its corners are held fast in the embrace of brick and stone, the flesh and spirit of encroaching walls. They are getting closer all the time. Though her journey from one wall to the other takes only a minute, she paces the room as if to take possession of every contested inch.

Night is almost here, night that lures virgins to sleep with the promise of sweet dreams, then claims the chosen bride with its probing fingers. Night is almost here, and Dunyazad knows there will be no sleep in it for her. Her aching feet must cover miles in a small room, all the way back to an interview that will change her life.

She has walked her way past many hours when she comes to a stop before the ivory-framed mirror on the wall near the bed. It is difficult to resist a mirror when it is so very small and innocuous. Or when a woman is alone. Or when the walls that surround her rise high and hard, cocksure of their victim. Dunyazad catches sight of herself in the dim gleam of glass. Only a few of her features are visible, and these, the large, staring eyes, the lips stretched thin with disappointment, are enhanced. It is as if she is looking at a secret image of herself. Or a selective montage of images, known only to a deaf-mute mirror, a thing that can crack, break into a thousand splinters. A thing that can, if she is not careful, cut into skin, draw blood.

The face in the mirror swells into a monstrous bubble that swallows all the air in the glass. Then it pops and the creature dissolves. Dunyazad's body is straight up against the wall now, her breasts pressed flat against it. Her nose brushes against the glass and a cloud of moisture hangs where her breath has met the mirror. She wipes it clean with her hand, steps back a little. Now the mirror presents her with another view, a hovering bird's view of a landscape. Far below is a lush, circular garden. At its very centre is its only eye, a palace so tall that the clouds rest on its domes in venerable bushes of white hair.

Dunyazad is high up in the air, looking down at the palace lightly crowned with clouds, at the garden that shrouds stony palatial skin in a protective green fur. But is the scene just empty spectacle? A pointless landscape of a fortress with a dead boulder for a heart? Dunyazad feels a sense of foreboding like a child who suspects the game may be too difficult after all. The stakes are too high, the rules and risks too unfamiliar and grown-up.

But she cannot retreat. She has just received a signal that the scene shelters somebody, many bodies. She can see a tiny firefly curve of light bobbing in the mirror towards her. With the moving light, a face, then a girl, floats up to the surface of the glass. Dunyazad's eyes are riveted. She has recognized the girl's stern face, her bony shoulders and tense neck. There *she* is in the mirror, the other half of herself she lost in the wazir's room many years ago. The girl walks past Dunyazad and turns right, going back into the mirror's recesses. Her destination is unambiguous. The palace gates loom in the distant background.

Young Dunyazad, with only a flickering lantern for guidance, is in the stretch of darkness that rings the forbidden palace. The grounds are within view, but to enter, slip into the palace before the favoured candidate, she must get past the old gatekeeper. As she comes up to him, he is taller, even more imposing than her father in real life. His robe covers all but his face in its thick armour, inscrutable as justice, dark as death.

'Father,' says Dunyazad, 'there is an hour left before you take her to the palace. There is still time – to choose another virgin bride.' She holds the lantern high above them. In its flimsy, diaphanous light his eyes pick up a glittering nest of gold and pearls. He takes in her new silky appearance, sees how she has emptied all the contents of her girlish boxes to satisfy her voracious appetite.

'You?' asks the wazir, his eyes widening with surprise. For an instant he seems suspiciously close to a smile, this man who has no time for small, insignificant gestures. Dunyazad is not fooled. Though the wazir is a distant father, he knows his household well enough to realize that there are two virgins who can save him and the city. Both of them are young and promising, both are his beloved daughters. But he must choose only one, or one first. Dunyazad brushes aside the thought that he has chosen her sister only because she is a year older. If he has already chosen one, it is because he believes that she is the better bet. But when he speaks in a gentle voice that sits strangely in his throat, he opts for the safe, lying words, 'You're too young. I can't spare you – you must see that your mother and I can't lose you yet.'

'But I am the eternal younger sister,' fumes Dunyazad. 'She goes every place first. She does everything before me, then tells me all about it. And when it's finally my turn, what will be left? All I can do is live out what she has already described and possessed completely.'

Dunyazad has never spoken like this before, never spoken like this to her father. But tonight she must seize something – a bundle of words and acts that are Shahrzad's by birthright – because it may never come her way again. 'I love my sister,' Dunyazad says in painful confession, her voice choking on that adamant, flinty intimacy tightening her chest till it is ready to break. 'I love my sister but I don't want to be her shadow.'

The wazir seems in danger of losing his newfound tenderness. The old eagle eye who can effortlessly penetrate the innermost skin of girlish dreams peeps out for a devastatingly shrewd moment. He says to her, with deliberate emphasis on each word as if he is spelling it out: 'Your sister, I think, has a plan. Do you know – or do you not know – that your sister has a plan?'

Dunyazad nods. He must know her answer anyway. If Shahrzad has a plan, how can Dunyazad not be part of it? Dunyazad who is marked out to be the perennial accomplice?

The wazir's words have brought her back to herself, to the face and body she must carry around all her life like hopeless scars. She can't rage or plead any longer, so she lets it go with a quick gulp of a parting sob. The wazir, equally deft with words and silence, now chooses the latter. In mute sympathy he moves closer to her and takes her lantern. Its flame, quelled into submission, goes out without a single protest. It dies with an easy, feminine grace. The wazir, having persuaded one daughter, dissuaded the other, is needed elsewhere; how long can he lurk at the palace gates when there is so much else to be done?

An hour later he is back, Shahrzad on one side, Dunyazad on the other. Shahryar is waiting for them in the room adjacent to the royal bedchamber. There have been so many marriages of late that there is no point in making a pompous ceremony of it all. Next door is the real point, a fat serpent coiled in its bed, waiting with its hood raised ready to strike. All three of them know this. Shahrzad walks away from the safety of the family trio. As she walks slowly towards Shahryar, her head held high, Dunyazad catches her out immediately. The walk, the way in which she holds her head, the expression on her face, the words that are bound to follow. With disbelief Dunyazad sees that her sister has borrowed her only successful scenario for that childish game they used to play with such yearning intensity. Dunyazad wants to look away but she cannot budge her eyes an inch. She must look, bound to the spot forever now, suspended in time by a partnership even more intimate than sisterhood. But she will never again play The Martyr's Walk, that foolish game for young women willing to be martyrs. This she promises herself.

*

Then there is no wazir, no Shahrzad. Only she and Shahryar are left in the world, the old world they knew, the one in which a thousand and one nights tailed a single day. Dunyazad, older, less unforgiving, wanders in the depths of the mirror, the mirror that has melted its glassy heart so she can plunge into it. Already she can see the palace gates, and this time there is no watchman, no glib-tongued father to stop her. She pushes a gate open, slips into the grounds, into the palace itself, as easily as the night that has draped itself about her. How easy it is to get into this palace! (For a minute she wonders whether getting out will be as easily accomplished. But why worry about that now, so many years later?)

Dunyazad, lone surveyor of palatial rooms empty of all but ghosts, wanders from one wing to another. Though there are no witnesses to praise or condemn the event, she has stepped on the line between male and female sanctuaries. She has stepped across it as if it is only a figment of some febrile imagination. Dunyazad is now in the men's wing, overlooking a secluded royal garden. There has always been something seductive about this garden; Zaman discovered that years ago, then Shahryar. Now the same window from which the brothers learnt of the world's treachery invites Dunyazad to partake of its forbidden delights. But when she looks out of the window, she does not find an orgiastic spectacle laid out for her. Though she has waited and watched for her turn for years now, all she is offered is the sight of a lonely silhouette, a flat shadow cut out of cardboard and topped with a crown. Dunyazad steals out of the room.

In the garden lit by a sliver of moon, they look at each other, Dunyazad and Shahryar. She is no virgin bride, this woman just past her prime who stands before him in challenging silence, her forehead and upper lip moist and shiny. He, God's gift to innocent and not-so-innocent brides, does not look surprised to see her there. They have left this matter unsettled for too long; he knows, better than anyone else, that appointments with a king cannot be deferred permanently. Silently they appraise each other. Then she turns towards the palace and goes to his bedchamber. The sultan follows.

It is all so very simple then. All these years, then a night, a banal piece of light pasted on the sky, a man and a woman, a bed. They have reached the door behind which the much-moulted serpent lies waiting still, the appetite of its raised hood immortal. Only its tail – and it is all tail below the hood – is brittle; perhaps in the cover of darkness, with the stimulant of urgency, it will make no difference. But there is a harem in this place, a harem that requires a ruby-tinged line to be drawn over and over again, dividing the world into two for ever. That senile old spirit of the bloody threshold, the palace-jinni, has already heard their conspicuous silence, woken up, yawned, stretched his limbs.

Then they see a sleepless Dilshad waiting for them at the door to Shahryar's chamber, ready to intercept them. It is for Shahryar to play sultan, dismiss her for the night, send her packing, but he says nothing. She steps aside to let them enter the room, then follows. She shuts the door behind her.

*

There are three of them in the room, a man and two women. Dilshad is playing Dunyazad to Dunyazad's Shahrzad. She goes about her business quietly, arranging cushions, chests, wine, a basin of fragrant, cleansing water. Dunyazad and Shahryar undress themselves like an old married couple expecting no surprises.

Dunyazad crawls under the sheets and waits. She remembers what the night contained for her early mentor: a bed, a sword, a tongue. Now Dunyazad is waiting for the night, *her* night, to come to her, reveal its insatiable appetite for unfamiliar skin.

Shahryar gets in beside her and moves the sheets aside. He is naked except for the rings on his fingers and a gold chain with a thick oval medallion hanging from it. He bends over her. His medallion is cold and heavy on her stomach, but it is he who shivers. Her eyes are too large, he can't go on while they lie there in wait, fixed and staring. He runs his hand gently over them. They close.

All candles, lamps and lanterns have been put out. Dilshad crouches on the floor in darkness. Dunyazad is waiting, eyes closed. Force of habit moves Shahryar's mouth to suck her nipples, his tongue to draw a wet trickle of a line down her belly. He can feel a dull fire seep into his skin from hers, the kind of fire jinn are made of. But it's an angel he needs, and angels are made of light. And what if he lights a lamp, gives up the comforts of darkness? He may see that this woman is that same cheating girl, doubled. Can one girl be two, two one, or is this just another clever, taunting notion? Shahryar's tongue pauses. The air smells of fear and saliva. This shape-shifting woman, the woman who turns into a shape-shifter the minute she gets into his bed: is she an invention of his? Or is it he who is a morsel of drifting bait in Shahrzad's oceanic imagination? He tenses his body, hoists it over hers, then lowers himself to meet her damp skin. The faint stirring between his thighs goes limp.

Dilshad has not learnt to wait as Dunyazad did. The bed is silent for so long that she gets up, gropes her way to the chest she has smuggled into the room, opens it. While Dunyazad and Shahryar find what comfort they can in the gifts of tongues, gentle tears and fraternal caresses, Dilshad undresses and slips on a dark, hooded robe. Once the ruby necklace is fastened round her neck and the rusty dagger tucked into the waistband of her skirt, she picks up a lamp and lights it.

Dunyazad and Shahryar do not protest. The night in this palace has always been divided into two. The first part, such as it was, is over and done with. Now the rest of the night must be whiled away, hungry bodies and bruised souls soothed into acceptance of the morning after.

Then Dilshad, Dilshad dressed in Shahrzad's leavings, says to Dunyazad: 'Tell us, my lady, a marvellous tale so the night will pass pleasantly.' Shahryar smiles a secretive smile of pleasure. He is the sultan once more; the rest – the rest was just a lying dream. He nods graciously, giving the women permission to continue.

Dunyazad looks at their expectant faces. On-stage at last, she can hear the restless crowd breathing heavily behind the screen: the wazir, Zaman, Umar, Mother Raziya, Nursemaid Sabiha, the freakish poet Satyasama, and her old lover and rival, Shahrzad.

'Once,' she begins, 'I heard a story about two sisters. You know the sort of thing: one was good. In her journey through life, she saved everyone from dangers, both real and imagined, and she was rewarded with a crown and a palace and a handsome, loving husband. The other sister – the irredeemable one – wasted her journey. It was doomed, you knew, from the very start.'

Dunyazad falters. Where does she go now? She turns to Shahryar and places a friendly hand on his naked shoulder. 'You finish it,' she says. 'You began the whole thing, now you complete it. Tell us a story – just one.'

Shahryar thinks. He has, after all, heard so many stories, a chain of them longer than the string with the hundred rings weighing them down. But wait a minute – who let *her* in here? There she is again, the ring-stealing jinni-woman, the shifty faithless bitch, slipping into the narrow, secret watering hole of his thoughts as if he is the woman, she the man. Now she taunts him under a palm tree by the seashore, now she has him hanging in the infinite threads of her sticky cobweb, now she feeds him tale and adventure, coaxing him back to laughter and sanity.

He turns to Dilshad and notices for the first time what she is wearing. The muscles on his face unknot into a smile. It is only a charade then; the woman is still only a woman. 'And you,' he says teasingly as you might to a pet monkey, 'have you learnt how to spin a magic web?'

'No,' replies Dilshad, lowering her eyes modestly to the ground. She runs a finger across the mark on her face. The bristly hair stands up on her skin like a little animal's tail. 'But there was someone else, a poet who wandered in and out of your harem, who gave me a small, magical gift. This is just for you, my sultan,' she says, sitting at his feet. 'But,' and she indicates Dunyazad, 'she may like to hear it too.'

*

'I met Satyasama,' says Dilshad, 'the woman with the monkey-face and the innumerable secrets, when I visited Monkey-Village many years ago. I arrived the week before the harvest, and found that the farmers of Monkey-Village had taken to spending all night in their fields to guard their crop. They found it terribly difficult to stay up. Soon a yawn would glide like a deadly snake from one to the next and put them to sleep. Every morning they woke to find a bald patch eating into their carpet of ripe cucumbers.

'Then one of the farmers' daughters, a young monkey-woman called Satyasama, came forward shyly to her elders. "I can tell the guards stories," she offered. "Not stories that flow like sleepy placid rivers, but stories which follow a rough path laid out with a winding rope. Every time I tie a knot or loosen another, my words will nudge you awake. With all that stumbling and prodding, no one will fall asleep."

'The farmers may have laughed at such an offer if they weren't so desperate. As it was, they agreed. Satyasama began that same night, and to their amazement they found she was right. Sometimes her story tickled their ears or the base of their spines so that it was impossible to settle down quietly. As the night wore on, and a farmer or two yawned, Satyasama began a story which teased their faces like a pesky fly; they were now afraid to yawn in case the pest flew into their mouths. And for dawn, for those still hours of the morning when dream and wakefulness meet like reunited lovers, Satya-sama saved stories that bit like bloodthirsty mosquitoes. Though they felt foolish about it, the farmers couldn't help slapping their arms and legs to kill the damn things.

'It was all worth it though. Night after night they stayed awake, listening. Night after night the thieves of the neigh-bouring Donkey-Village returned home disappointed and hungry.

'The donkeys held an emergency meeting; their chief spy, a jungle babbler, was called in to make a report. For the first time, they heard about Satyasama and her cunning, storytell-ing ways. The donkeys put their heads together and came up with a plan. Their handsome young hero, Prince Atbiq, was unanimously chosen to carry out the plot. (He was called Atbiq, or Prince "Close-it", because he often forgot to close his mouth and one of his slaves had the job of reminding him to close it.)

'Atbiq took to grazing just below Satyasama's tree. He spied on her when she sat there in rapt absorption, picking the lice out of her fur. His own face took on a longing look in response. In a few days Satyasama noticed her loyal admirer; as he gazed more and grazed less, it was clear to her that he would die if he did not get what he was yearning for.

'In a week or two they were inseparable. Atbiq felt he had never loved like this before. He was not worried about how it had all begun or where it was going to lead. They loved each other and lovers don't have secrets from each other, do they? And Satyasama: she was leading a full, rich life – Atbiq and love all day, the challenges of storytelling and wakefulness at night. Her blood raced as she swung from tenderness in secretive mango groves to a humble and rapt audience in the fields.

'Then one morning Atbiq stroked her furry shoulder with his hoof and asked in a low voice, "Will you share a secret with me? Do you love me enough?" Satyasama nodded, too wobbly-kneed with passion to speak.

' "Your stories," Atbiq whispered into her neck, "where do they come from? How do you do it?"

'Satyasama disentangled herself reluctantly. "Why do you ask?" she said, baffled. "What does it matter?"

' "I want to tell stories too," he mumbled, looking away from her loving, knowing eyes. "If you could teach me how it's done – stories that keep people awake and . . . and stories that put them to sleep . . ."

'The next morning Satyasama had a gift for her lover. She gave Atbiq a sealed envelope. "Take my secret," she told him. Atbiq kissed her tenderly, then added (with genuine tears) that they would have to part for some time. He had news that his mother was ailing. To his surprise, Satyasama seemed to know about it. "I thought you might have to go," she said as she embraced him and sent him on his way.

'In Donkey-Village, Atbiq called a meeting immediately, anxious to share the stolen formula. They sat around him all agog. He opened the envelope and pulled out a sheet of paper amid their cheers. He read it out, and as he read, they all grew more and more puzzled. Even worse, as they listened, the fat juicy cucumbers in their minds dwindled and shrank and dried up.

'I am told this is what they heard:

'Once there was a donkey who looked around him and

saw and thought things that absolutely needed to be expressed in song. Well, a donkey tends to bray as you know – and it was terribly difficult for our hero to tame and bend and modulate his voice into a singing one. When he was finally capable of melody, he acquired an audience. He wanted them of course – what is the use of a beautiful song if you can't share it? (And remember, he was no bird; he was not singing by instinct; and he was singing a design of all he had perceived, not a series of meaningless pretty sounds.)

'But once the audience had heard his songs, and word spread, and numbers grew, a few began to question him closely: how did he do it? It's not magic – there must be some explanation. Share your secret with us, they insisted. The donkey was flustered – he had been working so hard on his music that he, frankly, and somewhat to his shame, did not know. So he spent the next few years thinking about their question – and of course, there was no time to look around him and make new songs. And even worse, his voice, the carefully trained, disciplined voice grew rusty. You know what happened next. When his audience gathered again, he didn't sing. He brayed.'

*

Dilshad lets out a wonderfully full-throated bray. It fills the room, blows out the light in the lamp, flies out of the window and chases the night away. It is dawn now, the ancient hour of heart-stopping danger in this palace, but Dunyazad and Shahryar have not noticed. They are shaking with laughter like overgrown, breathless children, their arms round each other's waists for support.

Dilshad stops braying. She gets up, removes the dagger and necklace and puts them back into the open chest. She rolls the borrowed robe up to her waist, then her shoulders, and slips it off over her head. It is a crumpled mess but she throws it into the chest unfolded and shuts the lid with a bang. Then she sits on the bed, as naked as its other two occupants, and gently detaches their arms from each other. 'The night is gone,' she tells them. 'And we can leave it behind. We can now leave *her* behind too, to live out the rest of her days. Let her describe them in her own inimitable voice.'

Dilshad:

The Morning After

She lives in a corner room on the top floor of the palace, a spider on the fringe of the cobweb. She submits herself, this woman in the black hooded robe, to the servant girls as they carry out their night orders. The satin vest holding her drooping breasts in place is buttoned, the outer robe tightly fastened. The hood is momentarily pulled back. The wide-toothed comb runs through the stray tuft of curly grey on her head. Her itchy scalp tingles.

They help her on to the gilded chamber pot and she eases herself to the accompaniment of a secret, trickling sound, intermittent but endless. She watches herself in the care of these hired, ministering hands. Her eyes take in, with impartial detachment, two discordant images: their young hands, smooth, plump; lifting the robe to her waist, holding it there to expose a pair of flabby thighs. Her thighs, voluptuous battleground of a thousand and one intimacies, now fallow, creased; folds of flesh hanging loose from their pegs of sharp bone.

Her name is Shahrzad. Once the name was potent, a password that summoned, with its whispering, hypnotic sibilance, a jinni at the head of a caravan loaded with rich words. These words were hers, as good as live captives. Hearts racing, adrenalin flowing, they awaited her sharp, terse commands. She would shut her eyes for a moment to sort out the sunburst of patterns in her head; pick one out, link one with the other. Then open her eyes, her mouth, and they would fall into place, those words, breathing hard, sweating, building image, irony, parable. One story inside another inside another.

The girls hold her, one on either side, as she makes her journey from the pot to the bed. A groan she does not recognize, long, shamelessly unstifled, escapes her lips to hang in the room like an unspoken reproach. She stretches out on the bed and the two girls cover her. Now one girl has turned away from her; she is at the door. Before she blows out the lamp by the bed, the other girl looks at her. Their eyes meet, the girl's and the woman's, and the girl quickly looks away, afraid she will mouth the words she is thinking. 'Sleep well, Old Witch!'

*

Once she was Shahrzad the virgin. Her chastity was more than an invisible ideal – or a hidden undergarment. She wore it, this palpable badge, on the bold face with the crooked nose, and in the resolute eyes set a little too close to each other. When her father the wazir, indispensable minister to the king, came to her that morning, she had in fact been waiting for him. She knew, as he did, that not one family in the city would admit to harbouring a virgin daughter any longer. The king wanted a virgin every night. The morning after, his sword thirsted for a woman's neck, the neck of the girl who had shed a few drops of blood and grown into a woman overnight.

*

The girl puts out the lamp. Her hurried footsteps in the dark reach the door where her companion waits. The door shuts. Shahrzad lies in her bed, waiting for sleep. She knows she has only a few hours left; to sleep, to wake up fresh and ready for battle. In only a few hours it will be midnight again, and the familiar summons will take hold of her by the shoulders and shake her awake: 'Wake up, this is no time to sleep! A thin, sharp sword will rise from the horizon at dawn.' Shahrzad, past mistress of planning, courts sleep. She concentrates on one part of her body at a time – first the left foot to be relaxed, then the right; the thighs, the hips, the stomach. She moves up her body relentlessly, letting go of knots of muscles till she reaches the neck that escaped its fate; and the head that arranged for its salvation.

She first heard of salvation, met its stern demands, in her father's beloved face. Her father the trustworthy wazir, minister of justice. He and Shahrzad had exchanged a look that locked them together in a conspiracy. He sent her a quick signal; that she returned in a passing flash of understanding. Her father, pillar of public morality and private chastity, was now saying to Shahrzad: 'You, my first-born, have the razor-edged mind of a man and the cunning – the shrewd word-cunning – of a woman.' Her father, supreme pragmatist, did not say: 'But what's it worth if it's not put to good use?'

Then the first night in this room, in this chamber that encloses all earthly pleasures, the vast, full range of mortal horrors. In this chamber crowded with the ghosts of her predecessors, there was a large bed, low, bedecked with flowers, perfume. The sheets pulled aside suggestively, the goblet of wine within arm's reach. The girl-bride for the night, Shahrzad of the sloping hips took in the scene with a quick glint of an eye. She dismissed the servants for the night, moved to the bed, sat on it.

Alone, waiting, she could feel a dampness grow in her armpits, the back of her neck, and between her thighs. She could smell something heady – fear perhaps, or danger. Or the memories of the bed she sat on, which despite silken sheets changed twice a night, had soaked in blood, sweat, semen. Desire anticipated, desire satiated.

*

The girls know the old woman well. Or they are familiar, even intimate, with her body, and the needs of its sagging flesh, protruding bone, its swollen, creaky joints. And they know her distinguishing smell. Faint, lingering, a blend that suggests perfume, urine, old age – which smells, surprisingly, like something stale and forbidden.

As they hurry downstairs to their dinner in the palace servants' quarters, the first girl says to the other: 'Only a woman with a bad conscience would choose to sleep alone in that room.'

The second girl, the one who put out the lamp, shivers as the flame did before it died. She sees, in that instant, one silent hour stretching into another. 'Only a witch can stay awake like that,' she says. 'Night after night after night.'

*

'Sleep, Shahrzad!' she tells herself sharply, like a mother who knows how much her child has to do the next day. Her lips mouth the words. But the words have changed a little; so has their style of delivery. Though they must give voice to an impetuous command, her lips part hesitantly. And the two words hang out, like a stretching, elastic tongue, in a plea or a wail: 'Sleep, Shahryar!'

She hears her husband Shahryar's voice, muffled by time, travelling up the depths of an old well. 'But the dream, Begum! What if it comes again?'

Shahryar could not sleep. Or he was afraid to sleep. A dream lay waiting in the pit of sleep, and in the dream, blood. A gory swamp sucked him in. Not quickly, like the sword that detached girl's head from woman's body; but in inches, or seconds yawning into minutes and hours. Shahryar dreamt of blood. The air in his dreams was splattered and stained by it. Choked by blood, a mucus that mingled dispensable bodily juices, bits of flesh, trunkless heads, headless trunks. Shahryar drowned in his sleep; and in the blood of women he had killed, women he had to kill, women he desired to kill.

Shahrzad leant forward, drew his head towards her. His hair was flecked with grey. Without his royal robes and jewels, his naked neck and shoulders reminded her of a ragged, hungry crow. She stroked the head, then the thin, vulnerable neck that sheltered unprotected on her shoulder. 'One more story then,' she soothed. 'One more, and it will be dawn before you know it.'

She bent, picked up a large black robe from the pile of discarded clothes on the floor. As her back straightened, her hands found the shoulders of the robe. She shook it free of dust and crease. It flew through the air with a swift, liquid movement, a bird's dark wing in descent. She threw the robe round their naked bodies, his and hers. They sat huddled together under the robe, two children waiting for a storm to pass. Shahrzad began to speak.

*

Alone in her bed, Shahrzad remembers with a shiver: they are all dead! They are gone – Shahryar, the wazir, her interminable stories, the fickle sword sharpened every night. (And where is that sister who promised to be a better accomplice than a husband? Has she for once gone ahead of her mentor?)

A lullaby trickles into the room, an unexpected gift from the past. The old woman sleeps.

In her sleep she meets her father again. Dead, he is able to tell her: 'In the streets of the city, my daughter, you are a living legend. Your wit will live on, longer than any of your children or grandchildren. I see your name, Shahrzad, like a vine that creeps forward inch by inch, growing from one millennium to another.' She sees the embers in the old man's eyes, as if he has long ceased to separate his life and hers; or distinguish between his ambition and hers. But in his eyes *she* sees the reflection of her own old fantasy: that no story will be made, told, which cannot fit into the canvas she has stretched for a thousand and one nights.

Like all dreams, this too ends before desire is fulfilled. The old woman wakes, sits up in terror and excitement. She looks around, sees a dark empty room, sighs, feels the familiar pain and stiffness take hold of her again. It is useless to stretch out and try to sleep. Her night is over, though it is several hours to sunrise.

Shahrzad thinks of her dream and the unfinished conversation with her father. She remembers, with some reluctance, one or two stories that have trickled back to her with the obligatory postscript: 'This story, these words, Shahrzad told the Shah in their marriage bed.' She cannot place the story. A feature or two seem familiar, it is true; or a swift twist of irony. Could she have forgotten the rest? These stories, her illegitimate children. She can hear them now, beating their fists against her door, laying claim to a living mother with a bad memory. Go away, she wants to say. I've never seen you before. Is she, Wise Shahrzad, to play a commonplace step-mother out of a story?

The old woman has forgotten both dream and father, so enraged is she by this last thought. But she can't hold the anger for long. If she nurses it, it sits in her windpipe, a hard clogging pebble, making it impossible to breathe. And what does it matter? Does it matter if she thought the words, spoke those stories aloud? *She* bent her back and built the skeleton of enduring bones, the framework. Others stretched their canvas in *her* frame. They colonized her body, her skilfully planned design, to paint in their sticky colours and words, their own moral themes.

Through the window Shahrzad sees the sun rise as it has so many times before: the same story, different words, a new storyteller. The door swings open, and the two girls come in, one with a basin of warm water, the other with a freshly lit lamp no longer needed.

They move to her bed swiftly and begin their tasks for the morning. One wipes the night's crust around her eyes, nose, lips; the other chafes the cold, stiff hands between her own warm ones. She wants to say to these young girls who are even now suppressing impatience and revulsion: 'I, Shahrzad, saved your grandmothers from being beheaded. I saved them, and so your mothers and you. You would not be here if I had not done it!' The words ring in her mind, dangerously close to petulance. An inappropriate voice for a heroine, she thinks, and feels a twinge of shame at this slip into melodrama. She fought for her own head. For it to escape, to be saved. How are these girls to know? That while she fought furiously, mounted and rode her words with a life-and-death desperation, that she already carried their souls within her, the seeds of her descendants?

Warm, scrubbed clean of the night, the old woman looks at the girls, her patient, unknowing children, with indulgence. She smiles at them, the cunning smile of a wise old witch. 'Talk to me,' she suddenly croaks. Though they are only too willing to break the silence she has always demanded of them, the girls look shifty and embarrassed. They pause, their work unfinished.

Shahrzad sits in her chair by the window. The girls stand before her, hands hanging awkwardly, their faces eager and foolish. The open window, that old friend and messenger, tells her the day – and their silence, or their girlish yielding – cannot last for ever. Then her smile freezes into a grimace. She sees her past, their futures, curving one into the other, a circle with no beginning or end. She says to them, this old warrior in times of peace: 'I fought for myself, and yes, for you as well. And you – what will you do when your turn comes? When the drums roll, and the sword blunted with age, the rusty axe, wake up to be freshly sharpened?'